JK.

Death on a Golden Isle
A Max Hurlock Roaring 20s Mystery

By John Reisinger

JR R...ing...
2014

Glyphworks Publishing
www.glyphworkspublishing.com

APR /14

Death on a Golden Isle
A Max Hurlock Roaring 20s Mystery

This book is a work of fiction. Except for specific historic references, names, characters, places and incidents are products of the author's imagination and are not to be construed as real, and any resemblance to any actual place, event, organization or person living or dead, is unintentional and purely coincidental.

All rights reserved. No part of this book may be reproduced in any form or by any means without the prior written consent of the author or publisher, except for brief quotes to be used in reviews.

Copyright 2011 by John Reisinger
ISBN 978-0-9838818-1-0

Glyphworks Publishing, LLC
2012

To Barbara, for all her help and support

and special thanks to

Dr. Charles Tumosa for information on forensics

H.P. Ketterman

Gretchen Greminger, Curator
Jekyll Island Museum

The Jekyll Island Authority

The Jekyll Island Club Hotel

Jekyll Books at the Old Infirmary

The Chesapeake Bay Maritime Museum

The Town of St Michaels, Maryland

Barbara Reister,
The Claiborne Cottage by the Bay

Dunes Manor Hotel, Ocean City, Maryland

Andrea Gauger

Jan Behrens

The National Mah Jongg League, Inc.

Note:
At the time the story takes place in 1923, Jekyll Island was spelled Jekyl Island, the result of a misspelling of the original name. The name was changed to Jekyll Island by a state law in 1929 and is the name that is used today. To avoid confusion to readers more familiar with the present spelling, the name Jekyll will be used throughout the book.

Cast of Characters

Outsiders

Max and Allison Hurlock
Sean McCoy- Sheriff, Glynn County, Georgia
Peter Hamilton- Big-game hunter
Joe Campbell- Captain of the Sylvia

Jekyll Island Club members

Bradley and Eva Dawkins
Phillip and Millie Hester- Friends of Eva
Clarice Bailey- Local *femme fatal*
Charles and Albert- Suitors of Clarice Bailey
Colonel and Nancy McCormick
Robert and Theresa Woodson
Harlan and Darlene Caldwell
Dr. Culver

Jekyll Island Club staff and servants

Jason Williams- Club handyman
Alan McHale- Club gamekeeper
Harold Falstaff –Assistant gamekeeper
Carlos Sanchez- Woodson's Cuban servant
Mary Dooley- Maid from Ireland
Rosie and Mattie- Laundry workers

Note: A reading group guide is included at the back of the book.

Chapter 1

A dance at the club

The bouncy rhythms of Way Down Yonder in New Orleans drifted from the brightly-lit room and out into the balmy Georgia night. The music rose and fell, sometimes drowning out the sound of the breeze through the surrounding trees, before receding once again. Among the potted palms, men in tuxedos and women in pearls and ball gowns crowded the polished wooden dance floor as the clinking of champagne glasses, and the chatter of voices and laughter mixed with the music. Most women wore traditional long gowns in dark conservative shades, but a few of the more daring affected aspects of the new flapper look, with shorter skirts, long strings of pearls, and dramatic feathers or ostrich plumes in their hair.

A punchbowl in the corner was being emptied and replenished in an endless cycle. Pocket flasks with forbidden bootleg alcohol were everywhere, but kept discretely from view. A gaily-colored poster on the wall announced "Welcome to the Club Ball-1923."

On the wide veranda just outside, the lights from the dining room threw patches of illumination that just failed to reach the lone figure seated in a wicker armchair by the railing. The figure sat motionless, as if oblivious to the gaiety nearby. A door opened and a trim, dark-haired woman in a deep green ball dress appeared.

"How are you doing, Bradley? Are you feeling any better?"

Bradley Dawkins looked up from the wicker chair and smiled. He was square-jawed with curly brown hair and movie star good looks. "I think so, Eva. I guess once you pick up some damned bug in the tropics, it sticks with you. Fortunately these little relapses pass in an hour or so."

"I brought coffee. Do you feel well enough to drink it?"

"Oh, yes. It'll help me get back on my feet. Just leave it on the arm of the chair and I'll get to it. How's the dance?"

"Oh, pretty much as you'd expect. Peter is being very gallant, the Hesters are perfect dears, and Clarice Bailey is being insufferable. Everyone else is busy looking down their noses at me."

He grimaced. "They're a pretty conservative bunch, but they'll warm up to you soon enough. The season will be over in a few weeks in any event."

"I think you need a little more rest. Are you sure you don't want to go back to the cottage?"

"No, I'll be fine. You just go back in there and enjoy yourself. I'll be with you just as soon as this passes."

"All right," said Eva. She paused at the door of the dining room and turned back to him. "Enjoy your coffee, Bradley."

She reentered the heat and noise of the crowded dance floor.

"How's Bradley getting along out there?" asked a tall man with a reddish-brown mustache.

"Oh, I expect he'll be fine, Peter. He gets these relapses from time to time. They usually pass in less than an hour."

Part-time big game hunter Peter Hamilton, or Bwana Pete, as everyone else knew him, nodded sympathetically and gestured with his drink, causing the ice cubes to clink in the glass. "It's the jungle, I suppose. The place is crawling with diseases. More damned bugs than you could shake a stick at. I don't know how I've avoided it all this time, what with all my trips to Africa. I remember this one fellow over in Mombasa; got bit by something or other and swelled up like a balloon. Extraordinary. If you stuck a pin in the poor lad he would have burst. Anyway..."

"Is Bradley any better?" Millie and Phillip Hester appeared and interrupted the flow of Bwana Pete's safari reminiscences. Eva Dawkins did not look disappointed.

"He'll be fine in a little while."

Over in the corner of the room on an elevated platform decorated with paper streamers and red Chinese lanterns, Fred Dinkle's band was cranking out the Charleston with a somewhat ragged performance that made up with enthusiasm what it lacked in precision.

"Come on, Eva," said Bwana Pete, placing his drink on a table and wiping his mustache with the back of his hand, "let's show these stuffed shirts how to cut a rug. Maybe it will inspire Bradley to join us."

Bwana Pete and Eva joined the crowd on the dance floor making various attempts at the dance craze in a swirl of flailing arms and legs. The Hesters stood watching them for a few minutes, and then an anxious-looking young man approached and spoke loudly to be heard above the music.

"Mr. and Mrs. Hester, have you seen Clarice anywhere? She seems to have disappeared."

"Disappeared? What do you mean, Charles?"

"She was drinking a cup of coffee and said she was bored with it and would I go and get her some punch instead. When I got back she was gone."

"Well, the floor is pretty crowded," said Millie Hester sympathetically. "I'm sure you just got separated."

The band ended the Charleston to whistles and applause. Eva Dawkins and Bwana Pete rejoined the Hesters.

"That gets the old blood flowing," said Bwana Pete, wiping his forehead with a handkerchief.

"Charles is here with Clarice Bailey," Millie Hester explained, "but she seems to have gone missing."

"Oh, that's too bad," said Eva, in a flat tone that indicated it wasn't very bad at all.

The young man looked around the room.

"Anyway," Charles continued, "I just want to make sure she isn't seeing someone else."

Millie Hester pretended to be shocked. "Clarice Bailey interested in someone else? Why, that would be.."

"Fickle?" Eva finished the sentence for her.

"I was going to say awful."

"Ah, well. That too, I suppose."

"Here she is," said Charles in an excited tone more appropriate for announcing a Kentucky Derby winner.

Clarice Bailey swept into view in a cloud of blond hair, blue silk and lace. She eyed Eva Dawkins and gave her a brief, cold nod.

"Clarice; where have you been?" said Charles. "We've been worried sick."

"We?" muttered Eva Dawkins under her breath.

"Now Charles, a girl has to powder her nose once in a while," Clarice pouted. She turned to Eva with her most insincere smile. "Why Eva; wherever is that dear husband of yours? I was so hoping to have a dance with him for old time's sake. He was always so smooth on the dance floor. I do hope he isn't wandering already. Poor Bradley does sometimes get bored of the humdrum. Perhaps he met someone with superior.....typing skills."

"Your concern is touching," said Eva, with ice in her voice. "Actually, he said he was feeling nauseated by the atmosphere and needed a breath of fresh air. I know exactly how he felt."

"Well," said Clarice gaily, "if he needs cheering up, I'll be glad to help."

"I believe I could use a bit of fresh air myself," said Eva. "Peter, shall we go and check on Bradley?"

Leaving Clarice, Charles and the Hesters, Eva and Bwana Pete threaded their way through the crowd and headed for the veranda.

"Thank God the season will be over in a few weeks," said Eva, as she approached the doors. Just a few feet ahead, the doors flew open and one of the staff stood in the opening, a black man with graying hair, and an expression of alarm on his face.

"Why, Williams," said Bwana Pete. "What on earth? You look like you've seen a ghost."

Williams looked at them wide-eyed. "Mr. Hamilton, Miz Dawkins; you better come quick. I think something's wrong with Mr. Dawkins."

John Reisinger

Chapter 2

Dead letter

The town of St Michaels on Maryland's sleepy Eastern Shore of the Chesapeake Bay was a collection of weathered wooden buildings nestled up against the cannery and packing houses at Navy Point on one side and several church steeples on the other. White-painted Skipjack workboats, their wooden masts swinging slightly in the wind, crowded the piers and unloaded their cargoes of oysters at the cannery. Inside, teams of shuckers, their nimble fingers almost a blur in the dim light, shelled the catch and prepared the oysters for canning. Next to the packing houses were several busy boatyards humming with the almost constant sound of sawing and hammering.

On the main street several blocks away, at the St. Michaels Post Office, Max Hurlock was staring in amazement at the letter he had just opened.

"Aw, for Pete's sake; now I've heard everything."

The March day was cold and windy, with threatening clouds overhead. Several passersby on the gravel and oyster-shell street glanced at him curiously.

The bell tower clock in the nearby Episcopal Church began to chime the noon hour, momentarily drowning out Max's grumbling. Even so, it was evident that Max was exasperated about what he was reading.

"I solve a few cases and all of a sudden they expect me to work miracles...and this time the murder weapon is a coffee cup? And it's on an island, no less. They probably expect me to walk on water to get there."

"Hey, Max. You sound like a pig with his tail in a wringer." Local moonshiner Duffy Merkle, a tall bearded man in overalls, appeared by Max's side.

"What? Oh. Hey, Duffy. I just have a letter from someone who has an exaggerated idea of my abilities and wants a good bit more than I can deliver."

Duffy grinned, revealing a lifetime of neglected dental work. "Shoot. I know what you mean. Last week this old boy wanted 100 gallons of 'shine and I only had about 50. Well, you just cain't raise production that much without sacrificing quality."

Max looked at him. "Quality?"

"Sure. Hell, the stuff I make'll take the paint off a wall, but it won't kill you. I depend on repeat customers."

"Good to know the spirit of craftsmanship isn't dead."

"Yeah, I cut it with some branch water and you could hardly tell the difference."

"I hope the Prohibition agents are as impressed with your exacting standards as I am."

"Oh, I love them Prohibition boys. If it weren't for them eliminatin' the competition I'd have to cut my price in half."

"Keeping the spirit of free enterprise alive," said Max.

Duffy nodded. "Well, you got to keep up with the times I always says. Speakin' of which, I sure could use that airplane of yours once in a while. If you'd make a few deliveries for me, I could make it worth your while."

Max shook his head. "I'm sorry, Duffy, but Hurlock's Flying Service will have to stick to passengers, mail, and occasional barnstorming. Anyway, I think you're overestimating how much cargo a war surplus Curtiss Jenny can get off the ground, not to mention the fact that transporting white lightning is illegal."

Duffy shrugged. "Shoot, bein' illegal is what makes it pay so good. Way I look at it, the gummint's got no business tellin' average folks they can't have themselves a snort now and then just 'cause a few people are drunks."

"I have to agree, Duffy, but I also do some criminal investigating work from time to time and it wouldn't do for me to get in trouble with the law."

Duffy brightened up. " I heard about that case you did up in Jersey. Two people dead in a locked room? Whooee. Like one of them mystery stories. Guess that's why they call you Sherlock Hurlock."

"I was just helping out an old navy buddy," said Max. "Still, you never know when something like that might come up again, so I've got to keep my nose clean."

Duffy sighed. "All right, Max, but if you change your mind..."

"You'll be the first to know."

In the parlor of a white painted clapboard house just outside of St Michaels, Allison Hurlock sat in front of a typewriter staring at a blank piece of paper and sighing.

"Maybe an article on jazz? The problem is I don't know a thing about it, not enough to write an article, anyway."

She tapped her fingers on the table and stared out the window at trees still bare from winter. Her chestnut brown hair tumbled over the neck of the bulky white sweater as she huddled against the chill. She squinted in thought, making her brown eyes almost invisible for a moment.

Maybe evolution? William Jennings Bryan has everyone stirred up about it, so maybe...No; too controversial. My usual magazines wouldn't touch it."

A faint chugging sound through the trees told her Max was returning from town in the Model T. Max appeared in a few minutes, parked the car next to the barn with the hand-painted sign that read "Hurlock's Flying Service" and jumped out. He was up the porch steps and in the house in a few seconds.

"Hey, Allison; how's the article coming?"

She stood up and stretched. "If it were coming any slower, it would be going backwards. I'd be erasing things I've already written. Well, anyway, I see you're back from the pulsing metropolis of St Michaels."

"So how is the article coming along? Any progress?"

"At least I accomplished one thing; I proved that you can't write by simply staring intently at the paper."

"Did you really think you could?"

"I was sort of hoping."

"Life is full of disappointments."

"Oh, well. A little break and I'll be as good as new. So what's going on in town? Any exciting mail?"

"Peculiar is more like it," said Max. "I got a letter from a woman in Georgia named Eva Dawkins."

"Ah, a secret admirer among the southern belles?"

"Sort of, I suppose, except she's actually from Baltimore. It seems she heard about the Taylor-Bradwell case we just finished up in New Jersey, and figured I'd be just what the doctor ordered to get her out of a jam."

"She's from Baltimore? I thought you said the letter was from Georgia?"

"She's from Baltimore, but married a wealthy man who spends his winters at an exclusive island club in Georgia."

"That sounds like the kind of a jam a lot of women would like to be in. So what's the problem?"

"Death by coffee, apparently."

"What?"

"Here. Maybe you'd better read it for yourself." Max handed her the letter.

Dear Mr. Hurlock:

My name is Eva Dawkins and I am writing to appeal for your help in a life or death matter. I am originally from Baltimore and read the local papers occasionally. It was there that I saw an article about how you solved those terrible murders up in New Jersey, and I remembered you in my time of crisis. My situation is desperate; my husband has been murdered and everyone is pointing fingers at me.

My husband Bradley and I have been spending the winter here on the island. A week ago, we attended a dance at the club. Bradley died suddenly while sitting out on the club veranda after I brought coffee to him and now everyone is blaming me. They say I poisoned his coffee.

Allison looked up. "So Mrs. Dawkins would appear to be a damsel in distress, albeit a distress possibly self-inflicted. She would seem to be a pretty good suspect. Poison is usually a woman's weapon, and who else would be bringing her husband coffee?"

"I don't know, but I imagine anyone at that dance would have had the opportunity," Max reminded her.

Allison continued to read.

Mr. Hurlock, I appeal to you to come here and help me find the truth about Bradley's death. The people here have never accepted me because of my humble background. They refer to me as a gold digger because of Bradley's wealth, and actually think I murdered him for it. The local sheriff treats me as if I'm already convicted. Any day now, he could be coming to haul me off to jail.

I don't know who killed Bradley, but as sure as there is a God above, I am innocent. Bradley and I had a large joint bank account, so money is not a problem. I will pay whatever you wish, but please come at once, so this nightmare will end! Please contact me by telephone at Georgia 3094.

Sincerely,
Eva Dawkins
P.S.- The season will be ending in three weeks and almost everyone will be departing, so time is limited. Please hurry. I have made arrangements for you to stay at the Sans Souci.

Allison refolded the letter. "A damsel in need of rescue, it seems. What's the Sans Souci?"

Max shrugged. "The local hotel, I guess."

"Must be a pretty swanky place. Sans Souci is French for Without Care. And where is this island she's writing from? She never said."

Max picked up the envelope. "The postmark says Jekyll Island, Georgia. I'll have to check an atlas. I never heard of it."

"Jekyll Island? You're kidding. That's amazing." There was excitement in Allison's voice.

"You know about Jekyll Island?"

"And how. When I was at Goucher, one of my classmates was from Atlanta. She told me all about the place. It's an island off the Georgia coast and it's owned by a club made up of the richest people in America. They go there for the winter, often by private yacht or railroad car. They have mansions cheek by jowl, although they call then cottages. Just the place to live if you want neighbors with names like Rockefeller, Morgan, Vanderbilt and Pulitzer. It's like Newport with palm trees. Only the rich and powerful need apply. If our Mrs. Dawkins has run afoul of that crowd, God help her."

"Sounds like a delightful place."

"Oh, I'm sure most of the people are perfectly decent sorts, captains of industry and all that, but they live in a world of wealth and servants, insulated from the world around them. I think they are quite accustomed to having their way. There is a certain standard they expect, and I imagine some of them can be a bit cold if they don't get it."

"I suppose refraining from killing your husband is one of those standards," said Max dryly. "Seems reasonable enough."

"Do you think you're going to take the case?"

Max looked thoughtful. "Now that I think about it, I don't see how I can resist. After all, how many chances will I get to investigate a death by coffee? Still, it seems to be asking a lot to expect an outsider to pry secrets loose from so many rich and powerful people on their own turf."

"Not only that, but all the other suspects will be leaving the island in three weeks. That doesn't give you much time."

Max frowned. "That does complicate things a bit, but maybe in a tight little place like an island, it'll be easier to narrow things down. If we fly to Richmond and take the train from there it will save some time."

"Maybe." Allison did not sound convinced. "As long as Gypsy can stay in the air that long."

"I just gave Gypsy a complete going over yesterday. She's as ready as a war surplus Curtiss Jenny biplane can be."

"Oh, that's reassuring. Now she'll be good for at least another fifty miles, I'm sure. Well, assuming we actually manage to get there, I can gather some juicy material for another magazine article. I've been on a dry spell since that article on speakeasies. I worked up something on the Charleston, but no one has bitten yet. Maybe an article on one of the top secret enclaves of the rich would be cat's pajamas."

"I'll bet it would be darb, as I believe the expression is. And we'll be far away by the time the lawsuits start flying."

"Nonsense. They can't sue for libel if what you say is the truth."

"Correction; they can't prevail, but they can still sue, small comfort when the legal bills start fluttering in."

"Tush. I'll write an educational article, not a scandal. They're probably far too dull for scandal anyway."

"I wouldn't count on that," said Max, "Apparently one of them isn't too dull to commit murder."

"True. I don't envy you. All I have to do is find a topic for my next article. You have to find a homicidal needle in an exclusive haystack."

Max folded the letter and placed it back in the envelope. "All in a day's work. Besides, we have an advantage over the club members."

"Oh, really? What's that?"

"We don't have to worry about who's taking care of our polo ponies."

Max placed a phone call to Eva Dawkins, and though the connection was bad, was able to accept the case and make arrangements to travel to Jekyll Island. The next morning, Max and Allison packed their bags and were soon high above the Chesapeake Bay in Gypsy, passing over gray, white-capped waves under a threatening sky. In the passenger cockpit, Allison shouted into the speaking tube.

"Did you check everything on the engine before we left? That water down there looks way too cold for swimming."

"Of course," he shouted back. "Besides, we're crossing at Drum Point where it's only about ten miles wide. We could probably coast to land if we had to."

"Imagine my relief."

In spite of Allison's reservations, Gypsy performed flawlessly and they were in Richmond in two hours. Soon they were on the Southern Railroad rolling through Charlotte to Savannah, then changing at Jesup,

Georgia to the Georgia Southern train from Atlanta to Brunswick.

"So now we're headed to an exclusive island getaway for the wealthy and powerful," Allison mused as the wheels clicked on the tracks. "I have to admit I didn't anticipate anything like this when I pulled into that filling station for gasoline in my father's Model T a few years ago.

Max smiled. "Ah yes. The big scene where Juliet met her Romeo. I was working there part time to pay for my college tuition while you were a Goucher girl off on a jaunt. As I recall, I charmed you with my witty small talk."

"You asked if I wanted my windshield cleaned," Allison reminded him.

"Well yes, but what made it witty was the fact that it was pouring down rain at the time."

Allison made an exaggerated sigh. "Now I ask you; what girl could resist a line like that?"

"If you had known you'd end up marrying a future investigator, airplane pilot, engineer with an unfortunate habit of getting dragged into other people's problems, I'll bet you'd have kept right on going."

She leaned back in her seat. "Not a chance."

They traveled all that day and slept fitfully that night. The next morning they changed trains for the final leg south. Later that day, as they got closer to Brunswick, Max noticed some coastal fog.

"It's getting thicker," he remarked.

"Don't worry," said Allison, half-asleep beside him. "I doubt if the train will get lost."

"It's not the train I'm worried about," said Max, still gazing out at the thickening wet fog. "We have to make the final leg to Jekyll Island by boat."

Allison sat up in the seat. "So we're off to a great start. You need to find a killer but we may not even find the island."

John Reisinger

Chapter 3

The Fog

In the dense wet fog, beads of moisture hung on the railings, ropes, and overhangs of a small steamboat tied to the dock on Georgia's Brunswick River. The boat was plain, without the polished mahogany and shining brass fittings of a yacht. A painted headboard, barely visible in the gloom, carried the name Sylvia. Like the pier, the boat appeared deserted.

"This is our ride, apparently," said Max.

"And this looks like the River Styx," said Allison. "So where is Charon to take us across?"

"I don't know. I guess we should just get on board and see if anyone's about."

Warily, they stepped onto the glistening deck. The boat shifted slightly under their weight, then was still again. All around them was only a soft misty grayness. Max noticed a highly polished ships bell on the foremast and rang it cautiously. The tones of the bell shattered the silence and caused two loitering pelicans to fly away with a soft beating of their wings.

"I'll bet they get to Jekyll Island before we do," said Allison.

"Afternoon, folks," came a voice from the mist. Max and Allison turned to see a tall bearded man emerge from the fog and extend his hand. "You must be the people from up north that Mrs. Dawkins mentioned."

"That's us," said Max, "fresh from a very long ride on the train from Richmond."

"Joe Campbell's the name. I'm the captain of the Sylvia. I'll be taking you to Jekyll Island."

"Max and Allison Hurlock," said Max. "Is it just you, Captain?"

"Just me. I usually have a crewman, but he took off on me a week ago. It happens that way sometimes. They head back north when the season gets near the end. But don't you folks worry none. I can get the Sylvia to Jekyll in my sleep. Done it a thousand times."

"Even in this fog?" Allison asked.

"Oh, sure. Once we get to Jekyll Creek it gets so narrow you can't miss the pier at the island. We'll be there in an hour or so. Now if you could untie that stern line while I get the bow.."

With a deep throated chugging of the engine, the Sylvia pulled away from the pier and was swallowed up by the fog. Allison watched the pier fade and then vanish into the gloom behind them.

"I wonder if the Flying Dutchman started out this way?" she remarked.

Max was silent a moment.

"I think I'll have a chat with the captain. Maybe he can give me the lowdown on Jekyll Island."

Allison nodded. "Keep an eye on the compass while you're there. I don't want to wind up taking a transatlantic voyage in this tub."

"Aye, aye."

Max found the captain steering in a somewhat casual way, with one hand on the wheel and the other making an entry in a log book.
"Just making a note of your names and the date."
"You don't mean to say you keep track of every passenger?"
The captain nodded. "Sure do. That way the folks at the club can see what they're getting for their money. They pay for the service, you know, and you can take it from me they're mighty careful with a dollar."
"I assume you mean the Jekyll Island Club?" said Max.
"Right. Well, the board of directors actually."
"What can you tell me about Jekyll Island, Captain?"
The captain chuckled as he squinted through the fog. "Well, it's hard to describe to someone who's never been there, but it's basically just your garden variety private island for the very wealthy. They built cottages, mansions if the truth be told. Some of the members come for the season, and some only visit while their wives and families stay. Most of them bring servants with them, but others 'rough it' with just the seasonal help. It's a pretty place. Of course, all the islands in these parts are; St Simons, Sea Island, Little St Simons, and of course, Jekyll Island."
"What's the Sans Souci on Jekyll? The hotel?"
The captain shook his head. "They don't have a hotel, outside of some rooms at the clubhouse. The place doesn't exactly welcome casual visitors or tourists. No, the Sans Souci is sort of an apartment building for members who haven't built a cottage. Some keep an apartment there for friends and relatives. Is that where you're staying?"
"I think so."

"Nice place. You'll be comfortable."

Max decided to go for broke. "What do you know about the murder?"

For the first time the captain frowned. "Ah, that was a bad business. Poor Captain Dawkins. One minute he's at a dance at the club and the next he's dying. But it's Mrs. Dawkins I feel sorry for. You see, she was already something of an outcast. Now they think she's a criminal as well. She seemed like a nice lady to me. I hope you can find out the truth, Mr. Hurlock."

Max started. "How do you know why I'm here?"

"Oh, there aren't many secrets on Jekyll Island, I'm afraid. People watch each other and tongues wag. Yes sir; you're in for quite an experience."

Almost an hour later, the engines slowed and a ghostly pier and a small building materialized out of the fog. Several small sailboats were moored nearby, along with three speedy-looking runabouts. All the boats featured highly polished mahogany and gleaming brass work. Max thought of the contrast with the plain, white-painted workboats of the Chesapeake Bay. If he had known nothing else about Jekyll Island, he would have suspected it was populated by some very wealthy people.

The Sylvia's engines reversed to slow the boat then shut off as the Sylvia bumped up against the pier and the captain secured the lines. Everything was suddenly silent except for the gentle lapping of ripples along the hull Max and Allison looked at the still wall of grayness, then at each other.

"I assume this is the right island," said Allison.

Max nodded and gestured toward the wooden building on the pier. A small wooden sign said

Landing on this pier except by permission is strictly forbidden.

"You know," Allison said finally, "I expected a somewhat understated welcome, but this makes me feel like a burglar."

"The captain said they didn't welcome casual visitors."

"Here we are," boomed the voice of the captain, curiously muffled by the fog. "Welcome to Jekyll Island in the great state of Georgia. Now, Mrs. Dawkins's place is in that direction, just past the club house on Oglethorpe Road. That's the road that runs right along the waterfront here. The Dawkins' place has a sign in front that says Osage Cottage. It's a big gray house. You can't miss it. Watch your step please."

"No problem," said Max, helping Allison onto the pier. "We've gotten off of boats before."

"I wasn't talking about the boat. You watch your step on Jekyll Island."

"Don't worry," said Max. "We intend to."

Once Max, Allison and their luggage were deposited on the dock, Captain Campbell turned the Sylvia around and disappeared into the fog once more. In a few minutes, the sound of the engine faded and the mist-shrouded pier was silent once again except for the sound of a nearby sailboat rocking gently at its mooring.

"Well, here we are," said Max. "It's not exactly the end of the world, but I'll bet it's within walking distance. Do you see a telephone anywhere?"

"We're lucky there's a pier. The path away from here must lead to Oglethorpe Street, so I suppose we should see if we can find the elusive Mrs. Dawkins. Let's leave our luggage here. We can send for it as soon as we figure out where we're going."

The path was surfaced with crushed oyster shells that crunched as Max and Allison set off into the deeper gloom of overhanging trees half obscured by the fog. As they turned on to Oglethorpe Street, Allison stopped.

"Max, what is that?" She was pointing to a round, turret-like tower rising above the trees and barely visible in the mist.

"I don't know. It almost looks like a castle of some sort."

"An ominous castle looming dimly in the fog. Isn't this the way Dracula starts out? Listen, Max. Do you hear that?"

"The flutter of bat wings?"

"Very funny. It sounds like a car or a motorcycle, and it's getting closer."

"Good. Maybe Mrs. Dawkins is finally coming to pick us up."

They had come to an intersecting road, wider than the path from the dock. As the sound grew louder, they waited expectantly. Finally, something began to materialize out of the fog.

"What in the world is that?" said Allison, amazed.

"I don't know, but I'm pretty sure it isn't a vampire."

Slowing to a stop in front of them was a strange sort of small, two-seater automobile, its tiny engine chugging and sputtering. The vehicle consisted mostly of four bicycle wheels on a low slung, open wooden frame painted bright red. The apparition skidded to a stop and the driver looked at them in wonderment. He was a middle-aged man dressed in what looked like a hunting jacket, complete with leather elbow patches and a padded patch on one shoulder. He had a weathered and tan face with a trim, no-nonsense mustache that wouldn't have been out of place on a retired British general.

"Hello there. You folks lost? Haven't seen you around here before. I'd offer you a lift, but this is only a two-seater."

"Well, we.."

"Hamilton's the name; Peter Hamilton. Of course around here most folks call me Bwana Pete."

"Bwana Pete?"

"I do a spot of big game hunting, and the name stuck." The man grinned broadly, though his mustache seemed to move hardly at all.

"I see," said Max, doubtfully. "Well, I'm Max Hurlock and this is my wife Allison. We're looking for Mrs. Dawkins."

"Charmed, I'm sure. Eva's place is just down this road a bit. I've been out running various errands for the last hour or so, but I'm heading that way. This bug is too small to give you a lift, but if you like I could stop by her place and tell her you're coming."

"Thank you," said Max. "Say, exactly what kind of an automobile is this?"

"This?" Hamilton sounded as if he noticed the odd vehicle he was driving for the first time. "Oh, this is just your standard red bug. They're named after the gnats that fly around all over the place in these parts. Lots of people on the island have them. They're the bee's knees when it comes to getting around. A lot of people don't want to bother with cars in a place that's so small. Next year they're supposed to come out with an all-electric model. Well, must be off. I'll stop by Eva's place and tell her you're here."

He took off and the popping of the engine faded into the grayness.

"A big game hunter driving a toy automobile," said Allison. "I must say Jekyll Island seems full of surprises."

"It certainly was for Bradley Dawkins."

"Say, Max. Did you notice something strange?"

"I didn't notice anything that *wasn't* strange."

"I mean, we've been told how Eva Dawkins is a pariah around here. Supposedly no one speaks to her, but Mr. Hamilton seems to be on good enough terms with her to drop by her place unannounced."

"Yes, I noticed that too. I'm not sure just what it means at this point. We'd better get going."

A few minutes later they came to a rambling gray shingled house with a sign out front that read Osage Cottage. A red bug was parked out front.

Max felt the engine.

"Still warm. Either Eva Dawkins has a red bug of her own or our friend Bwana Pete is still here."

As they mounted the front stairs, the front door flew open and a small, dark haired woman appeared. She was wearing a black beaded dress, as if she couldn't make up her mind whether to attend a funeral or a party.

"Oh, Mr. and Mrs. Hurlock; I'm so sorry you had to walk. I assumed that the Sylvia wouldn't be running until the fog lifted. I never thought you'd be here this early. I'm Eva Dawkins."

The living room of Osage Cottage was large and comfortable in an overstuffed, Victorian sort of way. As they were ushered in, Max and Allison were only slightly surprised to see it was occupied.

"You've already met Mr. Hamilton, I understand."

Peter Hamilton stood up from the depths of the large chair in which he'd been sitting and smiled like an old friend. "Hello again. Sorry about the mix-up. You just never know when the weather will shut down the Sylvia. It reminds me of an old tramp steamer I took once in South America. It seems the.."

"Now, Peter," Eva Dawkins chided, "I'm sure the Hurlocks are too travel-weary for one of your big game hunting tales just now."

"Yes, of course. Well, welcome all the same."

Max and Allison sat in the large sofa by the fireplace, an accessory that seemed unnecessary in the warm climate. Eva Dawkins sat in an upholstered wingback chair and lit a cigarette. She had small features and an olive cast to her skin that, coupled with her dark hair and dark dress made her look like the tragic heroine in some gothic novel.

"Mr. Hurlock, I'm so glad you could come. I don't know where to turn. First I lose my husband and now the community that should be offering me comfort and support has turned on me. If it weren't for Peter here, I would have no friends at all on the island. I need you to find out the truth behind my husband's death, Mr. Hurlock. That's all I ask; the truth."

Max regarded her closely.

"If you want to find the truth, Mrs. Dawkins, I suggest you start by being truthful yourself."

Eva Dawkins looked startled. Peter Hamilton's jaw dropped.

"What..whatever do you mean?" she stammered.

"I mean," said Max coolly, "that you knew very well that the Sylvia was making its scheduled run today in spite of the fog, and our running into Mr. Hamilton was no accident, since you sent him to intercept us once we arrived. What I want to know is why the deception?"

John Reisinger

Chapter 4

The gold digger

The room was silent for several seconds until finally Hamilton spoke.

"You know, Eva, I believe this fellow really is quite a detective."

Eva Dawkins nodded. "He certainly is. I'm very impressed, Mr. Hurlock."

"And I'm very unsatisfied," said Max. "Why the deception? If I can't get the truth from my client, it isn't likely I'll get it from anyone else."

She sighed. "Very well, Mr. Hurlock. You are quite correct. I knew the Sylvia had arrived and I asked Peter to intercept you and make sure you didn't get lost. I would have come get you myself, but I wanted to avoid meeting anyone else who might have been on the same trip. I am referring to that awful Sheriff McCoy who is supposed to return soon from the mainland for another round of questioning about the murder. I had no wish to run into him and be examined about the detective I had hired and was meeting at the dock. So I asked Peter to come fetch you. I also asked him to pretend it was a casual meeting so you wouldn't draw any unworthy conclusions about our relationship. You see, Peter has been a frequent visitor since my husband was killed, and has been very supportive. I just didn't want it to look like...well..."

"But how did you ever guess?" Peter jumped in.

"It wasn't a guess," said Max. "It was a deduction based on the evidence."

"Evidence? What evidence? You've been on the island less than a half hour."

"The evidence presented itself in just a few minutes," Max replied. Allison sat back comfortably in her chair. She enjoyed these moments when Max used a few simple observations to wow an audience.

"Mr. Hamilton, you told me you had been running errands for an hour or so, yet when we arrived at this house, I felt the engine or your red bug and found it was warm, but still cool enough to put my hand on it. An air-cooled small engine like that would have been too hot to touch if it had really been run for an hour. I estimated that it probably hadn't gone more than two or three blocks at the most, almost the exact distance of a round trip from Osage Cottage."

Hamilton nodded. "Very good, but how do you know Eva knew about the arrival of the Sylvia?"

"That's even simpler. A sailboat is moored near the pier and when it rocks a little you can hear the rigging slapping and the gooseneck rattling. That's the metal fitting that attaches the boom to the mast. When we walked up the steps here I could still hear it faintly, so Osage Cottage must be close enough to the water that a motorized boat would be hard to miss, especially with the front windows open as they are. Therefore, it is unlikely anyone in this house would not know that the Sylvia had arrived."

Eva Dawkins smiled.

"Bravo, Mr. Hurlock. You are quite correct. I heard the Sylvia arrive and asked Peter to meet you and pretend it was happenstance. I'm sorry for the deception, but I'm afraid I've grown a bit paranoid with all the unfavorable attention I've gotten of late. I do apologize."

Max frowned. "One thing I must have from a client is absolute candor. You have to be honest with me if you ever expect me to find out the truth. Even something you think is insignificant might lead to something important, so you have to tell me everything. If not, remember that the Sylvia goes in both directions."

Eva Dawkins looked chastised. "Of course, Mr. Hurlock. What do you want to know?"

"Let's start at the beginning. How did you and Bradley Dawkins meet?"

She exhaled slowly as if thinking about her answer. "Bradley was an officer in the Marine Corps during the Great War, and then became an investor and financier in a company with a partner. His company manages hotels mostly; and builds them to take advantage of the increasing number of people with automobiles. Bradley believed that there would soon be a travel boom, and wanted to take advantage of it. I went to Rider Business College in New Jersey, and went to work as a stenographer at his company. I used to work late occasionally and so did Bradley. Before long we were meeting for dinner and things sort of progressed from there. We were married last year and he brought me here to the island in December. He had just bought this cottage the year before, and was considered a very eligible bachelor. Needless to say, some of the other women were not overjoyed that he was married and even less happy with whom he married."

"You were ostracized?"

Eva Dawkins smiled faintly, as if she were enjoying some joke the others wouldn't understand. "Oh no. The club members are far too well bred to act so crudely. They were all civil and polite, but that was as far as it went. I was seldom invited to any women's functions and I was aware of the gossip that was circulating."

"What sort of gossip?"

"The gist of it seemed to be that I was a nobody from the steno pool who set her cap for the rich company president and snared him through feminine wiles. The term gold digger was used occasionally. Of course most women here were born into wealth, so someone of humble origins who wasn't a servant was something of an enigma to them. Anyway, the season dragged on and I was increasingly unhappy. My only friend was Millie Hester, who has a somewhat similar background. Bradley was going back and forth to Baltimore and New York, so I was alone much of the time."

Allison looked around the luxuriously appointed house.

"A bird in a gilded cage?"

"Exactly. Well, it all came to a horrible end a week ago at the dance. They hold teas and dances here at the club and Bradley always insists we go. The odd thing was that most of the other club members were becoming more hospitable. We had several pleasant conversations. Soon, however, Bradley began to feel a bit ill. There was nothing unusual in that. Ever since the war he has been subject to headaches and fatigue whenever he is around crowds of people. Bradley picked up a touch of malaria or some such disease when he was in the tropics and had occasional relapses. I'm not sure what it was: perhaps the smoke or the noise set it off. At any rate, he went outside to sit on the veranda in hopes that the fresh air would clear his head."

"How long was he out there?"

"Perhaps an hour or so. I came out to check on him periodically and bring him coffee. He always loved his coffee."

"Just a minute," Max interrupted. "If your relations with the other club members were so strained, what did you do inside all this time?"

"I spoke with my friend Millie Hester and her husband Phillip."

"That's all?" Max leaned forward.

"Well, I...I did dance once or twice with Mr. Hamilton."

"And how did that go over with the others."

She shrugged. "I really don't care."

"You may not care, but I have a feeling the police may care quite a lot. So what happened next?"

"Mr. Hamilton and I started back to the veranda to check on Bradley and we were met at the door by Williams, the colored man who does a lot of the maintenance around the island. Apparently he had been passing by and noticed Bradley was in distress. He was on his way in to tell us that Bradley was very ill and needed a doctor. I shouted for Dr. Culver who was nearby and Peter and I went out to investigate. Bradley was slumped down in the chair and appeared to be asleep. I tried to wake him, but it was too late. He was dead. By then the other members were coming out on the veranda to see what the commotion was."

"So when the other members arrived they saw you and Mr. Hamilton bending over your dead husband?"

Eva frowned in thought. "Why, yes. I suppose they did."

Allison and Max looked at each other.

"I suppose you realize how suspicious that must have looked?"

"I...I suppose so. It really didn't occur to me at the time."

Peter Hamilton spoke up. "For heaven sakes; the man was dead or dying and we just discovered him. We hardly had time to consider.."

Max held up his hand. "I'm not criticizing, merely making an observation. Please continue, Eva."

"There's not much more to tell. Dr. Culver tried to revive Bradley, but had to pronounce him dead. The county coroner was called in the next morning and determined that Bradley died from poison, probably arsenic, in a cup of coffee found by his side. Several people saw me bringing him coffee and dancing with Mr. Hamilton, so some ugly assumptions were made. Now they are saying I killed Bradley to get hold of his money and possibly to marry Peter Hamilton. Clarice Bailey has been 'I told-you-so'ing to anyone who will listen. And that dreadful Sheriff McCoy from the mainland has been questioning me incessantly. You can tell what he thinks. I didn't know where to turn, so I contacted you, Max."

Max looked at her critically, as if making up his mind. "Did your husband have any enemies or anyone who would benefit from his death as far as you know?"

Eva Dawkins sighed. "No one. Everyone liked Bradley and no one benefited from his death."

"Which brings the suspicion right back to you," said Peter Hamilton. "Max, can't we do something about all of this? I mean, as a detective you should be able to set these people straight."

Max looked at him coldly.

"First of all, Mr. Hamilton, I am not a detective, I am an investigator. I don't work with the intention of proving or disproving anything, let alone to 'set people straight'. My object is to uncover the truth. If the truth is favorable, so much the better, but truth above all."

"Certainly, Mr. Hurlock," said Eva. "The truth will be more than adequate."

Max rose to his feet. "I'll want to know who might have information about Mr. Dawkins's business dealings and personal life, and a lot more information about the island and who does what around here. Right now, though, I just want to know where we'll be staying and I'd like a chance to freshen up a bit. We can talk more tonight."

"Of course," said Eva. "I have an automobile. I'll take you to the Sans Souci. There's an apartment there that my husband rented to accommodate visiting relatives."

"That'll be fine."

"Perhaps we should have dinner tonight; at the club. Have you brought formal evening dress?"

"A monkey suit?" Max looked pained. "I don't even own one."

"Not to worry, old boy," said Bwana Pete. "We're about the same size. I'll loan you one of mine. I'm dining in tonight anyway. It'll just be you and Eva at the club."

Max frowned at Eva Dawkins. "I thought you were an outcast around here? I would have thought you might be uncomfortable eating at the club under the disapproving gaze of the others."

She smiled.

"On the contrary, Max. I'm looking forward to it."

The fog had started to lift and soon they were in front of the Sans Souci, a three story apartment building not far from the main clubhouse. When they found their apartment, Max threw a suitcase on the bed and turned to Allison.

"Well, what do you think?"

She looked out the window. "I think you have a talent for landing in the soup, and I'm not talking about the fog."

Max sat down heavily in an overstuffed chair and put his feet up on a side table.

"And you have a talent for understatement. There's a lot more happening around here than a simple murder; Bwana Pete for one. What do you suppose is going on with him and my client?"

Allison turned from the window and sat in the other chair. She took off her hat and lightly tossed it on the bed where it came to rest next to the suitcase.

"Hard to say at this point, but I think they're *very* good friends, maybe even lovers."

Max acted surprised, though he really wasn't. "Just because he stopped by her house today?"

"He didn't just stop by her house. He had already been there for a good while. Otherwise the engine on his red bug would have been hotter."

"I agree. Besides there were the glasses."

"Glasses?"

"You couldn't see from where you were sitting, but I noticed several pairs of used glasses on the sideboard. Apparently Bwana Pete had been there long enough to have a few rounds of drinks with the bereaved widow. I'd say that means several hours at least. That's hardly a neighborly drop in. And why do you suppose she's so anxious to be seen at the club? That doesn't seem to fit with the social outcast scenario."

"I think I know," said Allison. "The club members have been looking down on her from the beginning, and she's had to take it for her husband's sake. Then when he was murdered the disapproval got even worse. But now that she's hired you, she's fighting back to protect herself. Showing up with us at the club is her way of sticking her thumb in their eyes; her way of refusing to be intimidated."

Max nodded. "Yes, of course. Sounds like the sort of thing you'd do."

"I would have done it long before this."

John Reisinger

Chapter 5

The club

The clubhouse was a rambling tan brick Victorian building dominated by a round tower near its center, the tower that had loomed out of the fog earlier. The club sat confidently in a park-like area of shaded paths and carefully tended plantings on acres of green lawn that ran a few hundred feet down to the riverfront. Twisted oak trees surrounded the building, their branches hung with gray clouds of Spanish moss. Well dressed and well-heeled ladies and gentlemen strolled the grounds or lingered on the wicker furniture on the clubhouse porches and verandas. Max and Allison approached the main building with some trepidation. Allison moved easily in a form-fitting blue silk gown cut just below the knees, while Max was obviously uncomfortable in Bwana Pete's tuxedo.

"I feel like I've fallen into a Seurat painting," Allison remarked. "Lucky I brought my evening gowns."

"Why exactly would you bring evening gowns?" said Max, trying to loosen his tie.

"I girl likes to be prepared. Besides, you remember my friend from Goucher, the one who told me about Jekyll Island? Well, she used to talk about how formal and stuffy the place was at dinner time, so I decided to play it safe."

"Great. Why am I always the last to know?"

"Now, Max, what would you have said if I had told you to buy a tuxedo? I have enough trouble getting you to wear your straw boater."

"Point taken. Well, I think this is the dining room."

They had crossed a wide porch at the top of the front entrance steps. Just inside the front door was a long wood-paneled room divided into thirds by a double line of Greek columns and full of people seated at tables covered with white tablecloths gleaming with china and silver. The diners looked up at the strangers with a mixture of curiosity and annoyance.

"Look at all those overdressed people," said Allison. "We seem to be as welcome as a caterpillar in the soup."

Max took a deep breath. "Well, in situations like this, there is only one thing to do; walk in as if you own the place."

A dignified maître d' materialized from behind a potted palm and viewed Max and Allison curiously.

"Good evening sir...madam. May I be of assistance?" He spoke in an undertone that implied that being of assistance was the last thing he wanted.

Max turned an expressionless eye on the waiter. ""Why, yes. Would you direct us to Mrs. Dawkins's table?"

"Mrs. Eva Dawkins, sir?"

"That is correct."

"Are you guests of Mrs. Dawkins, sir?"
"That is also correct."
"And would you be..'"
Max smiled. "The table?"
"I was merely..'
"The table...please."
The maître d' hesitated, and then bowed slightly. "Of course. This way please."
Eva Dawkins was seated at a table next to a column, and greeted Max and Allison warmly as they sat down. "Oh, Allison. You look stunning. I just adore that gown. Who is your seamstress?"
"Hochschild Kohn in Baltimore. You know; the department store."
"Well, it looks lovely. And Max, you look so dashing in a tuxedo. So what will you have?" Eva Dawkins was now looking through a large, leather-bound menu. "The veal tends to be a bit dry but the game hen is usually excellent."
When they had read over the menu, Max spoke. "Eva, are we really free to talk here? It's not exactly private."
"I just wanted to show how much I appreciate your coming here. This will get you off to a good start so to speak; maybe give you a little of the flavor of the place."
Max looked around the room at the disapproving faces. "The flavor of the place would seem to be somewhat on the sour side at the moment."
Allison raised her menu slightly to hide her smile.
"All right," Max continued. "Maybe you can tell me some more about Bradley's acquaintances around here."
Eva leaned back slightly and looked around the room. "Over at that table on the left are the McCormicks, Nancy and the Colonel. They're from New

York; he made his fortune in real estate and she tries her best to spend it. Sitting with them are the Woodsons. Robert is in the plumbing products business and Theresa is active in charities and amateur theater. I believe they're from Atlanta. She's sort of the Grande Dame around the club."

Max and Allison regarded the four rather plain-looking people with interest.

"Colonel McCormick looks like the man who owns the dry goods store in St Michaels," Allison remarked.

Eva motioned toward another table at which sat three couples. The ladies all looked ordinary and similar, but the men were a study in contrasts

"Now, over at the far table are the directors of the Jekyll Island Club, Tim Morrison, he's the thin one with the beard; Charles Andrews, the heavy set, bald one; and Herbert Davis, the one with all the white hair. Those rather gray looking ladies with them are their wives, but frankly, I could never tell them apart."

A waiter glided up to the table and coughed softly.

"Hello, Charles," said Eva, smiling at him. "Is there any fresh game tonight?"

The waiter nodded. "Why yes, madam. Mr. McHale brought us two fine pheasants this afternoon, and we still have some good cuts of the wild pig from yesterday."

"We'll all have the pheasant, then," said Eva, snapping the menu closed.

"Very good, madam," said the waiter, before silently backing away.

As the waiter gathered up the menus and disappeared between the tables, Max and Allison looked at each other.

"I hope that was all right?" Eva asked.

"Oh, yes," said Allison. "We haven't had a good pheasant in days."

Max poked her gently under the table.

"Pheasant will be fine," said Max.

"Yes," said Allison, "it will be so nice not to have to pry dinner out of a shell."

Eva looked confused. "A shell?"

"We eat a lot of crabs and oysters where we live on the Eastern Shore," Max explained.

"Oh, of course," Eva smiled. "Not much of that here, but our gamekeeper, Mr. McHale is really a marvel. Even Peter says so, and he tends to be critical of other hunters. Between Mr. McHale and his assistant, we usually have the most wonderful meals here."

"I wouldn't have thought there'd be much game on an island this size," said Max.

"Oh, yes. We have sea turtles, deer, several varieties of birds, and the wild pigs."

"Where did the wild pigs come from?" Allison asked.

"The theory is that a Spanish ship had some pigs on board and was shipwrecked. Most likely, however, they're the result of some careless long-ago farmer who didn't keep his pens in good repair. Either way, there are so many that it's always open season on them. The things can be a nuisance. You should see what they can do to a garden!"

"Hello, Eva," came a voice. Max and Allison looked up to see a middle aged couple standing behind them. The man had short blond hair and a thin mustache, while the red haired woman was short and energetic.

Eva Dawkins smiled with delight. "Good evening Phillip and Millie. Max and Allison Hurlock, these are my friends the Hesters."

"Ah," said Phillip, shaking Max's hand, "you must be that detective fellow from up north."

"Actually I'm just an investigator.."

"And you.." Phillip Hester had turned his attention to Allison. "Why, Millie; do you know who Mrs. Hurlock looks like?"

"Why sure enough,' said Millie. "She looks like that movie star. What was her name again?"

"Yes," Phillip agreed. "Mary Pickford! Of course."

"America's sweetheart," Millie gushed. "Has anyone ever told you that?"

"Well,.." Allison began.

"Phillip said I look like Mabel Normand," said Millie. "Can you imagine? Why she's a comedian!"

Eva laughed, earning disapproving looks from adjoining tables. "You'll have to excuse Millie. She's a dear, but sometimes gets carried away."

"Yes; well. How you like our little island so far, Mr. and Mrs. Hurlock?" said Phillip.

"It's very interesting," said Max. "We hope to see a lot more of it."

Millie nodded vigorously. "I hope you can find out what happened to poor Bradley."

Max looked around nervously. "Mrs. Hester, I really..."

"Not to worry, Millie," said Eva. "Everything will be fine."

As the Hesters made their way out of the dining room, Max and Allison looked around and saw that everyone was looking at them.

"Eva, did you tell everyone we were coming?" said Max.

"Oh, Millie's a dear. I had to tell her."

"And she had to tell the world," Allison remarked.

"It doesn't matter," said Max. "They'll know soon enough anyway. On an island this small I imagine everyone knows when you sneeze. Do you think they'll cooperate?"

Eva shrugged. "You never know. They don't talk to me much, but you're someone new. They might all talk to you if only to assure you of my guilt."

The dinners arrived just then. Two waiters expertly and quietly placed them on the table under shiny silver domes. The head waiter removed the domes with a flourish to reveal the perfectly cooked portions underneath

"Bon appetite."

"So, Eva, who was your husband friendly with around here?" said Max, digging into his pheasant.

Eva dabbed daintily at her mouth with a spotless linen napkin. "Oh, I suppose he was closest to Peter Hamilton. They both shared an interest in guns and hunting. Peter had been an avid hunter all his life and got interested in big game from some of the British officers he met in France when he was in the army."

"Anyone else?"

"Oh, Bradley was outgoing and on good terms with everyone. I suppose that's why everyone has reacted the way they have."

"How about the staff around here? Was Bradley friendly with any of them?"

Eva nodded. "More or less. He was on good terms with Mr. Grob, the club manager, and the gamekeepers of course."

Max was taking notes. "That would be Mr. McHale?"

"Yes, and of course his assistant, Mr. Falstaff. They both took out hunting parties on request and Bradley and Peter went occasionally. Oh, and there's Mr.

Williams, that nice colored man that does a lot of the maintenance around here. He and Bradley used to get in deep conversations all the time."

Max looked interested. "Deep conversations about what?"

Eva shook her head. "I have no idea. I just noticed them from time to time. They got quite animated."

Max and Allison looked at each other.

As Max questioned Eva Dawkins, several couples finished their dinner and left the dining room. Each couple nodded politely to Eva Dawkins as they passed the table, but no one stopped to chat.

"I've seen friendlier crowds at a hanging," Allison remarked. "If I didn't know any better, I'd think this was an undertakers' convention."

Eva chuckled.

"Yes, I'm afraid it's as I told you earlier. I am persona non grata around here, but I hope Max can fix that."

Allison reached over and patted Max's hand.

"I wouldn't be at all surprised. Don't let his modesty fool you; when it comes to digging up the facts, Max is the bee's knees."

A young couple passed by the table. The man was sallow and nondescript, but the woman was tall, and strikingly beautiful. She had pale blue eyes and hair so blond it was almost white. The vision looked as if she, or her servants, had spent the afternoon perfecting her hair, makeup and dress. She looked to be in her twenties, and in spite of her good looks, had a certain aspect of coldness about her.

"Evening, Mrs. Dawkins," said the man, nodding as he passed. The woman glared at him a moment, then at Eva Dawkins and her table. She did not speak, but her eyes lingered a moment on Max.

"I suppose they were from the welcoming committee?" said Allison.

Eva laughed. "That rather frosty lady was Clarice Bailey, our local femme fatal. The men around here dote on her something shameful."

"She's not one of your fans, I take it," Max asked.

"Hardly. It seems that last season, before I met Bradley, the fair Clarice had her hooks in him. They were never engaged or anything formal, but she came to think he was hers for the taking. When she found out he had married me, she became the head of the 'gold-digger chorus'."

"So I suppose she'd be happy to see you go to jail," said Max.

Eva sighed. "She'd be happier to see me hanged, but I suppose she'd settle for jail."

"Where was she the night your husband died?" Max asked.

"She was at the dance with one of her admirers."

Max looked thoughtful. "At the dance, do you think she'd have been able to...well, that is, could she.."

Eva finished the question. "If you're wondering if she had the opportunity to poison that coffee, the answer is yes."

Allison was surprised. "You really think she was mad enough with Bradley to want to kill him?"

Eva took a sip of tea.

"Probably not, but there is a far more likely possibility."

"And what would that be?" Max asked.

"The poison was meant for me," Eva said quietly.

An hour later, Eva Dawkins and Max and Allison rose and made their way to the door. The remaining

John Reisinger

diners watched them discretely. Eva Dawkins walked proudly and completely unrattled.

Until they reached the porch.

A tall thin, slightly shabby looking man was waiting at the head of the porch steps smoking a cigarette. Eva Dawkins froze when she saw him.

Evening, Miz Dawkins," the man said, removing his battered fedora.

"Good evening, Sheriff McCoy. It's a little late to be out, isn't it?"

"Law enforcement hours can be a bit irregular, Miz Dawkins. It's sort of like huntin'. You can't tree a coon when the sun is shinin'. Ah need to ask you a few more questions if you don't mind. Ah'm sure you folks'll understand." He was nodding toward Max and Allison.

"Good evening, Sheriff," said Max. "I'm Max Hurlock and this is my wife Allison. I'm assisting Mrs. Dawkins."

McCoy nodded. "So you're Mrs. Dawkins's lawyer, Mr. Hurlock?"

"I'm an investigator, and I'm trying to help her gather information and put the pieces together."

McCoy nodded slowly in a sizing-up sort of way. "Is that a fact? Well, Mr. Hurlock, you go right ahead and lend a hand to Miz Dawkins, long as you don't interfere in police business. You hear?"

"I wouldn't dream of it, Sheriff," Max replied coolly. "I might even be able to help you. In fact, I've helped your investigation already."

McCoy snickered. "Help me? How you figure that?"

"If I wasn't here, Mrs. Dawkins would probably have had her attorney here by now. He might have advised her not to cooperate."

"Would he now? And what are you going to advise her?"

"Since I am as interested in getting to the truth as you are, I've advised her to answer all pertinent questions as well as she can."

McCoy nodded. "Well then here's her chance. I've got a few now."

"Please, sheriff," said Eva, "could we do this at my house? There are too many prying ears around the club."

"Why not? Let's go then."

As they walked to the cottage, they passed under the long branches of oak trees heavy with Spanish moss.

"I suppose you don't have many murders on Jekyll Island, Sheriff," Max ventured as they walked.

McCoy shook his head. "No, the club members usually save any lethal impulses for the business world. Still, there's a first time for everything. I aim to make it the last."

Max took Eva aside.

"Eva, at some point in the questioning, I want you to object to a question and turn to me for support."

"Why?"

"I'll tell you later."

John Reisinger

Chapter 6

The law

A few minutes later, they were all seated in the sitting room of Osage Cottage. In the elegant setting with Max, Allison, and Eva Dawkins in formal attire, the sheriff looked shabby and out of place. He didn't act like it, however.

"Now, Miz Dawkins, if you want Mr. Hurlock to sit here while we chat, that's your right, but I'm the one doing the questioning."

"Of course," said Eva, "but I'd be interested in Max's views."

"Well I'm not. If anyone tries to interfere, we can always do this over in Brunswick instead. Now, let's go over the night in question once more. I've had a chance to talk to that colored fella, Jason Williams. He was the first to notice your husband was in distress. He's got some pretty good powers of observation it seems. He noticed some things everyone else seems to have missed."

"What sort of things?" said Eva suspiciously.

"Well, for instance, how many times did you bring your husband coffee?"

"Just once..around 10:00 or so."

"Once?" said McCoy. "Well now that's a mite peculiar, seein' as how there were two cups next to his chair when he was found."

"Two?"

"That's right; one on the arm of his chair and one on the floor under the chair. They both had a little coffee in 'em, but the one on the arm was the only one everybody noticed. That was the one that was poisoned."

"What about the one on the floor?"

"It just had coffee in it."

"Then what difference does it make? For heaven's sakes, why badger me about it?"

McCoy smiled slyly. "Now, Miz Dawkins, you know we have to keep the details straight in a murder investigation."

"Yes, but you're trying to trap me with a silly detail!"

She turned to Max sitting in an adjoining chair. "Max, this is outrageous. Isn't it bad enough I've lost my husband? I shouldn't have to..."

"I'm afraid I have to agree with the sheriff here," said Max. "It could be an important point. If there was more than one coffee cup, there could be more than one person bringing it."

McCoy nodded his approval. "Now y'all just listen to Mr. Max. He knows what he's talking about."

Max stole a glance at Allison, who was standing in the doorway. She smiled faintly.

"Eva, I really think you need to cooperate with the police," Max continued. "Sheriff McCoy has a job to do and as far as I can tell, he's doing it. Just because a question sounds like it's a small detail doesn't mean it's not important. His questions have a purpose. He wants to get at the truth, just as we do."

"I'm sorry, sheriff," said Eva softly. "You may continue."

"Much obliged, Mr. Hurlock. Now, Miz. Eva, you and Mr. Dawkins have been married for how long?

"About nine months."

"And you're the beneficiary of his life insurance and his will?"

"I suppose so. I'm his wife."

"And Mr. Dawkins was quite well off?"

"So is every other club member. That doesn't make their wives murderers."

"Now, where was Mr. Hamilton during the dance?"

"He was there as well."

'Did you speak with him there?"

"Yes. He was telling me about a wild boar hunt he had been on. I also danced with him several times."

"Uh huh. And just how did you first meet Mr. Hamilton?"

"He was a friend of my husband's. They met in France. Bradley invited him to visit the island for a few weeks. He stayed with us at first, but moved to the clubhouse after Bradley's death."

"You got along well with Mr. Hamilton, did you?"

From her perch in the doorway, Allison could see Eva's fists clench.

"Yes. He has been very supportive since Bradley died, and yes I see him often. He's one of the few around here who support me and isn't talking behind my back."

"And you and Mr. Hamilton aren't, well.. you know..."

"I really resent that question, Mr. McCoy."

53

"Come on now, Eva," Max intervened again. "You know the sheriff has to ask."

Eva took a deep breath, as if stifling her rage. "No, sheriff, we are not... 'you know' and never have been."

McCoy consulted a notebook. "Now you said your husband got on pretty good with everyone around here."

"That's right."

"But Mrs. Woodson tells me he had an argument with her husband just two days before the murder. What was that all about?"

"I have no idea. Perhaps you should ask Mrs. Woodson, since she's the one who started that particular rumor."

As McCoy thumbed through some notebook pages, Max discretely cleared his throat.

"Excuse me, sheriff, but do you know what poison was used?"

"The doc seems to think it was arsenic, but he isn't certain. He hasn't seen a whole lot of poisoning cases round these parts."

Max nodded. "Assuming it was arsenic then, have you found any around here?"

McCoy looked up. "We searched the dining room and it was clean, but that doesn't mean much. It's easy to get rid of."

Max nodded. "Of course, but I meant on the island itself. Just where would one go to get it?"

"Shoot, you can buy that stuff in a drugstore. Anybody can."

"Are there many drugstores on the island?" said Max.

"Not a one," McCoy admitted.

"So anyone who wanted to use arsenic to poison someone would have to bring it on the island ahead of time?"

McCoy shook his head. "Not necessarily. They keep a bottle in the maintenance shed for poisoning varmints and cleaning. The place is locked at night, but other than that anyone could have gotten to it."

"Anyone who knew about it."

"I found out easy enough, and I ain't even a member. Now, Miz. Dawkins, can you think of anyone else who had it in for your husband?"

She sighed. "Not that I know of, but we've only been married less than a year. He might have something in his past I am not aware of, I suppose. Let's just say there was certainly nothing obvious. My husband was a fair-minded man, a man of integrity. Everyone knew that."

The sheriff asked some more questions about the domestic life of the Dawkins household and dropped a few more hints that he was not entirely satisfied with the apparent innocence of Eva's relations with Bwana Pete, but finally he snapped his notebook shut.

"That's it for now, Miz Dawkins. I'll be back when I need some more information. But first I need to talk to Mr. Hurlock here."

"Of course, sheriff," said Max. "Whatever I can do."

Max and Sheriff McCoy went out on the porch where the sheriff lit another cigarette.

"Now I gotta be honest with you," McCoy began, "I came here tonight intending to arrest Miz Dawkins and take her back to Brunswick. I'm getting' a lot of guff from people about lettin' a killer run loose on the island. The local reporters are nippin' at my heels somethin' fierce. They can't get on the island and pester people here, so they rag on me instead. Some folks say island people are so rich they get a new boat when the old one gets wet. Mainland folks figure that kinda money buys a certain amount of favoritism."

Max nodded sympathetically. "The public can be hard to please."

"Daggone right. Some of those people would still be unhappy with a ham under each arm. Still, they got a point, but I'm leaving Miz. Dawkins here provided she doesn't leave the island."

"A wise decision, Sheriff McCoy," said Max. "Even if she did kill her husband, she'd be no threat to anyone else."

"That's right, but that's not why I'm leaving her here. The information about the second cup of coffee has clouded the issue a mite, and so have you.'

"Me?"

"Sure. If you're investigatin', you can keep an eye on Miz. Dawkins for me. You can be responsible-like."

"Me?" said Max. "Why should I accept that responsibility? I could just look the other way and let her take off."

The sheriff exhaled a smoke ring that drifted lazily in the humid night air. "You could, if you'd like to be arrested for aiding and abetting a fugitive and obstructing justice."

Max smiled. "Well played, sheriff."

The sheriff smiled slyly and touched the brim of his hat. "Now you folks have a real good evenin', y'hear?"

Max, Allison and Eva stood at the window watching the sheriff disappear in the darkness. Max told them what the sheriff had said.

"So what do you think, Max," Allison asked.

"I think that behind the good ol' boy act, our sheriff is a shrewd lawman."

"Let's hope he's an honest one as well," Allison said. "He's under a lot of pressure to haul Eva off to the clink."

Eva turned toward Max. "Why did you tell me to object to a question if you were going to take his side?"

"Sorry I didn't have time to explain," said Max. "That was just a ploy to get him to start to rely on me to help his investigation. It also helped to convince him that I'm not just here to be a mindless advocate, but to find the truth. It might help to loosen his tongue about what he's found."

Eva nodded. "Well, it certainly seems to have done the trick. He was eating out of your hand, and decided to leave me in your care, so to speak. That was a nice touch on his part, threatening to arrest you if I take a powder."

"Yes," Max agreed. "A wise precaution, I have to admit. The sheriff is a man who believes in hedging his bets, it seems."

"After that," said Allison, "I'm going to be watching you myself."

Back at the Sans Souci, Max and Allison stepped through the front door of the lobby area to meet a couple going out. He was stocky and had a gray handlebar mustache. She was of average height and had thick blonde hair.

"Good evening," the man said. "You must be the Hurlocks, Eva Dawkins's guests."

"News travels fast. I'm Max Hurlock and this is my wife Allison."

"I'm Harlan Caldwell and this is my wife Darlene."

"Are you the Allison Hurlock that wrote the article about crossword puzzles in Today's Life magazine last month?"

"That's me," Allison beamed. "You have a good memory."

"That's what Harlan says."

"You know, Mrs. Hurlock, you're a dead ringer for that movie actress. Oh, what's her name, Darlene?"

Darlene looked Allison over carefully. "I know; Mary Miles Minter!"

"That's the one. Most extraordinary. And quite lovely." Harlan Caldwell gazed at Allison the way a dog looks at a steak.

"You'll have to excuse Harlan," said Darlene Caldwell with a slight edge of annoyance in her voice. "He's always had an eye for the ladies. I've spoken to him about it before."

"I have an eye for her myself," said Max, attempting to pour some cool water on Mrs. Caldwell's annoyance. "So, are you visitors, too?"

"Us?" Harlan Caldwell asked, as if the room was full of couples waiting to be called on. "Oh, no. We just have a place in the Sans Souci while waiting for our cottage to be renovated. So I understand you're the detective Mrs. Dawkins called in."

"I'm not a detective," said Max. "I'm an investigator."

"Is there a difference?"

"I'm not advocating for anyone and I'm not trying to track down anyone. I'm just gathering the facts and trying to make sense of them."

The Caldwells nodded politely. "Well, I don't envy you, Mr. Hurlock. You've got an uphill battle on your hands."

"Oh? Why is that?"

"Isn't it obvious? Young woman married to wealthy man. Wealthy man is murdered just a few months later on an island where everyone else is an old friend. You have to admit it looks suspicious, especially after that argument he had with Eva just a few weeks ago."

"Argument?"

Darlene Caldwell took over the narrative. She looked almost embarrassed. "I don't think anyone heard it but us. It was just after dinner one night. They were sitting under a tree near the water and were engaged in a very lively argument as we strolled past them. They weren't loud, but they were talking in those low growling voices that sounded like they were gritting their teeth in anger."

"What were they arguing about?"

"We couldn't hear the particulars, but it seemed to be about money," said Harlan Caldwell, shaking his head. "Bad form, really. It's an unwritten rule around here that we don't talk about money or business in public. After all, this is a place to get away from all that."

Allison snapped her fingers. "At the risk of breaking the rule, are you the Caldwell of the Caldwell's Chocolates they served after dinner tonight?"

Harlan Caldwell laughed. "Yes, that's me. The Caldwell Corporation imports all kinds of goods from all over the world, but the chocolate is about the only product we process and sell directly. The club was buying it long before we became members, so there's no favoritism."

Allison smiled. "And how do so many people from so many different industries get along on the island?"

"Quite well, actually. Oh, there's sort of a hierarchy, but it revolves more around how long you've been a member than how wealthy you are. That being said, the names Vanderbilt and Rockefeller carry a good bit of weight around here of course. Still, it's as informal and egalitarian as possible."

"And how egalitarian is it as far as Eva Dawkins is concerned?" Max asked.

Harland Caldwell shrugged slightly. "The members are all good upstanding Christian citizens; accomplished, civic-minded, responsible and so on."

He hesitated a second. "What you have to understand, Mr. and Mrs. Hurlock, is that any brand new spouse is viewed with a certain degree of, well.."

"Suspicion?" Allison suggested.

"I was going to say wariness, but even that is too strong a term. What I mean to say is that with powerful and wealthy men, there is always the possibility that when a new spouse from an unknown background suddenly appears, she might be a gold-digger. People say the wealthy are inbred because they marry among themselves, but that is one of the main reasons. Unless a spouse has wealth of her own, how do you know whom to trust? So to answer your question, Eva Dawkins was accepted, but certain members were alert for any signs of gold digging on her part."

"I see," said Max. "And were there any?"

Mrs. Caldwell chimed in. "Well, Eva talked about money more than she should have, but that's common with people who suddenly become wealthy. The real questionable area was her relationship with that Peter Hamilton. He was supposed to be Bradley's friend, but many times I've seen him strolling with Eva. Since Bradley died, it's been worse than ever."

"Now, Darlene; I'm sure Eva just needs some companionship about now," Harlan assured her.

"Maybe."

"Were you at the dance the night Bradley Dawkins died?"

"Oh, yes," said Harlan Caldwell. "It was terrible. There was a commotion out on the veranda and we went to see what was going on. One of the help had come running in looking for a doctor, then Eva Dawkins ran out. By the time we got there, a crowd had gathered and Bradley was dead. Terrible business. Terrible."

"So now I suppose everyone thinks Eva Dawkins killed her husband?" Max asked.

Harlan Caldwell suddenly looked stern-faced. "What's that you detective fellows say? The killer is someone who had the motive, means and opportunity. Well it seems to people in the club that pretty near everyone had the opportunity at that dance. Arsenic is easy to find, so I guess you can say everyone had the means as well. That leaves only motive."

"So who had the motive?" Max asked.

Harlan Caldwell put his hat on and guided Darlene to the door. As he opened it, he turned back to Max and Allison.

"Only two people: Eva Dawkins and Peter Hamilton. Good evening."

John Reisinger

Chapter 7

Islanders

Green manicured lawns and sprawling painted "cottages" touched with long morning shadows gleamed in the rays of the rising sun as Jekyll Island awoke to another day. Allison looked out the window and saw the castle-like bulk of the club building to her right and the dock on the water straight ahead. Spanish moss hanging like gray beards from the branches of stately oaks swayed slightly in the soft breezes. A few couples strolled on the paths looking like a painting come to life.

"Now why can't St Michaels look like this in the morning?" she said, shaking her head.

Max sat at a small table making notes. "What was that?"

She turned away from the window. "I have to admit; if you have to get murdered, you could hardly find a nicer place for it. So much better than a squalid alley or a vacant lot. So what's on your agenda for today?"

Max looked up. "I have a list of the Dawkins' friends and neighbors. I thought I'd look them up and see what they know. First, however, I need to have another chat with Eva about that argument she had with her husband just before he was murdered. I also want to look up this Jason Williams, the staff member who discovered the body. How about you?"

"I thought I'd talk to some of the women about life at the club. It might make a good magazine article. I'll never get this chance again. Besides, I might learn something to help with the case."

"That's the spirit. But don't hesitate to chat up the men as well. Somehow most men that meet you get struck with the overwhelming desire to tell all."

Allison smiled. "I guess I'm just a good listener."

After a quick breakfast at the clubhouse under the curious eyes of other club members, Max and Allison split up. Max walked toward the staff buildings behind the club in search of Jason Williams, the handyman who discovered the body. The road from the pier went between the clubhouse and the Sans Souci and continued between two rows of small wooden buildings that were clearly shops and other buildings used by the staff. As he strolled down the lane, he passed staff members coming and going. Some, such as kitchen help and chauffeurs wore uniforms, while others seemed to be dressed in neat work clothes. He got several curious glances, but no one stopped to talk.

"Ah, Max. There you are! Stop in here a minute. There are some fellows here you should meet."

Max looked around and saw Bwana Pete in the company of two other men standing just inside the door of a small building that looked like a shop. He strolled over and found himself in a one-room shed of sorts. The walls were hung with various pelts and several baskets of long feathers stood in a corner. In the center of the room was a table where Bwana Pete had been talking to the two other men.

"Max, this is Alan McHale. Alan's the gamekeeper for the club."

The gamekeeper looked to be in his forties. He was sandy-haired, burly, and red faced, as if embarrassed about something. Max noticed a pronounced limp as the man stepped forward.

"Glad to meet you, Mr. Hurlock. Mr. Hamilton was telling us all about you and how you saw right through him last night. You'd probably be a good hunter."

"Well, I.."

"Oh, and this is my assistant, Harold Falstaff."

The assistant had bushy dark hair and a similar mustache. In spite of Falstaff's horn-rimmed glasses, Max could clearly see the beginnings of crow's feet at the corners of his eyes as he smiled eagerly.

"We were just talking of organizing a wild pig hunt. What do you say?"

"Well, I really don't have a lot of time, but.."

"We can do a short hunt, maybe two or three hours, tops. You won't regret it."

"I don't have a hunting rifle with me."

"Not to worry," said Bwana Pete. "Alan here has several sporters for loan. I think we can fit you up with a .303 Enfield. It's converted from the British infantry rifle. The bolt action cocks as you're pushing the bolt forward instead on as you pull it up. That makes it easier to keep the sights on an animal while you're setting up a second shot."

"Why would I need a second shot?" Max deadpanned. The others laughed.

"I think Mr. Hurlock is a natural," McHale laughed. "He already has the bragging down pat."

"Well, you let me know when and we'll see," said Max. "Is there really that much game on the island?"

"What do you mean?" said McHale.

"The island is only about eight miles long," said Max, but the club employs not only a gamekeeper but an assistant. How come?"

"Two reasons, Mr. Hurlock," McHale said. "First off, the gamekeeper not only provides sport, but meat for the club's table. They love fresh game and they save a lot of uncertainty and expense by not having to ship so much meat to the island. As a side benefit, we collect fancy feathers from the birds we shoot." He motioned to the baskets of feathers Max had already noticed. "Half the fashionable feathers you'll see in the ladies' hats around here are from birds we shot."

Max nodded. "I see. What is the other reason?"

"It's to help me out. I've been the gamekeeper for years, usually alone. During the war, however, I picked up some shrapnel in my leg and I can't get around as well as I used to. Since then I've had a series of assistants. I couldn't get along without Harold here. He's eager and hard working. Plus he's an old farm boy so he has a feel for animals and wild game."

Harold Falstaff beamed proudly. "You want to see that Enfield, Mr. Hurlock? It's one pretty rifle."

"Maybe later. I've got to get going. By the way, were any of you near the dance when Bradley Dawkins was killed?"

McHale shook his head. "I was home in bed. The shrapnel wound was acting up a bit and when that happens, rest usually does the trick. I didn't hear about it until the next day."

"I was here cleaning some pelts we shot that day," said Falstaff. "I closed up around nine or so and went and sat by that tree outside listening to the music from the dance. Then I went home maybe a half-hour or so later. I didn't hear about what happened until the next day either."

"While you were sitting there, did you see anyone going to or from the veranda?"

Falstaff shook his head. "No. There's not many people up and about that time of night around here. Everyone was either at the dance or home getting ready for bed."

"Did either of you have any dealings with Bradley Dawkins?" Max asked.

"Sure," said McHale. "He hunted occasionally, and he stopped by to pick up some feathers for his wife once in a while. Seemed like a nice fellow. Other than that, I really didn't know him very well."

Falstaff nodded agreement. "I used to see him strolling a lot, and he always said hello, but that was about it. I still can't believe Mrs. Daw..er, I mean *someone* wanted to kill him."

"Interesting slip of the tongue," Max remarked.

Falstaff reddened and started stammering. "Gee, I'm sorry, Mr. Hurlock. I didn't mean...well it's just that everybody is saying that...I mean.."

"It's all right," said Max. "A lot of tongues seem to be slipping in that direction around here."

Allison couldn't get over the profusion of gnarled oak trees everywhere and the garlands of Spanish moss hanging from their branches. When she added in the palmetto palms scattered about and rustling in the wind, she felt as if she had been transported to some beautiful, but alien world.

She strolled up the main street, notebook in hand and paused several times to make notes. Soon she came to the attention of a group of women having tea on the lawn of a mansion with a sign out front that said Goodyear Cottage. Several servants in white linen jackets scurried about to keep the tea flowing, but what Allison noticed most was a rich looking oriental carpet laid out on the lawn.

"You there!" one of the ladies cried. "Young lady! Would you come here please?"

The tone, though a bit peremptory, was friendly enough, so Allison strolled over. There were five women dressed for a garden party and sitting in wooden lawn chairs with several tables laden with tea and cakes. Apparently the flapper look had not yet penetrated the island very deeply, for the women wore ankle length white dresses and broad brimmed "garden" hats decorated with lace and feathers. Allison made no effort to conceal or even close her notebook, figuring it would be a conversation starter.

"Are you a reporter, young lady?" one of the older ones asked.

Allison smiled. "Not at all. My name is Allison Hurlock and I am making notes for a possible magazine article."

"Oooh; a magazine article," several of them cooed.

"Exactly what sort of an article?" the oldest one asked in a stern tone.

"I'm not sure just yet, but I think an article on the club might be of great interest to readers everywhere."

The women looked at each other.

"Something telling the fascinating history of the club, what it's like in season."

There was still no response from the lawn party. The ladies simply sat staring at Allison, though whether from hostility or fascination she couldn't tell.

"..and maybe something about local hospitality."

The women looked at each other, and then several of them suddenly remembered their manners and asked Allison to sit with them. She found and empty wicker chair and obliged.

"And what magazine do you work for, Allison?"

"I'm a freelancer, but I've written for Modern Girls, Southern Life, American Family, and several others."

"Thank heavens," one of them said, reclining in her chair in relief. "I was afraid you were going to say National Geographic."

"Do have some tea, Allison," said a small woman with jet-black hair and pince-nez glasses on a black ribbon. "I am Nancy McCormick. This is Henrietta Morrison, Maggie Davis, Clarice Bailey, and this rather stern lady is Theresa Woodson."

Allison recognized Clarice Bailey as the cold beauty from the club dining room the night before.

Theresa Woodson looked annoyed. She was a formidable looking older woman, with severely coifed gray hair and several ropes of pearls looped around her neck and draping over an ample bosom. Allison half expected her to produce a lorgnette and peer at her disapprovingly through it. "I'm simply trying to find out why a complete stranger should be wandering around spying on us. This is a private club for a reason. Since when do we invite magazine writers to visit?"

"A reasonable question, Mrs. Woodson," Allison said. "The answer is simple. I am here with my husband, Maxwell as guests of Mrs. Dawkins."

Everyone froze and looked at Allison as if she had just belched out loud. Finally, Mrs. Woodson broke the frosty silence.

"As guests of Mrs. Dawkins? I thought I saw you with her last night at the club. I assume you are aware that Mrs. Dawkins has just murdered her husband?"

Allison smiled sweetly. "I'm aware that her husband was apparently murdered, but I was certainly not aware that there has been a trial of Mrs. Dawkins, let alone a conviction."

Nancy McCormick spoke up. "Well, there hasn't, but you must admit it seems likely. I mean, no one else would want to kill poor Bradley."

"Why?" said Allison. "Was he well liked on the island?"

"Oh, he was quite popular," gushed Henrietta Morrison, who was still holding her teacup in midair where she had it when Allison announced she was Mrs. Dawkins's guest. "Bradley was such a dear. And so dashing. He was a war hero, you know. Why, I believe half the women on the island were secretly in love with him."

Allison raised her eyebrows. "What about the other half?"

"They made no secret of it whatsoever," said Nancy McCormick. "Why, Clarice here was especially..." She stopped, suddenly aware that Clarice Bailey was glaring at her through narrowed eyelids.

Clarice Bailey spoke. Her voice was soft and delicate, but had a curious edge of hardness to it, like that of a queen in the habit of ordering executions while having breakfast.

"Nancy was about to say that I was especially close to Bradley Dawkins. Well you might as well know. You'll hear it from someone else soon enough anyway. I met Bradley here at the club the previous winter. We saw a lot of each other..."

"They were practically engaged," Henrietta Morrison added, earning her a frown from Clarice Bailey.

"I wouldn't go quite that far," Clarice continued, "but we were close, and it is quite possible we would have become affianced this season, but that Eva woman got to him first; straight from the steno pool and into the marriage bed. Who knows what revolting things that gold-digger did to turn his head. That was all bad enough, of course, but then she went and killed him...all for the money. And I must say I consider it perfectly foul that you and your husband are here as the guests of a murderess, as if nothing happened. Poor Bradley is barely cold in his grave and you are enjoying the hospitality of the woman who killed him."

"Extraordinary," said Allison, in a level voice. "Do you mean to say that you can read minds; that you somehow know what Eva was thinking?"

"Of course. What she was thinking is so obvious a child could see it."

Allison held her gaze. "Well, then you must know what I'm thinking."

"Never mind all that." Mrs. Woodson was determined not to be distracted. "Why did Mrs. Dawkins invite you when she is at least under suspicion of murder?"

Allison picked up a cup of tea and took a sip before answering, leaving the circle of ladies sitting in silent anticipation.

"My husband Max is an investigator. Mrs. Dawkins asked him to come and see if he could find out the truth about her husband's death."

"That is up to the local authorities," Mrs. Woodson harrumphed.

Allison shrugged. "Officially, yes, but it never hurts to have another set of eyes on the problem. After all, everyone wants the truth to come out, don't they?"

"I doubt that the murderer does," Nancy McCormick said quietly.

"So now we have someone else around here twisting the truth," sneered Clarice Bailey. "I suppose Eva thinks she has covered her tracks sufficiently to fool everyone."

"All nonsense," Mrs. Woodson huffed. "In the end, they will find that Mrs. Dawkins is guilty. That's the truth, pure and simple."

"Well, we will see," said Allison, "but remember what the late Oscar Wilde said; the truth is rarely pure and never simple."

"Wasn't Mr. Wilde jailed for indecency?" said Mrs. Woodson, with obvious distaste.

"He was," said Allison. "His works were not."

Nancy McCormick spoke up. "Mrs. Hurlock, do you and your husband really believe Mrs. Dawkins might actually be innocent of this terrible crime?"

"Yes," chimed in Maggie Davis. "Could someone else have done it?"

"Oh, this is just like those terrible mystery novels one reads about," said Henrietta Morrison, excitedly. Just when it looks like one person did it, the detective proves it was someone else altogether!"

Maggie Davis jumped back into the conversation. "Yes, it turns out to be a long lost twin,,"

"Or one of the servants!"

Suddenly everyone was talking at once, excited by the prospect of a juicy mystery in their midst. Mrs. Woodson clapped her hands to stifle the enthusiasm.

"May I remind you ladies that there is a reason those dreadful mystery novels are classified as fiction? In the real world, murder is a sordid business, and usually the perpetrator is obvious. I seriously doubt that there will be any long lost twins, killers in disguise or homicidal butlers to come to Mrs. Dawkins's rescue."

Allison looked around at the sea of disappointed faces and smiled. "I'm afraid Mrs. Woodson might be right in the end, but my husband and the police will explore all the evidence first. If Mrs. Dawkins turns out to be the killer, so be it, but it's only fair to investigate all the possibilities before coming to such a conclusion."

"I suppose if you want to postpone the inevitable..." mumbled Clarice Bailey, daintily sipping a cup of tea.

Henrietta Morrison spoke up in a quiet voice. "Well, if your husband wishes to investigate other possibilities, he might take a look at Mr. Hamilton."

Allison looked at her. "You mean Bwana Pete? Why do you say that?"

Henrietta Morrison looked from side to side, as if afraid of spies lurking in the hedges.

"Well, just a few nights before Bradley Dawkins was killed, I saw Eva Dawkins and Mr. Hamilton strolling along by the water. It was twilight, but I saw it quite distinctly. They stopped and embraced."

In the silence that followed, Mrs. Woodson spoke up in a somewhat more conciliatory tone. "Now, Mrs. Hurlock...may I call you Allison? I think I need to take you under my wing, so to speak. With all this loose talk and speculation about, I wouldn't want you to get the wrong impression and make us look provincial in whatever article you write."

Allison hesitated. "Oh, I wouldn't want to trouble you, Mrs. Woodson, but I wouldn't mind someone taking me on a tour of this lovely place."

"Very well," said Mrs. Woodson, "but I'm afraid I have engagements for the next two days."

"I can take you," said Nancy McCormick, earning a frown from Mrs. Woodson. "How about at one today? We can meet for lunch at the club."

Allison rose to leave. "I'll look forward to it. Mrs. Woodson, I'll keep you informed of whatever I find out. May I call on you when I have questions or problems?"

Mrs. Woodson was somewhat appeased. "Of course, my dear. I'll be glad to help you understand our little club."

I think I'm already starting to, Allison thought.

"Ladies, I understand your views" she said, rising, "but I can promise you that my husband will pursue only the truth and do it scrupulously. If Eva Dawkins really did kill her husband, Max will be the one to prove it."

"Let us hope so," Clarice Bailey said. "People will be watching."

After Max left the gamekeeper's shed, he strolled down the path leading further away from the water and the clubhouse. Soon he came to a maintenance shop and poked his head in. The room was well lit and split by a long table. Behind the bench were shelves with tools and a row of old books. On the table, two black men were busy repairing an ornate wooden bench. The older man wiped his hands on a cloth and greeted Max. He had the beginnings of gray hair around his temples and a small, trim mustache.

"Mornin' Suh. What do you need fixed? We're just finishin' this bench."

Max looked at the bench. It was decorated with rich carvings.

"You carved that?" he asked.

The man laughed. "Oh, no suh. We jus' fixed it. See, the leg there was loose and we had to fit it up with some dowels and glue. 'Course, the tricky part was doin' it so's the repair don't show."

Max nodded. "Good work. The repair is almost invisible. Do you usually fix furniture?"

"No, we usually just keep the buildings and piers in good shape, but this is for Miz Woodson."

"I see," Max replied. "Well, I'm looking for a Mr. Williams."

The man smiled. "That's me; Jason Williams at your service. You must be Mr. Hurlock."

Max was startled. "You know who I am?"

Williams chuckled. "My cousin works in the dining room. Ain't much 'round here that's secret for long."

"I'll be getting' over to the dock to repair that plank, Jason," the younger man said. Williams nodded and the other man left.

"So this is your shop?" Max asked.

"Well, it's the club's shop, but Mr. Grob the manager pretty much lets me take care of it. Anything needs fixing or buildin' round here, they all calls for Jason. Yessuh, I suppose I done fixed near every building round here. Why there was this one ol' place got a leakin' roof. Well, I says to myself..."

"All right," Max interrupted. "You can drop the act, Williams. I'm on to you. You're an intelligent and well-read man. There's no need to talk like you're a field hand."

Williams, who had been smiling, suddenly became serious. "Well, seems you really are a detective, Mr. Hurlock. How in the world did you know?"

"Mrs. Dawkins told me you had long conversations with Mr. Dawkins before he was killed. There's only so much maintenance any house needs, so what could those conversations be about? Something no doubt of interest to you both, but what could that be? Then I noticed those books on that shelf in the back. I can't read all the titles from here, but I can make out a biography of George Washington and a copy of Plato's Republic. I'm betting those are your books and there are more where they came from. What's more, I'll bet Bradley Dawkins was one of the few people you could discuss those books with and that's what the long conversations were about."

Jason Williams shook his head. "They said you were a detective and they weren't fooling. Yes, it's true. I read when I can to improve my mind. Mr. Dawkins came in and saw me reading Shakespeare's Julius Caesar one day and said 'He reads much. He is a great observer, and he looks quite through the deeds of men.' I was amazed; that was a direct quote. Well, we got to talking and it seems he was a big reader as well. He used to read a lot when he was in the marines and stationed in Haiti for a while after he got back from France. Julius Caesar was one of his favorites and he had half of it memorized. Well, from then on, he'd stop by every week or so and say 'Williams, what are you reading?' Most times it was something he'd read too, so we'd have a long talk about it. I really miss those talks."

Max nodded.

"See, being a Negro round these parts means your opportunities are limited. The best I can hope for is to become a clerk or teacher in a colored school somewhere and that doesn't pay as well as this. Well, in the off season I can read the books in the club library, and they give me any of the old ones they're throwing out. So I do my job here and travel the world when I read. It's not a bad life. I figure I've been able to see and know things most of the club members never will, even with all their money."

"Well, Mr. Williams," said Max, "I for one am very interested in the things you've seen and know, and I don't mean from books. Tell me about the night you found Bradley Dawkins after he had been poisoned."

Williams looked grim. He exhaled softly and sat down on a wooden chair as if suddenly weary.

"That was a terrible thing, Mr. Hurlock; it really was. That Mr. Dawkins was a good man. Everybody liked him. There are a few around here I could name that are nice folks to their friends, but mean to everyone else. Mr. Dawkins was good with everybody. Now he's dead. It's a dirty shame."

"So will you tell me about it?"

Williams stood up and put on a hat. "Why don't I show you? It's not very far away."

After a short walk, they came to the front veranda of the clubhouse, the same veranda where the sheriff had been waiting the night before. The wooden veranda was about eight feet above the ground. As they approached, Williams stopped on the gravel pathway.

"The dances here are usually held in the dining room up there off the main lobby. It was around 10:30 or maybe a little after. I'd been at home but came back to the shop to put another coat of varnish on a length of ship's railing I was finishing. That way it would have two coats all dried by the morning. Anyway, I heard the music from the club and thought I'd take me a look. You can see how close it is. I got near the porch and stood about here, under that light." He indicated a Victorian-looking streetlight by the side of the path.

"I had a good view of the people through the windows and I could hear the music just fine. They had just finished up playing the Charleston. I listen to the phonograph records in the off season, too, so I recognized it, even though the band seemed to have their own version of it. Anyway, standing here under the light, I guess I was in plain view because I heard someone speak my name. I looked up at the porch and saw someone slumped in a chair. I couldn't tell who it was at first, since the veranda was pretty dark compared to the bright lights of the dining room next to it, but it sounded like Mr. Dawkins. His voice was all scratchy, like he was sick or in pain, so I wasn't sure."

Max nodded and they walked up the stairs to the veranda. In the daylight, Max noticed it was large and had a sweeping view of the river. Several white painted wicker chairs stood empty by the railing. Williams indicated one of the chairs.

"I went up to see what he wanted and he slumped down in this chair even more just as I got there. I noticed there was a half-empty cup of coffee on the arm of the chair and another one underneath. It was Mr. Dawkins all right, and he looked real sick. I could see he was in a bad way, so I bent down and told him I was going for help."

"He was still alive?"

"Just barely. I turned to run in and get help when Mr. Dawkins spoke one last time."

"He spoke? What did he say?"

"His voice was faint and sort of rough and scratchy, so it was hard to make out, what with the wind and all, but he only said one word: 'cocoa'."

Chapter 8

Last words

"Cocoa? Are you certain that's what he said? Could you have misunderstood him?"

"Like I said, his words were hard to make out, so I can't be certain, but that's sure what it sounded like to me."

"Had he been drinking cocoa?"

Williams shook his head. "He only had two cups and there was coffee in both. I smelled them both. I thought maybe there was something in the cups that had made him sick, but it just smelled like coffee to me. It wasn't cocoa, that's for sure. Besides, I remember one time he told me he didn't care for chocolate."

"Cocoa. What could that mean? Does that fit in with anything you discussed with him from one the books?"

Williams shook his head slowly. "Not unless he was reading a cook book I didn't know about. No, Mr. Hurlock; I've been wracking my brain trying to think of what it might mean, but I have no idea."

"Did you tell this to the sheriff?"

"I told him, and he said not to tell anybody. But I figure I should tell you since you're investigating too."

"What did the sheriff think of the word?"

"When I told him, he says I must have misunderstood. He figures what Mr. Dawkins really said was 'go, go', meaning go get help."

"Is that possible?"

Williams sighed. "He might be right at that. It sounds similar, and go, go sure makes more sense than cocoa. Either way, it's not much help, is it?"

"No, not at this point," Max had to admit. "So then what happened?"

"I went to get help, but just as I got to the door of the dining room, Mrs. Dawkins and Mr. Hamilton were just coming out. I told them Mr. Dawkins was sick and they should get a doctor. They called out to Dr. Culver in the dining room then went to Mr. Dawkins's side, but he was dead by that time. A few seconds later, people started coming out and gathering round. Everything got real excited after that."

"I can imagine," said Max. "Do you know anyone on the island that had a grudge against Mr. Dawkins?"

"No, but then I don't know all of the feelings of the members. All I can tell you is that I never heard anyone bad-mouthing him."

"How about Mr. Hamilton? Do you think he has an interest in Mrs. Dawkins?"

Williams looked wary. "Oh, I don't get involved in gossip, Mr. Hurlock. I'm just glad Mrs. Dawkins has someone to look after her now that her husband is gone."

"I appreciate your diplomacy," said Max, "but I want to find out who killed Mr. Dawkins and if you have some information that would help, I need to know about it."

Williams was unshaken. "I understand, Mr. Hurlock. I'll do what I can, but I can't be spreading rumors about club members. There's plenty of other folks doing that already."

Max looked around the veranda again. "Fair enough. All right, if you hear anything or think of anything else, you let me know. All right?"

"Of course."

Williams walked back toward the maintenance shop while Max stood on the veranda thinking about the night Bradley Dawkins died. Max was lost in thought when a voice called to him. "You there. Mr. Hurlock!"

Max turned to see Robert Woodson coming up the walk from Pier Street dressed in a business suit and looking annoyed. He soon caught up to Max.

"You are that Hurlock fellow, aren't you?"

"All my life," Max assured him.

"My name's Woodson and I'm one of the directors of the club. I believe I have a responsibility to ask just what your business is on the island."

"Max Hurlock; pleased to meet you. It's no secret what I'm doing here. I'm a guest of Mrs. Dawkins and I am looking into the circumstances surrounding her husband's tragic death."

"We already have the local sheriff doing that, sir. Are you a private detective?"

"I'm an investigator," Max explained for what was not the first time. "I assemble the facts as I find them. I am not trying to prove or disprove anything at this point."

"But to what purpose? The local sheriff has the situation in hand. Do you expect to come to some different conclusion?"

"At this point I have no idea, but if I do then we'll just have to see who has the better evidence. I'm sure you all want this investigated as thoroughly as possible, so having another perspective can't hurt."

"Well, don't expect to give me the third degree. I don't have to answer any questions from an outside amateur and I don't intend to. I'll have no part in spreading rumors, or helping anyone else spread rumors."

There was that reference to rumors again. Max decided to try a little finesse.

"A little late for that, I'm afraid," Max said with a faint smile. "Someone has already told me about...well, you know."

Woodson looked wary. "Do you mean to tell me..."

"I hear things. It's part of the job." Actually, Max had heard nothing about Woodson, but thought he'd cast some bait and see if he got a bite.

Woodson was flustered. "Good God; are they talking about it to you, too? It's bad enough I have to suffer that fool sheriff, but.."

"I'm afraid so," Max said sympathetically. "You can't really afford to dismiss all rumors, though. The strange thing about rumors is that they're sometimes true."

Woodson frowned and turned a somewhat deep shade of pink. He removed a handkerchief and mopped his brow, mumbling to himself.

"All right, Hurlock. You might as well hear the proper story at least. It's true I had an argument with Brad Dawkins two days before he was murdered, and a rather loud one at that, but it had nothing to do with what came afterwards. I was as flabbergasted as anyone."

Max nodded. "Well, you know how people talk. They'll take any little thing and stretch it. By the way, what was the argument about, exactly? Someone said it was money." Max had no idea what the argument was about since this was the first he had heard there even was an argument, but money seemed likely.

"I'd rather not say. You can be assured, however, that it did not have any bearing on the murder. It was just a disagreement between club members."

"A loud disagreement?"

"Let's just say it was spirited. Still, gentlemen can disagree and remain friends."

"Of course," Max agreed. "It just looks a bit awkward when one turns up dead afterwards."

"Mr. Hurlock, since you are a guest of a club member, you have every right to remain here, but I'd advise you to be careful. There are laws against slander and I do not intend to allow loose tongues to sully my good reputation. Good day."

Woodson stalked off, leaving Max to wonder just what the loud argument had been about.

Allison met Max outside the clubhouse on the croquet lawn. She flagged him down before he could get to the steps to the club dining room.

"Max; over here."

"Ah, there you are, Allison. Ready for lunch?"

"Not today, Max," she replied in a whisper. I have a date with Nancy McCormick. We're having lunch, and then she's taking me on a tour of the club."

Max nodded appreciatively. "Good work. One day and you've already punctured the bubble that seems to surround this place. Maybe you can find out something useful."

"I already have," she replied. "Mrs. Dawkins and Bwana Pete were seen embracing just a week before Bradley Dawkins was poisoned. It seems to be common knowledge."

"That doesn't sound too good for my client. Maybe I should insist on payment in advance."

"Just one more little thing she omitted to tell us, I suppose."

"I found out something as well," said Max. "It seems Bradley Dawkins had a loud argument with Robert Woodson just two nights before the murder."

"Interesting. What about?"

Max's face fell. "I don't know. Woodson wouldn't say."

"Too bad. Well, I have to go. Maybe Nancy McCormick might know. See you at dinner."

"I wish I had a photograph of the look on Theresa Woodson's face when you strolled by today," said Nancy McCormick over her third glass of wine. "She doesn't like strangers of any kind on the island, let alone one who shows up asking questions."

Allison sipped a cup of tea. "But why? She seems almost belligerently respectable. She didn't strike me as a woman with guilty secrets."

"Oh, it's not *her* secrets she's worried about," Nancy chuckled. "It's the isolation of the club."

"The isolation?"

"She's afraid that any publicity and especially any scandal could undermine the club's privacy from the rest of the world. After all, that's the whole reason for the club in the first place. The fact that her husband is one of the club directors this year makes it even more important to her."

Allison nodded. "But as this is a private club on an island, it seems unlikely they'll be overrun with curiosity seekers."

"Probably, but the less said to the outside world the better. If you're ready for that tour, you'll see what I mean."

"Tally ho."

"The island's plantation economy was wrecked in the Civil War and had never recovered, and the previous owner wanted out, so some New York businessmen bought the island for a winter retreat. That was in 1888 and was the start of the club. Soon they attracted more members and set up the club building and hired the help. In a few years, the Jekyll Island Club became the place to be for wealthy people who didn't want all the flashy balls and obligations of Newport or Bar Harbor. Since the entire island is owned by the club, it's private property and casual visitors aren't allowed. That's why you may have noticed a cool reception when you arrived."

"Oh, it wasn't that bad," Allison laughed, "but it wasn't exactly warm either."

"So here we are. That's the Sans Souci as you already know," said Nancy McCormick. "It's a lovely place. They built it so that members would have a place to stay while waiting for their cottages to be built."

"Not exactly roughing it," said Allison. "Our apartment is a lot more luxurious than our house back in Maryland. The furnishings look like they're all antiques, and there's a vase in the sitting room that looks like it belongs in the palace of a Chinese Emperor"

Nancy smiled. "That's probably where they got it. Bradley Dawkins's father was at the siege of Peking during the Boxer Rebellion on 1900. I understand he picked up a few souvenirs."

"Did you know Bradley very well?"

"Oh, well enough, I suppose. Bradley was a dear and most of the women admired him."

"Anyone dislike him?"

But Nancy McCormick just shrugged.

"Now this is Riverview Drive where some of the nicest cottages are located. This is Indian Mound Cottage, home of the Rockefellers (not John D. but his younger brother), then Mistletoe, home of Henry Kyle Porter, a locomotive manufacturer. He died recently, so I suppose it will be sold. Then there's Goodyear Cottage, where we were this morning. The Goodyears are actually in lumber, not rubber as you'd think. Let's see, then there's Moss Cottage, though some call it the Macy Cottage after the family that lives there now, then Pulitzer Cottage. That was built for the publisher, but a coal magnate named Albright lives there now."

Allison was still admiring the cottages. I suppose this is where the grandest cottages are located."

"Oh, I guess that's mostly a matter of taste," said Nancy, "but most people think the grand prize, if there were such a thing, would go to Crane Cottage. That's the white Spanish-looking place just on the other side of the clubhouse."

"Oh, yes,' said Allison," I saw that this morning. It's stunning."

Nancy laughed. "It certainly stunned people around here. The board thought it was too ostentatious and were afraid it would overshadow the clubhouse, so they pressured Richard Crane to tone it down a bit. He removed a marble floor and put in wood, and made some other changes, but it's still the fanciest place here."

"What business is Mr. Crane in?"

"Plumbing fixtures. You know; sinks, bathtubs, toilets."

Allison shook her head. "He must sell an awfully lot of them."

They were approaching the white walls of Crane Cottage, but Nancy was looking ahead. "Now just up the road is Darlene Cottage. Harlan Caldwell named it after his wife to make it up to her for his interest in other women. Poor Darlene has to watch him every minute."

"Does he chase the other members' wives?"

"He doesn't dare or Darlene would strangle him. He was very interested in Eva Dawkins, though."

Allison perked up. "Really? How do you know?"

"I hear things and I see things as well. Eva is a good-looking woman and a lot of fun besides. Harlan Caldwell used to flirt outrageously with her around the club until Darlene saw him and lowered the boom. I didn't see it, but I understand she threatened him. She said if he didn't stay away from Eva Dawkins he would regret it the rest of his life."

"That sounds serious," said Allison. "What do you suppose she meant?"

"Who knows? The funny thing is that this all happened just a few weeks before Bradley Dawkins was killed. Quite a coincidence if you ask me."

Allison stopped and looked at Nancy. "Are you saying there's a connection somehow?"

"All I'm saying is that Darlene Caldwell was mad enough to do something to somebody."

Allison considered this for a moment, then thought of something else.

"How about Clarice Bailey? I understand she had her sights on Bradley as well. Was she mad enough to do something drastic?"

"As far as I can tell, she still is. She had it all figured out. She was going to meet up with Bradley again this season and he was going to ask her to marry him. The only problem was that Eva got there first."

"So Clarice was pretty unhappy, huh?"

"Unhappy? She was spitting fire. She was furious with Eva, of course, but I think she was just as mad at Bradley."

Chapter 9

Around the club

The Jekyll Island Club didn't have an infirmary, but relied on one of its members, Dr. Culver for the occasional medical problem. For more serious ailments, there were doctors and a hospital in Brunswick. Dr. Culver's cottage was one of the smaller ones, but still rambling and comfortable. Max stepped onto the porch and knocked on the door. A woman who appeared to be a housemaid answered. She seemed startled to see someone who was not a club member.

"Oh...Hello. May I help you?"

"Hi. I'm Max Hurlock and I'd like to see Dr. Culver."

The woman was still not up to speed. "What seems to be the problem?"

"Well, you might say I've noticed a symptom and I'm trying to find out what caused it."

"Oh? What symptom exactly?"

"The death of Bradley Dawkins."

"Oh...well, I..."

Mercifully, a thin gray haired man appeared in the doorway. "It's all right, Mary. This gentleman must be the private detective I've heard about." He walked up to Max and extended his hand. "I'm Dr. Joe Culver. Come on in."

Culver led Max into a room toward the back of the house that looked like a rudimentary medical office.

"I expect you want to talk about Brad Dawkins's poisoning?" Culver said when they were settled. The place smelled of equal parts mold and various liniments. A stethoscope was lying casually on the desk, like some exhausted snake.

"I appreciate your cooperation, doctor. As you may have heard, I am investigating at the request of Mrs. Dawkins, but I am only gathering the facts, not trying to prove anything."

Culver nodded. "Ah yes; the scientific method. Most commendable. If more people indulged in the spirit of free inquiry, it would be a better world."

Max nodded. "Amen. Now tell me about what happened when you were called out to check Mr. Dawkins."

"He was still warm, but his vital signs had pretty much shut down. If he wasn't dead he was about an inch away."

"How did you know he'd been poisoned?"

"The symptoms are somewhat similar to a massive coronary, but I noticed his tongue and lips were swollen and there was a bluish tint under his fingernails. That would indicate something highly irritating that upset his metabolism and deprived his blood of oxygen. Also he seemed to be clutching his stomach, his tongue was swollen, and there were traces of redness around his mouth. Poisoning seemed the most likely cause. I suspected arsenic simply because it is so common and easily obtainable."

"Did you test for it later?"

"I'm not set up to do any proper forensic analysis. Most of the year I'm at Johns Hopkins in Baltimore; during the season at Jekyll I usually only deal with minor medical problems, not murder."

"So you couldn't determine what kind of poison was used?" Max asked.

Culver shook his head. "My equipment is fine for cuts, bruises, stomachaches, and even the occasional pregnancy, but that's about it. We don't have much need for crime detection around the island, you see. So I took samples of the coffee and gave them to the sheriff. He's going to have them analyzed by the coroner in Atlanta as part of the autopsy."

"So it might not be arsenic?"

"Very possibly. We'll just have to wait and see."

Max thought a moment. "One more question; if it isn't arsenic, what other kinds of poisons might be available around the island?"

Culver shrugged. "Why limit your attentions to just the island? If the murder was planned in advance, anyone could have brought a small bottle of who-knows-what along with them."

"Has anyone shown an interest in such things around here?"

Culver frowned. "Well, just about a week before Dawkins died, I was talking with Darlene Caldwell and she was asking about poisons and what kinds were the hardest to detect. I asked her why in the world she was asking and she said she was just curious. I sort of forgot about it until you asked."

"What did you tell her?" said Max.

"I told her the only poisoning we've ever had was that time little Billy Clemet ate all those green apples and had to have his stomach pumped last season. She just laughed and said it didn't matter. Then she walked away. Well, Darlene Caldwell reads those mystery stories, and she's interested in things like that. I'm sure it's harmless."

Allison and Nancy McCormick had reached the north side of the residential area and were circling around toward the stables. The day was cool, but pleasant, with a breeze rustling the trees.
"Now that green painted place with the turret is Excelsior Cottage, owned by Robert and Theresa Woodson. It has probably the best landscaping around here. Just look at the Hibiscus and Bougainvillea."
"Looks like they have a gardener to keep it up, too," said Allison. "Well, well. Who is that with him? It looks like Clarice Bailey." Allison gestured toward a trim female figure standing and another figure kneeling by a flowerbed. The woman had her back to them, but the man looked at them briefly. He was dark, with a black mustache and think black hair. After staring at them for a moment, he turned back to the standing female next to him. Nancy shivered.
"That's Sanchez, Mr. Woodson's personal man. He doesn't talk much and smiles even less. Rumor has it that Mr. Woodson picked him up in Cuba while he was down there last year. He's a hard worker and extremely loyal and protective of the Woodsons, but he gives me the creeps."
"But why would Clarice talk to a gardener? It doesn't seem like her style."
"Oh, she does have an interest in growing flowers, and she stops to ask his advice occasionally. And since she also likes to play with men the way a cat plays with a mouse, by talking to him she can indulge both her interests."
Allison nodded. "I see. Very efficient."

They kept walking.

"Here's the stable. Some of the members bring horses down and keep them here, along with carriages and such. We don't have one ourselves. They're too much of a bother."

"And what is that area back there through the woods; the one with the rows of red houses?" asked Allison.

"That's Red Row, where most of the help lives, the married ones at least. Mr. Grob, the club manager built them a few years ago. The red color is from the tarpaper that covers the roofs and the walls."

"They look pretty basic," Allison remarked.

"Believe me those places are a lot better than the houses of most of the colored in these parts and a lot of the whites as well. They even have stoves for heat."

"How do the members and the help get along?"

"Very well. We're pretty much the only source of steady employment for miles. Of course most members bring some staff down with them, like the Woodsons with Sanchez over there. The Vanderbilts always had quite a few as well. This causes some friction occasionally between the year-round staff and the big city staff, but it all works out."

"This is a quite a set up," said Allison. "It's almost like some kind of social experiment. There are different types of servants and different types of millionaires all living on an isolated place. The interaction between the wives alone would be a fascinating study based on what I've seen so far."

Nancy laughed. "And how! You still haven't seen Mrs. Woodson at her indignant best. That woman could strip the bark off the trees with one of her disapproving glares."

"She seemed nice enough after a while today. She offered to take me under her wing."

"...said the spider to the fly. I think she was just trying to put a leash on you. She's not well disposed toward outsiders."

Perhaps better than Clarice Bailey, at any rate," said Allison.

Nancy chuckled. "Oh, yes. Clarice has always been a head turner and is used to men falling all over her. She'll never forgive Eva for snatching Bradley away from her."

"It doesn't sound like she'll ever forgive me either," said Allison.

"Probably not. She almost had Bradley in her clutches last season, but then Eva came along. She pretty much led the whispering campaign against Eva around here...claimed she was a gold digger."

"I suppose it's easy to look down on someone else as being a gold digger when you've already got plenty of gold yourself," said Allison.

"You said it. I'm surprised Clarice didn't get one of the servants to do it for her. Now she's hell bent on seeing Eva sent up the river."

They came to an ornate wooden bench under the shade of a large oak. They sat down under a waving beard of Spanish moss. Around them club members were strolling and servants were bustling back and forth on various errands.

"How about the others?" Allison asked.

"Well, you know about the Caldwells and the Woodsons. Millie and Phillip Hester are friends of Eva's even after the murder. They seem to have this curious idea that Eva is innocent until proven guilty."

"Oh? Is that a radical concept around here?"

"No, of course not. It's just that things do look rather black for Eva Dawkins at the moment. Besides, Phillip Hester has been trying to get a piece of Bradley Dawkins's business all winter. Being friendly with Eva doesn't hurt, especially now that Bradley is dead."

"What is Mr. Dawkins's business exactly?"

"He builds and owns some hotels located near railroad terminals and new roads. He does a booming business with long distance passengers, business travelers, etc. Phillip Hester's bank does financing of commercial construction. He'd love the finance some of Dawkins's hotels."

"So maybe he has a chance with Bradley gone?"

Nancy McCormick shrugged. "Who knows? The point is that there are a lot of conflicting little dramas going on around here."

As they sat contemplating the dramas, Bwana Pete sputtered by in his red bug. He waved, but didn't stop.

Little dramas indeed, Allison thought.

The section of lawn that meandered along the river and beneath the trees was a popular promenade for the Jekyll Island Club members, and it was there that Max spotted the Caldwells. As he started in their direction, however, he heard a voice behind him.

"Mistah Hurlock."

Max turned to see the familiar figure of Sheriff McCoy on his way up from the boat dock.

"Afternoon, Sheriff," said Max. "Any new developments in the case?"

The sheriff pushed his hat back on his head and regarded Max for a moment. "I'll bet you been nosin' around the club some, haven't you?"

"Of course," said Max. "I told you I'm trying to find out what happened. Naturally I'd be glad to share any information I come across."

"And what information would that be?"

Max told him of his conversation with Jason Williams and the 'cocoa' remark. McCoy was unimpressed.

"I heard that story, too, but I ain't bitin'. Now that Williams seems like he's level-headed, but he admitted the word wasn't all that clear. I figure Dawkins said go, go, not cocoa."

Max nodded. "Well, I admit that makes more sense, still, it's something to keep in mind. Now maybe you can tell me something. Is the autopsy done?"

McCoy nodded. "Yup. Got me the report right here. I was on my way to discuss it with Miz. Dawkins. It says Mr. Dawkins died by poisoning. Now that there's no doubt it was murder, I also got me a subpoena for Miz Dawkins to testify at the hearing. It's at noon tomorrow at the Brunswick courthouse. You can come along if you'd like, long as you don't interfere."

They set off for Osage Cottage along the riverfront.

"I thought you weren't going to arrest her as long as I was here?" Max protested.

"It's not an arrest, just a way to make sure she appears at the hearing tomorrow."

"So did they determine what poison was used?"

"Now that's a little mystery of its own," McCoy replied. "Seems it wasn't arsenic, but the coroner wasn't sure just what it was. He said it looked like some sort of toxin from a plant, but he was jiggered if he could tell which one. He's lookin' for some other chemist who's more familiar with that sort of thing."

"How about Edward Heinrich?" Max suggested.

"Who?"

"He's a chemistry professor at the University of California. From what I've read he's the best criminal analyst in the country. Maybe if you have enough samples left he could figure out what poison was used."

"Now don't you worry none. We got our own local boys can figure it out. This is a job for professionals."

"But I can help.."

"Don't need any help. No offense, Mistah Hurlock, but too many folks read a few detective stories and think they can do just as well. They don't realize it ain't all that cut and dried, so they think they can tell me my job. Most of 'em couldn't track a muddy hound dog 'cross a white linoleum floor. They'd waste a lot of my time iffin I'd let 'em."

"Sheriff McCoy!" came a voice in the distance. They turned and saw a figure running up from the boat pier.

"That looks like 'ol Dewey, one of my deputies. Now what's he doing here?"

A man with a floppy hat and a badge caught up to them.

"Sheriff, I grabbed another boat right after you left. You got to get back right away."

"Get back? I just got here and I gotta subpoena to serve. What's goin' on?"

The man gasped to catch his breath. "We got a call from somebody over on Bodie Road by the dump. Seems there's a dismembered body out there. Right now they only found the hand, but the rest is sure to be there. What's more, the hand's been surgically removed; cut at the wrist just as clean as you like. Looks like it's been there a while, too. It's all black and shriveled like. You got to get out there quick."

Max thought about it a minute, then smiled. "Looks like you got a real crime wave going here, sheriff."

The sheriff looked at him. "Ain't got time to jabber with an amateur. I got some serious work to do. Here's the subpoena. You give it to Miz Dawkins, seein' as how you're her representative and all. Otherwise, I'll have to come back to arrest her if'n she don't show." He turned toward the pier and started to walk away. Max decided the time had come to try a long shot. He had a strong feeling about what that "hand" really was and he prayed he was right.

"I wouldn't be in too big a rush, sheriff," said Max, calling after them. "It's not a human hand."

The sheriff and the deputy stopped in their tracks and turned back toward Max. The sheriff's face had an expression that was halfway between disbelief and outrage.

"What?"

"I said that thing they found is not a human hand."

"Not a... And just what do you think it is?"

Max didn't reply. Instead he took out a piece of paper from his pocket and wrote on it. Then he fumbled in his jacket pocket. "Now I think I have.. ah here it is."

Max produced an envelope, put the paper inside and sealed it. He handed it to the sheriff.

"Now when you get there and investigate, what you will find is written on the paper inside. Please, no peeking before then. Oh, and there's no dismembered body, either. Sorry."

The sheriff grabbed the envelope, stuffed it in his pocket, and turned back toward the pier shaking his head.

"Yankees."

Max just smiled.

Allison left Nancy McCormick and started wandering on her own. She saw Max talking with the sheriff and headed that way, arriving just in time to hear the tail end of the conversation without being noticed by the sheriff. As the sheriff stalked away, Allison came up alongside Max watching him go.

"So what was that all about? If you're still trying to charm the local constabulary, you might want to polish your technique."

Max turned to her. "Oh, I just went way out on a limb with a deduction."

"Why?"

"If I'm right, the sheriff should be so amazed he'll keep me informed of every detail of his investigation just to get my opinion."

"And if you're wrong?"

"Then I'm going to look very foolish."

Allison shook her head. "That's my Max; the riverboat gambler spinning the wheel with all his chips on the red."

"McCoy came to subpoena Eva Dawkins for the hearing tomorrow, but an emergency on shore diverted him. The hearing will determine if they should proceed to a trial."

"What actual evidence do they have against her?"

"Other than the finding of murder by poison, I doubt they have very much, but I don't know at this point. McCoy doesn't want to tell me anything. That's why I took a chance to try to dazzle him and get him to open up."

"You should talk to the ladies as I have," said Allison. "They'll talk all day long. I turned up three more suspects without even trying."

"Oh? And who are they?"

"Phillip Hester wanted to finance Bradley Dawkins's hotels, but Bradley was cool to the idea.

Maybe Hester thought he'd have better luck with Eva with Bradley out of the way."

"Interesting," said Max. "Who else?"

"The ever-charming Clarice Bailey, who seems to be living proof that sometimes beauty isn't even skin deep, was counting on luring Bradley to the altar this season. When she found out someone from the steno pool beat her to the punch it made her feel like a dog whose bone was taken away. She could have wanted to poison either one of them."

"Delightful. Money can't buy happiness, but it can sure spread the misery around. Who else?"

"Well, Darlene Caldwell was angry with her husband for his attentions to Eva Dawkins and threatened to make him pay."

"By poisoning Bradley?"

"No, but maybe she was really trying to poison her husband but somehow Bradley Dawkins got the coffee by mistake."

Max nodded. "Maybe, or more likely, she gave Eva poisoned coffee to remove her husband's temptation and Eva gave it to Bradley without knowing it was poisoned. There are all sorts of possibilities."

"So it looks like there are alternative solutions besides Eva Dawkins being the killer. I wouldn't be surprised if we didn't turn up even more possibilities."

"Here's one," said Max. "According to Jason Williams, who first discovered Dawkins in distress, Bradley's dying word was cocoa."

"Cocoa?" said Allison. "Well, I'd hardly want that on my tombstone. What do you suppose he meant?"

Max shrugged his shoulders. "At the moment, I have absolutely no idea."

Chapter 10

Whispers at twilight

The Jekyll Island Club in the late afternoon is a place of great beauty and quiet contemplation. The deepening shadows through the trees and across the marshes alternate with streaks of fading reddish sunlight crossing the green lawns and everything seems to have a softer edge to it. Couples drift along as if floating through the air. The only sound is the soft hissing of the wind in the trees and the occasional sputtering of a passing red bug. In the living room of Osage Cottage, however, the four people meeting ignored the restful scene outside. All were dressed for dinner at the club, with Max and Bwana Pete in black ties, Eva Dawkins in an embroidered yellow silk gown and Allison in a plain blue dress that made her look more like a movie star than ever. No one, however, was feeling hungry.

Eva Dawkins placed the telephone receiver back in the bracket with a sigh.

"Well, that's it. My attorney in Baltimore can't come down, but he says there is nothing we can do to avoid the arrest if the inquest leads to an indictment. He'll call the local judge and see if he can get an expedited bail hearing if that happens, but he's not optimistic. I wonder what the jail is like in Brunswick, Georgia?"

"They always have an inquest or a hearing when there's been a suspicious death," said Max, "but there won't be an indictment if there's no evidence. What you and Bwana Pete have to do is try to reconstruct the events of that night and see if there is another reasonable explanation."

"But, damn it all," said Bwana Pete, "that's what your investigation is supposed to do."

"No it isn't," said Max firmly. "I'm looking for the truth and that takes a little more than one day. Besides, at this point you both know a lot more about what you were doing that night than I do."

"Isn't there anything you've found out that could help us?" Eva asked.

"There are several people here who might have had motives to want Bradley out of the way, but the information I have is pretty vague."

"How about the arsenic?" Bwana Pete asked, snapping his fingers. "Can't we show that Eva had no access to arsenic and kept none in the house?"

Max shook his head. "That wouldn't help. The sheriff said the autopsy determined it wasn't arsenic."

Eva looked interested. "Not arsenic? Then what was it?"

"Some sort of plant poison, apparently. They couldn't tell for sure just what it was beyond that. I went back and checked with Dr. Culver after the sheriff left yesterday and he said there are dozens of poisonous plants on Jekyll Island, plants like Monkshood, Hemlock, or Castor Bean. Most of the plants will make you sick, but not kill you. Of course, a big enough dose..."

"So anyone could have poisoned Bradley?"

"Maybe anyone with a knowledge of plant poisons, but that doesn't narrow it down much, I'm afraid. Eva is still the center of attention."

"A lot of tongues are wagging about Peter and me," said Eva. "I doubt that a court would consider that evidence, but around here it's 'eyewitness testimony'".

"Never the less," said Max cautiously, "a jury might consider that motive enough, especially if you are in the habit of embracing in public."

Eva went pale. She put down her drink and sat up rigidly straight in her chair. "Who said that?"

Max looked at her directly. "It doesn't matter who said it. Is it true?"

Bwana Pete looked deeply into his drink and frowned. He cleared his throat to speak, but Eva beat him to it.

"Max, I don't know if you can understand, but have you ever met someone who is perfectly compatible? Someone who thinks as you do and values the things you value? Someone who almost knows your thoughts and laughs at the same things you do?"

"Yes," said Max. "I married her."

Eva was unfazed. "Of course Bradley was like that. I loved him deeply, but Peter is very similar and I do enjoy his company. Even Bradley perked up when Peter was around. Now that Bradley is gone, I admit I find Peter's presence comforting. I miss having a male presence to depend on. This cottage has an emptiness that is a constant reminder. So yes, I do see Peter frequently, and when things are particularly dark, we embrace occasionally. This is how I cope, and I don't need instruction on how to be a widow from those who have never had to face the prospect."

Max nodded. "Very well put, Mrs. Dawkins, but did you ever embrace <u>before</u> Bradley died?"

"Now, look here, Max," Bwana Pete started, but Eva held up a hand to calm him.

"As a matter of fact, I did. One day a few weeks ago, Bradley was finishing up some work at the cottage and it was a warm afternoon, so I went for a walk along the riverfront under the trees around twilight. As it happens, Peter was sitting on a bench, going through his mail. The Sylvia had just made a run from Brunswick and had dropped off several days' worth of mail at the pier. When Peter saw me he tipped his hat and rose. We walked together as he finished the mail."

"What about the embrace?" Max asked.

"I can explain that," Peter interjected. This time Eva made no move to stop him. "When I was in Africa there was this British chap by the name of Reggie Collingsworth, one of the best hunters on the continent. We got to be good friends and he taught me what I needed to stay alive in the bush country. Anyway, about a month earlier I had gotten a letter from one of the guides. It seemed Collingsworth had been badly mauled by a lion as he was sleeping in his tent. One of the bearers heard the screams and dispatched the lion with a well-placed shot. Turns out it was a lioness that was too old to hunt and was starving. Otherwise she'd have never come right into camp that way. Well, the damage was already done. I'll spare you the details, but even an old injured lion can wreak havoc in a short time and it looked like old Reggie was a goner. They got him to a hospital in Nairobi, but the doctors didn't have much hope. I'd been sick about it for weeks until I got a letter that afternoon."

Bwana Pete paused for dramatic effect. "It was from Reggie himself, sitting up in bed and dashing off letters to his friends to let them know he was all right. I should have known it would take more than a lion to put Reggie out of commission. Well I read the letter out loud as we were walking and I was so happy I grabbed Eva and hugged her. I'm not sure I didn't kiss her as well."

"You did," Eva interjected.

"Well, there it is then," Bwana Pete concluded. "I was overcome by the relief of it. If that's a crime, I'll plead guilty every time."

"Obviously some prying eyes saw the whole thing and mistook relief for lust," said Eva.

Allison sank back in her chair and let out a sigh of relief.

"All right," said Max. "I'll assume that is the sole cause of the speculation at the moment. Now, so far, between Allison and myself, we've turned up several more people with a hint of a motive to want Bradley out of the way. It's all pretty thin, but at this point all we need is enough alternate possibilities to keep you out of jail until I can complete my investigation."

"Fine by me," said Eva, picking up her glass again. "Who are they?"

"First we have the Caldwells. It seems Harlan was attracted to you, Eva, much to his wife Darlene's displeasure. It's a long shot, but Darlene might have poisoned your coffee to remove you as a temptation and you unknowingly gave it to Bradley instead."

Eva laughed. "If that's the best alternative we have I should throw myself on the mercy of the court right now. Harlan Caldwell is attracted to every woman on the island. If his wife is miffed at him it's not because she feels threatened, but because she's tired of him acting like a fool. She's not the murdering type in any event. She can't even bear to poison the mice when they appear."

Max was not too surprised. "Then there's Clarice Bailey, who doesn't seem to possess enough milk of human kindness to lighten a cup of tea. She hasn't forgiven you for getting Bradley before she had a chance to."

Eva chuckled bitterly. "If only she knew. Bradley saw right through her. He once told me there were some women who were beautiful on the outside and rotten on the inside, and that Clarice Bailey was that type of woman. She thinks she's irresistible, but Bradley just wanted to run for the hills when he saw her. He tried to be civil, of course, because Bradley was a gentleman, but he considered her more of a nuisance than anything else."

"That may be, but someone forgot to tell Clarice just how resistible she was to Bradley," said Allison. "Did she ever threaten you?"

"She never spoke enough words to me to threaten me. If looks could kill, however..."

"All right," said Max. "Then we have the Hesters."

"The Hesters?" Eva looked as she was ready to explode. "Good heavens, they're about the most loyal friends I have. Why in the world would you suspect them?"

"I didn't say I suspected anyone," Max explained patiently. "These are simply people that might benefit in some way from Bradley's death."

"Benefit? How in the world would the Hesters benefit?"

"Allison has heard that Phillip Hester has been after Bradley to let his bank finance Bradley's hotel expansions, but that Bradley wasn't interested. With

Bradley out of the way, it could be worth millions to the Hesters and people have killed for far less."

To Max's surprise, Eva did not dismiss this idea out of hand, but looked thoughtful and troubled.

"You know, now that you mention it, Phillip has mentioned the financing several times. Still, that doesn't mean that he did anything wrong."

"Of course not, but it does mean that there are several other people with motives and that's what we have to bring out at the inquest. Then there are the Woodsons."

"Robert and Theresa?" said Eva. "I admit Theresa's a bit imperious at times, but murder? Whatever for?"

"Apparently," said Max, "Robert Woodson had some sort of a loud argument with Bradley shortly before he died. This is not just a rumor; Robert Woodson confirmed it."

"I wasn't aware of that," said Eva. "What was the argument about?"

"Woodson refused to say, but he insisted it had nothing to do with your husband's murder."

Eva sank back in her chair and shook her head. "Jekyll Island is supposed to be a place people come to get away from things like that."

"Bah," said Bwana Pete. "People are people. They don't change their personalities just because they change their address. The tiger doesn't change his stripes wherever he is."

" Say, did you ever bag a tiger on one of those African safaris of yours, Peter?" Max asked offhandedly.

"A tiger?" Bwana Pete looked momentarily confused, then smiled knowingly. "Always deducting, eh, Max? Always checking stories and alibis. Well, that's fine—shows you're on the ball."

"Am I missing something here?" Eva asked.

"Max is testing me," said Bwana Pete. "He knows very well there are no tigers in Africa; they're in India and Southeast Asia. He just wanted to see if I knew. He wanted to find out if I'm a big game hunter or just a fortune hunter."

Max blushed slightly. "I'm afraid he's right. The Germans have a saying that trust is good, but verification is better."

"They would," said Allison.

"Well," said Eva. "You've only been here one day and you have four suspects already? I call that fast work."

"They're a long way from being suspects," Max corrected her, "but they're the best we've got right now."

Chapter 11

Inquest

The next morning, Allison saw Max, Bwana Pete and Eva off on the Sylvia for their trip to the inquest in Brunswick. Jason Williams was already on board. As the boat pulled away from the pier and chugged up the river, Allison sat on a bench on the waterfront promenade with her notepad and began to write.

The Millionaires Club
By Allison Hurlock

Just a mile or so off the coast of southern Georgia is a place few have heard about and even fewer have visited. Amid tidal flatlands covered with stately oak trees, pine, and palmetto palms is a beautiful island that is home to the most exclusive club in America. Sprinkled among the trees, manicured flower beds, and well-tended lawns are large, comfortable homes the members call cottages, each one the winter residence of an American captain of industry or finance and his family. Here you will find Vanderbilts,

Rockefellers, Morgans, Pulitzers, and others who come to the Jekyll Island Club to get away from it all in a way only those with wealth and servants can.

Allison read over what she had written. It sounded pretty good so far; it gave something of the flavor of the place without sliding into a bash-the-rich screed. She unscrewed her fountain pen and resumed.

For three months each year, some of the biggest names in American industry and finance live, hunt, play and just enjoy a relaxing break from the headlines in a place few others can go. Some come by private yacht or private railroad car, but once on Jekyll Island they are just part of the crowd. A large and luxurious clubhouse that also houses the exclusive restaurant anchors the stately cottages. Some members take all their meals at the restaurant and others bring their own cooks with them for the season.

The entire island becomes a single isolated community of club members, their servants, club support staff and their children. If you can picture a Garden of Eden, where everyone is fully clothed, and where half of the residents work for the other half, you have some idea what Jekyll Island is like.

"Working on your article, Mrs. Hurlock?" came a voice from behind her. Allison turned and saw Theresa Woodson looking down on her.

"Oh, good morning, Mrs. Woodson. Yes, I'm just setting it up, so to speak."

"My dear I do hope you will avoid the sensationalism that characterizes so much that is written about the club. I can well imagine what they are saying about the death of Bradley Dawkins. I understand the hearing is being held in Brunswick this morning."

"Yes, my husband Max is on his way there now."

Mrs. Woodson shook her head slowly and gazed out toward the north, as if she could see Brunswick from where she stood.

"This will be very bad for the club, very bad indeed. One reason we are all here is to escape the public eye for a while, and now look. I suppose there will be newspaper coverage and sensational stories everywhere. I can see the headlines now; Murder among the Millionaires, or some such sensational drivel."

"Perhaps," said Allison, "but crime pops up nearly everywhere from time to time."

"Not on Jekyll Island it doesn't," said Mrs. Woodson stiffly. "We are supposed to be setting the standards here. For better or worse, people tend to look up to us. If we become known as just another place seething with vices and base passions, well then something very important will be gone, and the world will be a poorer place."

"Oh, I'm sure people will forget about it and focus on the next scandal somewhere else. After all, it's just a club."

Mrs. Woodson looked at an old fashioned watch on a ribbon. "I'm almost late for an appointment, Mrs. Hurlock, so I really must be going. I still would like to take you on that tour I promised. I think I can show you a side of the club you might not have considered. If you're a really good journalist, my dear, you'll soon find there is a lot more to the club than leisure and luxury. You've seen the surface, but I can show you what lies beneath."

"That would be splendid, Mrs. Woodson. I'm looking forward to it."

"Well, I must be going. Good morning."

Allison watched her walking with a leisurely, almost regal gait and thought to herself that Theresa Woodson was almost surely right; there was a lot more to the Jekyll Island Club than meets the eye.

As the Sylvia chugged its way across the smooth waters toward Brunswick, long straight ripples from its wake spread out all the way to the muddy banks on either side. After they were well underway, Max sought out the captain and found him in the wheelhouse.

"Ah, Mr. Hurlock," said Captain Campbell, recognizing Max right away. "How are you finding Jekyll Island?"

"Complex," said Max. "It's like one of those Russian dolls that have another figure under the surface, then another one after that."

Campbell smiled knowingly. " It's an interesting place, all right. There's more undercurrents there than in this river. Not that it's a bad place, mind you. Most of the people there are good folks, all in all, but..."

"But what?" Max asked.

"They're still people," said the captain, "and where you got people, you got some friction. And where you got friction, well, sometimes it can get out of hand."

The captain shrugged. He suddenly seemed to be aware that he might have spoken too freely. "Aw, don't you pay me no mind now, Mr. Hurlock. I'm just a boat driver round here. Shoot, by this time, you probably know more about the club than I do."

"Captain, I wonder if I might have a look at that logbook you keep, the one I saw when we came over."

"Sure thing. It's right on that shelf. Anything in particular you're looking for?"

Max started thumbing through the pages. "Well, assuming Mrs. Dawkins is not the poisoner, then someone else is, and that someone might have wanted to get off the island before the police started getting too nosey. So I'm looking at your passengers to Brunswick starting the morning after the murder to see who might have made a quick exit."

"We have members and the help going back and forth to Brunswick all the time," said Campbell. "They're always getting supplies or shopping, or some such thing. After all, that's why they have the Sylvia."

"I know," said Max. "That's why I'm comparing the names of people going to Brunswick with the names of people coming back to see if anyone made a one way trip."

"I can save you the trouble," said Campbell. "Other than one of the maids who's in Brunswick to visit a sick mother, everyone I brought over went back the same day. There were only six of them all told."

Max closed the log book. "Is there any other way off the island?"

"Besides swimming, you mean? Well, there are some small boats on the island, so someone could take one of those, but it would be noticed. Not only that, in a tight little place like Jekyll, people would notice if someone ups and takes a powder. No, Mr. Hurlock, I'd say that whoever was on the island when Mr. Dawkins was murdered is almost certainly still there."

The Glynn County Courthouse is an old stone structure with a small dome and a clock outside. As Max, Bwana Pete and Eva Dawkins approached past several shaggy palmetto palm trees, Sheriff McCoy appeared. He seemed to be confused and flustered.

"Mistah Hurlock!"

"Oh, hello, sheriff," said Max. "Found the rest of that body yet?"

"That's what I want to talk to you about. How the blue blazes did you know?" He was waving a slip of paper about as he spoke.

Max tried to hide his relief. "So I was right?"

"It says right here on that paper you gave me 'It's not a human hand. It's a bear paw. Check with local taxidermists.' So how in the hell did you know that? It couldn't have been a guess."

"Did you check with local taxidermists?" Max asked.

"Of course. We found this ol' boy lives nearby. He skinned a bear to make a rug. He took off the claws and cut off the paws after he skinned it. He threw the paws in the dump and the thing must have dried out. It looked just like a human hand. But how did you know that?"

Max shrugged. "Just a little deduction, sheriff."

"Don't give me that. It was the dangdest thing I've ever seen. Not even Sherlock Holmes could deduce a thing like that. So how did you know? Somebody out there told you, right?"

"No. I picked up a copy of the Brunswick News when we came here several days ago. The paper was several weeks old. One of the articles told about a bear that was raiding the garbage cans of some woman on the mainland. She had children in the house so she shot the bear. Now what would you do if you had a bear carcass to get rid of? Well, one thing you might do is get a taxidermist to make a rug for you. Then he has to get rid of the rest. The fact that you found the thing at the dump was the first clue. A bear paw without the skin and claws looks very similar to a human hand. The same thing happened in Maryland a few years ago. So you see I didn't really *know* it was a bear paw, but it seemed like a pretty good possibility, so I took a chance."

McCoy nodded his head slowly. "Well, I'll be. For an amateur, you got a pretty good way of puttin' things together."

"That's what I've been telling you, sheriff," said Max, pressing his advantage, "and what I'm putting together now is a bunch of people who might have benefited from Bradley Dawkins's death; people other than Eva Dawkins."

"We'll see what the judge has to say about it, but at this here moment, I'm a ready to place Miz Dawkins under arrest."

He tipped his hat. "Sorry, Ma'am, but you're the most likely suspect and the season ends in a couple of weeks. Can't have the killer escaping justice."

"Sheriff," said Max, "we all know you have to do your duty, but as you said, there isn't much time left before everyone involved is gone."

"Ah'm glad you were listenin'."

"So why not let me help you gather the facts in the time that's left? If Mrs. Dawkins really did do it, then the evidence should support that conclusion. If not, then it becomes even more important to investigate thoroughly."

McCoy squinted at Max suspiciously. "So what are you sayin'?"

"Let me help. After all, maybe that hand everybody thinks they see is really a bear paw."

McCoy smiled. "Wooeee. Mr. Max, I believe you could talk a coon out of a tree, but I reckon you do make sense. Let's see what the judge says then we'll see."

When the participants had seated themselves on the hard wooden benches in the courtroom, a bailiff called for order and the hearing began. Eva Dawkins testified about the events of the night of her husband's death and insisted on the solidity of her marriage, her voice echoing slightly in the cavernous room. Bwana Pete testified about his actions. Max testified about the other people who stood to benefit from the death of Bradley Dawkins, being careful not to actually accuse anyone. Sheriff McCoy testified to the conditions when he investigated, and Jason Williams appeared to testify to the circumstances in which he found the victim. Finally, the judge retired to consider, promising to return within the hour with a ruling.

Allison put her notebook away and walked back toward the Sans Souci. The clubhouse, with its imposing round tower stood reflecting the morning sun. On a flagstaff at the top of the tower, the club flag snapped in the breeze, giving the place the effect of some storybook castle. A few gardeners were weeding the flowerbeds and a few club members came and went. She noticed Clarice Bailey seated on a bench in the shade under a tree holding court with several male admirers. She was fanning herself like a southern belle in a novel, and one of the admirers was actually serenading her on a ukulele. Fortunately, Allison was too far away to hear.
"Well," she murmured to herself, "I suppose every Eden must have its serpent."
In the distance, she could faintly hear a red bug, the sound mixed in with the hiss of wind through the

Death on a Golden Isle

trees and Spanish moss. All in all, not a bad place to come in the winter, Allison thought. It sure beats shoveling snow and shivering. As she was admiring the ambiance of the club, Harlan Caldwell came into view.

"Ah, Mrs. Hurlock...Allison," he gushed as they met on the pathway. "How delightful to see you here."

"Good morning, Mr. Caldwell."

"I hope you're finding our little island to your liking."

"The island is extraordinary, and very beautiful. Anyone who isn't happy here wouldn't be happy anywhere."

Caldwell smiled wolfishly. He was looking her up and down as he spoke. From his manner, it was clear that he liked what he saw. "How true. You have a fascinating way of expressing yourself, Allison. Have you had lunch?"

"It's 10:30."

"Oh, so it is," said Caldwell. "Well, perhaps you'd like me to show you around."

"You know, for such a small place, the island seems remarkably well supplied with tour guides," Allison remarked. "Nancy McCormick has already shown me around and Theresa Woodson has threatened to do the same. If I get shown around much more I'll have to get my shoes resoled."

"Well how about an interview, then? I understand you're writing a magazine piece of this place. I could tell you tales."

Allison was suddenly interested. "What sort of tales?"

"Oh, secrets, scandals and the like. Believe me, I've seen them all."

"Then maybe you could tell me why Eva Dawkins would have any reason to kill her husband?"

"Eva?" Caldwell acted as if he were hearing the name for the first time. "Well, the usual motives, I suppose."

"There are usual motives for murdering your spouse?"

"Oh, you know; a young wife with a wandering eye perhaps. It happens, I'm afraid."

"Are you saying that Eva Dawkins was seeing another man?"

Harlan Caldwell looked flustered. "Well, I'm not in a position to know for sure, of course, but she has been seen with that Bwana Pete fellow quite a bit."

"At the moment you can be seen with me," said Allison, "but that certainly doesn't mean anything more, necessarily. I certainly hope a man of your standing wouldn't spread idle gossip."

"Oh, of course not. I mean.."

"Who else had reason to want Bradley Dawkins out of the way?"

"Bradley? Why no one; no one at all," said Caldwell. "That's why everyone says Eva did it."

"How about the help?"

"The help?"

"Yes. The staff people. Did he mistreat any of them in some way?"

"Why, no. He seemed pretty levelheaded toward everyone. Of course you have to know how to handle these subordinates, or they get above themselves. Why I remember on my last trip to South America there was this chauffeur. Well, one day.."

"South America?"

"Of course. I go there every year or two to meet with our suppliers for our chocolate business. We can't grow the beans here in the states very well; they need a tropical climate. Well, anyway, it seems they were having this revolution you see, and people were reluctant to go out in the streets. It happens every couple of years. I think it's their national sport. So the chauffeur..."

"Wait a minute," Allison interrupted. "What kind of beans are you talking about?"

"Beans?" Caldwell chuckled. "Why Allison, in the chocolate business there's only one kind of bean that matters; the cocoa bean."

In Brunswick, The judge reentered the courtroom to read his findings.

"In the matter of the death of Bradley Dawkins on Jekyll Island, this court finds that Bradley Dawkins was poisoned by a "person or persons unknown" and that there was sufficient cause to recommend continued investigation of the matter until sufficient evidence against the culprit is found."

Eva looked at Max, but Max was still looking at the judge.

"The court duly notes the evidence of Maxwell Hurlock that there were others who would benefit from the death of Bradley Dawkins, but also notes that when anyone dies there are always those who might derive some benefit. Deriving an incidental benefit, however, is a long way from committing homicide, so the wife, being the victim's most frequent and intimate contact is often the prime suspect. At this time, however, there is not yet sufficient evidence to go to trial. Therefore the court will hold this matter in abeyance until such time as the sheriff's office concludes its investigation. Eva Dawkins is hereby instructed to remain in the county and be available until the investigation is officially closed. The sheriff's office is urged to conclude its investigation with all deliberate speed. To that end, later today I will be issuing a search warrant for the Dawkins house, AKA Osage Cottage."

With a rap of the gavel and a swirl of his black robes, the judge concluded the hearing and rose to adjourn. Sheriff McCoy dutifully rose, and then turned to Eva Dawkins.

"Well, Mrs. Dawkins, looks like I'm not going to be arresting you just yet, but I'll be back to ask you some more questions just like the judge says."

Eva nodded. "That's fine, sheriff."

"And Mr. Max," the sheriff continued. "looks like I got to get me some more evidence. I'll bring a couple of my boys over to search Miz Dawkins's house tomorrow. I'll expect you to keep me up to date on your findings as well. No reason why we can't work together on this."

Max smiled faintly. "No reason at all, sheriff."

"Good. Now maybe you can look into those folks you mentioned, and anybody else who got somethin' hidin' under the leaves."

"Of course, sheriff, and I expect you'll be telling me what you've found out as well, just to keep us from duplicating efforts of course."

The sheriff took out a pack of Lucky Strikes and prepared to light one. "Of course. Oh, by the way, what was the name of that chemistry professor in California you mentioned?"

"Edward Heinrich, at the University of California at Berkeley."

The sheriff took out a pencil and paper and noted the name. "Well, don't see as how it would do any harm to let him look at a sample of the coffee. We need to know just what that poison was. Some of the lab boys around here ain't so sure."

Chapter 12

Cocoa beans

The Sylvia arrived back at the Jekyll Island pier at 1:30. Allison was waiting, and anxiously paced the dock as the boat was eased along side

"I guess we did all right," Max said as he got off. "Eva wasn't arrested and McCoy is cooperating."

"That's good, isn't it?" said Allison. "That's what you wanted."

"Yes, but the judge made it clear that Eva is the one and only suspect and that this is just a breather to give the sheriff time to gather enough evidence to bring her to trial. That's why McCoy and his pals will be here tomorrow to search Eva's cottage."

"That doesn't worry me, aside from the damage they might cause," said Eva. "There's absolutely nothing in the cottage that will interest them, but I suppose it's something they have to do."

"Yes," said Bwana Pete. "But this is just the beginning. From now on McCoy will be here so much we might as well book him a room at the club. Every time you look out a window the sheriff will be there with more questions and more suspicions. It was bad enough before, but with that search warrant he now has a blank check for snooping and harassment."

"Well, we have just as much time as he has," said Max, "so I'll continue with my own inquiries and see where they lead."

"Max," said Eva, "I want to thank you for your efforts on my behalf today. You may have kept me out of jail...for now. We're going back to the cottage."

Max noticed Allison was quietly pulling at his sleeve. "I'll keep on trying to get to the bottom of the case," he called after them. "You go on ahead. I just want to talk to Allison a moment."

"I thought maybe they shouldn't hear this, Max," said Allison. "While you were gone I ran into Harlan Caldwell."

"Ah, yes, our would-be Lothario," said Max with a smirk. "Did he ask you to come up and see his etchings?"

"Not quite, but he mentioned he took occasional trips to South America to buy cocoa beans."

"Cocoa beans? Now that's interesting."

"Maybe that was what Bradley Dawkins meant when he said 'cocoa' as he was dying."

"Could he have been pointing the finger at Caldwell?" said Max. "But if Caldwell was the killer, why not just say Caldwell? Why make a puzzle out of it?"

"I don't know, but who else could be connected with cocoa around here?"

"It could be just a coincidence," Max mused. "The man manufactures chocolate products. Of course he needs cocoa beans. There's nothing sinister about that."

"All I can say is, if it's a coincidence, it's a doozy," said Allison, shaking her head. "Bradley Dawkins' last word points to the one product associated with Harlan Caldwell."

"I'm glad you didn't tell me in front of them," said Max. "I'd just as soon keep the whole cocoa thing a secret until I have a better idea what it means."

"That's what I thought, too," said Allison. "No sense showing your hand just yet."

They walked over to a bench and sat down watching the ripples in the water.

"So what is your plan, Max?"

"My plan? I suppose my plan remains as it has from the beginning. I keep digging and poking around until I get a lead I can pursue to the truth. So far I haven't found it, but I'll keep looking."

Allison was silent a moment, then spoke. "I hope you haven't told Eva Dawkins about your plan. She has enough to worry about."

"Hey, don't complain about my plan. I can assure you that Sheriff McCoy is doing the same thing."

"Oh, well, that raises my confidence. The killer is as good as convicted."

Max rose and stretched. "Enough of this shop talk. I understand there is a meeting of the club directors in about a half-hour. I'm going to drop by and see if I can get any information out of them."

Allison reached down and picked up a small stone from the gravel pathway. "While you're at it, why don't you squeeze this and see if you can get blood from it?"

"Very funny, but I have to try. I don't expect any revelations, but I want to get their support so the others will know it's all right to tell me what they know. I intend to use McCoy's agreement to work together to put me on the same official plane in their eyes. It might help loosen some tongues around here. See you at the Sans Souci around five so we can dress for dinner."

As Max walked away, Allison sighed and looked back at the water. She took out her notes again and looked them over without enthusiasm. She began to write.

Jekyll Island is not a place of secrets so much as a place of discretion. The club members tend to be wary of outsiders that might disturb or disrupt the world they have created. The members are polite, but are seldom anxious to reveal much that is below the surface. Still, a visitor cannot help but notice that there are certain rhythms to life on the island, and traditions that have developed over time. This is a place where public opinion doesn't matter because it doesn't penetrate, where..

"Are you still here working on your article, my dear?" came a voice from behind her. Allison turned and saw Theresa Woodson looking down on her once again.

"Oh, hello again, Mrs. Woodson. No, I haven't been working the whole time, I've been roaming a bit then came back. I'm just looking over what I have so far and adding a bit."

"Nothing scandalous, I trust."

Allison smiled. "Oh, no. The truth is interesting enough. This really is a unique place and I think people will find it fascinating."

Mrs. Woodson sat down next to her and looked out at the water wistfully. "It really is, isn't it? Robert and I have been coming down here for the last ten years and I always get the same thrill when we arrive. I always feel rejuvenated just to be in this wonderful area. Jekyll, Brunswick, St Simons, Sea Island, Little St Simons... The local people call them the Sea Islands, but to me they are the Golden Isles, glowing with both beauty and promise.

"We live in New York, you see, and our life there seems to be consumed by a constant round of business, benefits, formal dinners, and charity events. It's a life most people would envy, but it can be tedious and exhausting at times. Sometimes when I'm at some stuffy formal affair in New York, I wish I could be back here just sitting on a bench like this one. You see, here in the Golden Isles, we can get away from all that. We can shape our own world, so to speak. What's more, we can see the good we're doing."

"The good?"

Mrs. Woodson smiled. "Oh, I'm not claiming we're here for philanthropic reasons. It's pure self-interest, I'm afraid. But I believe we bring a little bit of stability and economic well-being to the local people in the process. We do a good deal of charity work in New York of course, but it's a bit impersonal. We never see who might benefit, but here we see them every day. We even know their names. It gives one a good feeling to see all the people on the island who have employment and decent homes because of the club. Does that sound paternalistic, my dear?"

Allison made a slight shrug. "Maybe a little, but in a good way."

"Well, it seems we have a bit of time. Are you ready for that tour I promised you?"

Allison screwed the top back on her pen. "Sure thing. Let's go."

Max walked down the wood paneled halls of the Jekyll Island Club's clubhouse until he came to a well-appointed room on the water side. The room had damask wallpaper, heavy wainscoting, and dark

John Reisinger

Victorian overstuffed furniture. At the center was a fireplace, giving the room the appearance of a parlor in the home of a wealthy man. The Jekyll Island Club board members were standing around the fireplace smoking cigars and holding small glasses of either wine or brandy, Max couldn't tell which. When Max walked into the room, all conversation stopped and every head turned his way. Max had once had a Jewish friend who used to refer to something being "as popular as a pork chop at a Bar Mitzvah". Suddenly, Max knew exactly how that pork chop must have felt.

After attempting to wither Max with their eyes, the group shuffled a little and one spoke. "This meeting is not open to the general public, sir."

"Of course," Max replied. "Gentlemen, I mean no disrespect to the club or its traditions, but would ask to be permitted to briefly address the honorable board members on a matter of great import to the club and its future."

The members stared at Max, then began to talk among themselves. Finally, Robert Woodson spoke.

"You may introduce yourself to he board."

"I'm Max Hurlock and I'm an investigator. I'm here at the request of Mrs. Dawkins to look into the death of her husband. I am also working with the full cooperation of the Glynn County Sheriff's Office. I have only one purpose and that's the same as their purpose; to find out what the evidence will tell us about the death of Bradley Dawkins."

"Do you mean to say you're not here to get her off?"

"Only if the evidence says I should. If the evidence points to her guilt, I will share that with the sheriff as well. All I want is the truth. I am not an advocate. I'm no more anxious to see a murderer walking free than you are."

"Fair enough," said another board member, crushing his cigar stub. "I say we hear him out."

"Second," said another member.

"All in favor?"

The ayes were unanimous and Max was given the floor. "All right, Mr. Hurlock, what do you have to tell us?"

"Thank you," said Max. "As you all know, the club has recently been the scene of a murder and it has caused a certain amount of confusion and tension here. I think it's fair to say that many members suspect Eva Dawkins of the crime. I can't blame anyone for suspecting her, since the spouse is always the first suspect in a case such as this. Right now, I have no idea if they are right or not, but one thing I do know is that we need more evidence to bring the killer to justice. The sooner this is done the sooner the killer can be removed from your midst and the glare of the curious lifted from the club. It's one thing to have an opinion as to who is responsible, but what's needed is evidence."

"So what are you suggesting, Mr. Hurlock?"

"You gentlemen are the backbone of this club. You are respected and looked up to. I'm suggesting that you take the lead in spreading the word about the necessity to cooperate with those who are investigating, and to think back on this season and try to remember the social interactions that took place. Even the smallest detail might contain a vital link to the crime. Someone had a reason to want Bradley Dawkins dead or at least out of the way and we need to know who."

The members looked at each other. "What you say makes sense up to a point, Mr. Hurlock," said Robert Woodson, "but we don't want members turning on each other and spreading gossip."

Max nodded. "Of course. We don't want gossip and finger-pointing. That's why I'm asking you gentlemen to help make the case to the rest of the members. I don't expect people to turn in their neighbors, but I do expect them to willingly answer questions from the sheriff or myself."

The members nodded in agreement. "That sounds reasonable, Mr. Hurlock. We will inform the members, and we will discuss among ourselves any unusual, er...incidents we can recall. But in return, we expect you to make due allowances for our members' privacy and dignity. The sheriff is a public official. He has the authority to be here and pry into things, and he has to answer to the local taxpayers if he doesn't get results. You, however, are a guest, and every member on this island is your host. We ask that you remember that."

Max rose. "I will remember. Thank you, gentlemen. I hope your actions will help lead to a speedy resolution of this matter. And now I've taken enough of your time. Good afternoon."

"I'm sure Nancy showed you the clubhouse and the cottages, and all the trappings of luxury around here, Allison," said Theresa Woodson as they walked, "but I want to show you another side of the club. This is the Pier Road and it runs from the pier past the clubhouse and the Sans Souci then past these buildings you see in the back here. These are shops and small offices of the staff. Just look around you at the activity and the industriousness; people with honorable and productive jobs and a steady source of income."

It was true. All along the section of road past the clubhouse men and women were coming and going along the crushed oyster shell road and carrying various bundles and packages in and out of the shops and offices. Some people were black and some white, but they all moved with purpose.

"Over on your left is a sort of dormitory for the unmarried seasonal help. The club provides jobs and income not just for local residents, but for others as well. None of this would be here if not for the club. In addition, we often order supplies and hire contractors from Brunswick as well, so the benefits are spread more widely than people realize."

Allison nodded. "Very impressive. How many people work here?"

"That's hard to say. Maybe Mr. Grob, the manager would have some figures, but it depends on whom you include. Most members bring some of their own staff down with them, so the numbers swell and vary in season, but there are several hundred year round."

"What's that shop over there? I see a container of what looks like ostrich feathers."

"That's the gamekeeper's office. Come on. You can see for yourself."

A lone figure was bending over the table with his back to the door. He was cleaning a rifle.

"Mr. McHale?" said Theresa Woodson.

McHale's assistant, Harold Falstaff turned around. He was sweating with the effort and hastily rolled his sleeves down when he saw the women. "No, I'm his assistant, Harold Falstaff, Ma'am. Mr. McHale's out with a hunting party. He should be back any minute now."

"Oh, yes, Falstaff. I remember now. Well, I just wanted to show your office to Mrs. Hurlock here. She was attracted by the feathers."

Falstaff adjusted his glasses and grinned. "Oh, the feathers. Well, take a look. We save the longer feathers from the game birds we shoot. The ladies all like them."

Allison looked through the feathers. "Quite a variety. I'm surprised there's a bird left around here."

Falstaff laughed. "Oh, no worry about that, Mrs. Hurlock. The sky's black with birds most of the time. We couldn't put a dent in them with a Lewis."

"With a what?" said Allison.

"Machine gun."

"Oh."

Allison continued to look through the feathers.

"Your husband was by here yesterday, Mrs. Hurlock," Falstaff remarked. "Mr. McHale and I are going to take him and Mr. Hamilton out hunting soon. 'Cause I suppose he's pretty busy what with investigating the murder and all."

"News travels quickly around here," said Allison.

"Has he found out anything yet? If you don't mind me asking."

Allison turned from the feathers and looked at him. "It's very early yet. You never know what he'll find. Do you know anything about it, Mr. Falstaff?"

Falstaff looked embarrassed. "Me? Oh, no. I'm just as much in the dark as anyone else around here. I was just wondering. I mean, it's terrible and all, but it's sort of exciting, too."

"I'm sure it's very exciting to Mrs. Dawkins."

"Aw, gee, Mrs. Hurlock. I didn't mean anything by it. I was just curious. I suppose everybody around here is."

"Yes. Well perhaps we should be going Allison," said Theresa Woodson. "Good day, Mr. Falstaff."

"Afternoon, ladies. Stop in again any time."

"It looks like the murder is a popular topic of conversation around here," said Allison as they walked away.

Theresa Woodson shrugged. "Understandable, I suppose. We get very few sensational crimes around here, or crimes of any sort, come to that. Falstaff is young yet. He'll learn a little discretion in time."

"He's probably just saying what the others are thinking," said Allison.

"No doubt. Now we're coming up on the married employees' quarters. These are the year round staff that keeps the place running. We call it Red Row."

Allison saw a line of small cabin-like houses, all covered with tarpaper with a reddish tint.

"All these houses were built by the club. The houses are simple, but top notch for the area. So you see the club does a lot of good. It's true the club members are wealthy, but most of that wealth came through hard work and by building businesses that employ people and provide goods and services people need. We feel that with wealth comes responsibility. Wealth makes it possible for us to do a great deal of good and we spend a considerable amount of time and effort doing so. We make a tremendous difference in many people's lives, either through charity works or through the economic opportunities we generate. That's why I tend to be defensive about the club and its members sometimes, especially if I think someone might sensationalize our problems. I don't want one ugly incident crowding out the rest. If the club were to be undermined or damaged it would be a great loss; not just to the members, but to all the people here in the Golden Isles and in the club who depend on us."

"Mrs. Woodson," said Allison, "the sooner Max gets to the bottom of the case the sooner all the rumors will be dispelled."

Theresa Woodson stopped and looked at Allison sternly. "The bottom of the case? My dear, we are already at the bottom. Eva Dawkins poisoned her husband. I'm sure one can dream up all sorts of fanciful alternative solutions, but in the end, Eva Dawkins will be the one in jail."

"But do you have any idea why she would kill her husband?"

"Of course. Eva Dawkins was after his money."

"She was married to him," Allison insisted. "She already had his money."

Theresa Woodson looked surprised. "Oh, my dear. Didn't she tell you? Bradley Dawkins was about to file for a divorce."

Allison was stunned. "A...a divorce?"

"I'm afraid so. And because of the family business, most of his money was in a trust fund where Eva couldn't touch it. She'd have been cut off with a small stipend. If you're looking for a motive, you'd have a difficult time finding a better one."

Chapter 13

The bottle

Back in their large and luxurious apartment at the Sans Souci, Max and Allison dressed for dinner. Max reluctantly and painstakingly put on a tuxedo, while Allison slipped into a shimmering white dress with a single strand necklace. Max, who had been admiring the view out the window toward the clubhouse and the croquet lawn, suddenly stopped to admire his wife instead.

"You look sensational, Allison. They might throw you out for showing them up so badly. What was it that Romeo said when he first saw Juliet? So shows a snowy dove trooping with crows, as yonder lady among her fellows shows."

"Well, I'm impressed, Max. You don't know much Shakespeare, but what you do know is the real Tabasco. As the Bard himself might have said, Verily, Milord, thou art the ocelot's elbows."

"Forsooth, Milady," said Max, bowing.

"Speaking of Shakespearean tragedy," said Allison cautiously, as if reluctant to break the mood, "I hate to tell you, but I found out something today that doesn't help Eva's case one bit. Theresa Woodson told me that Bradley Dawkins was contemplating a divorce."

"What? Just how in the devil could Theresa Woodson know that?"

"I asked the same question," said Allison. "It seems Bradley had consulted with the club's attorney and the attorney told Robert Woodson as board chairman so he'd be prepared in case a scandal resulted."

Max sat down on the bed. "For the love of...When will I get a client who tells me the truth?"

"The most charitable explanation is that possibly Eva didn't know about it," said Allison, wriggling her fingers as she slid on an elbow-length glove.

"Yes, that's possible, but if she did know about it, we've got a motive that makes Eva Dawkins an even better suspect than I thought she was. Whether she knew about it or not, they must have been having marriage problems. When was she planning on telling me about that?"

"Are you going to tell Sheriff McCoy?"

"McCoy? No, I don't think so. Not yet at least. I'll have to consider this and see if Eva wants to come clean on her own. You've done some pretty good detective work without even trying."

Allison slipped on the other glove and stood in front of the full-length mirror smoothing her white dress.

"It would be a shame to spill anything on that dress," said Max, looking over her shoulder. "Maybe you should take it off."

She turned and kissed him. "Maybe you could help me take it off," she whispered seductively.

"Now you're cooking with gas.."

"But first we've got to get to dinner."

"Business before...oh, you know," Max sighed. "Let's go."

At the club dining room that evening, Max and Allison noticed that the other members were, if not actually friendly, at least not openly hostile to Eva and her friends. Whether this was because of Max's talk with the board or a growing familiarity was hard to say. All through dinner, Max hinted and probed about possible marital friction between Eva and her now deceased husband. Eva shrugged it off and continued to insist the marriage was a happy one. It was clear either Eva didn't know about her husband's inquiry into divorce, or she wasn't going to talk about it. Finally, as they were leaving the dining room, Max got impatient. They had just stepped onto the broad veranda facing the water. The moon was starting to rise, casting a pale gray light over the trees and flower beds.

"Eva, the sheriff will probably be here tomorrow to search your house, and that's just the beginning of his efforts to hang the crime on you. If I don't look into any rumors, you can be sure McCoy will, so I have to check out everything, no matter how trivial. One of the rumors we've heard is that Bradley was looking into a divorce. What can you tell me about that?"

Eva looked ashen-faced. "Oh my God. Is that what they're saying? Well, it isn't true, at least not the way they say."

"So in what way *is* it true?" Max asked.

Eva frowned in a look of someone trapped. "About a month before he died, Bradley and I got into a fearful row about the cottage. He wanted to expand it and I thought it was plenty big enough as it was. I know it sounds silly now, but in a place like this, small problems can seem big. Anyway, one thing led to another and in a fit of anger, I lost my head and mentioned the word 'divorce'. He stalked out and I didn't see him again the rest of the day. When he returned I embraced him and apologized for being so stupid as to ever mention divorce. We reconciled and were happy after that. I didn't realize he had actually looked into it."

"And just why didn't you tell me this earlier?" Max asked.

Eva slumped into a wicker chair on the veranda and put her face in her hands. "I was too embarrassed at my own stupidity. Besides, I didn't know that he had told anyone; I thought it was just a foolish incident that was forgotten."

"If I found out, you know McCoy will and then you have a prime motive. Are there any other foolish incidents I should know about?"

Eva just shook her head, sobbing slightly.

"I'd better get her back to the cottage," said Bwana Pete. "Tomorrow could be a trying day, I'm afraid."

Bwana Pete and Eva slowly disappeared into the dusk as the lamps were coming on. When they were gone, Max turned to Allison.

"Do you believe her story?"

Allison crossed her arms and cocked her head, a pose she often took when pondering a problem. "I think so. It has the ring of truth to it, especially since she took the blame. If she had been making it up, I think she would have said Bradley mentioned divorce, so I think it's the truth. Whether the sheriff will believe it, of course, is another matter entirely."

At that moment, Clarice Bailey appeared, escorted by one of the younger club members. She was wearing a dark blue gown with black trim. Even Allison had to admit that she looked stunning.

"Why, hello, Mrs. Hurlock." Clarice acted as if she was glad to see Allison again, although Allison was pretty sure she wasn't. "Why, this must be your husband."

"Er, yes," said Allison. "This is Max. Max, this is Clarice Bailey."

Clarice extended a lace-gloved hand, apparently offering Max the chance to kiss it. Max just shook it warily.

"Oh, and this is Albert Fuller." Clarice gestured toward her companion. "His father is William Fuller of Fuller Industries. He's celebrating tonight because daddy just bought a railroad."

"Well, it wasn't actually a railroad, more of a rail siding for one of his factories..." Fuller began, but Clarice ignored him.

"So, Maxwell, how is your investigation going? I think it's thrilling to have a real detective on the island to find out the truth about Eva Dawkins. That bumpkin sheriff never will; he hasn't even arrested her yet."

"Actually..."

"It's really so tragic when a wife kills her poor husband, but I'm sure a fine detective like you will solve the mystery of why she did it and see that justice is done." She was talking directly to Max now and ignoring everyone else. She actually batted her eyes at him.

Max smiled slightly. "Sometimes human behavior is the greatest mystery of all."

She gazed at him. "Oh, I think so, too. Some people can be so intriguing."

"People like Bradley Dawkins?"

She smiled slyly, as if Max had said something daring. "Oh, poor Bradley and I were very close, but this isn't the time or place to discuss such things. We should meet some other time and discuss it in private. Would you like that, Maxwell?" She batted her eyes again.

"Oh, I intend to talk with all the suspects in this case."

For the first time, Clarice seemed taken aback. "S...Suspects? What do you mean, suspects?"

Max was still smiling. "Oh, did I say suspects? A slip of the tongue. Maybe I should have said 'people who knew Bradley Dawkins'."

"Yes...well come along, Albert. Good evening Allison, Maxwell." Clarice retreated from the field of verbal battle as Max and Allison watched her go.

"Charming girl," said Max. "I can't understand why you don't like her."

Allison bit her lower lip, a sure sign of storm clouds gathering. She opened her mouth to reply, but Max laughed.

"Come on, Allison. I'm just pulling your leg a bit. I have no doubt she is every bit as vicious as you said. She certainly knows how to manipulate, although she's not very subtle about it."

"Maybe we should meet and discuss it in private," said Allison in a high and whiny voice. "Why didn't she just drop her house key in your pocket? It would have been less obvious."

"Now, now," Max chuckled. "I want you girls to play nice. After all, maybe she can't help herself."

"Can't help herself?" said Allison. "On the contrary, it seems to me she was trying to help herself to my husband."

"I mean." said Max, "that she strikes me as a woman who routinely uses her charms to get what she wants from men. When she's around men she reflexively turns on the allure. It's second nature. You met her among a group of women when she could let her true personality out."

"So you think she was pitching the woo to you out of force of habit?" Allison asked.

"Well, yes. Don't you?"

"Max, your insightful analysis of the feminine mind let you down. You missed the most obvious reason for her little charade."

"My irresistible charm?"

"No; your irresistible investigation. She wants Eva put away for the twin crimes of murder and the far more serious crime of standing between Clarice Bailey and something she wanted. If she charms you and gets you to want to make her happy, you might be more likely to do that. Manipulating men is her business and as far as I can tell, business is good."

"She does have a certain knack, although she didn't seem to care for my referring to her as a suspect. Are you ready to go?"

Allison rose. "Maybe we better, before some other woman comes by our table trolling."

They were out on the veranda in a minute and paused to look at the moon over the trees.

Max looked at her. "My God, you look even better by moonlight."

She leaned over and whispered in his ear. "You should see me when the moonlight is coming through a window of the Sans Souci. Are you ready to help me out of this dress?"

Max embraced her. "The sooner the better," he said.

The weather was cooler the next morning, with a chilly wind from the ocean side rustling the trees. At around nine, the Sylvia arrived, bringing Sheriff McCoy and two deputies. They stepped on to the pier, and then walked toward Osage Cottage, search warrant in hand.

Max and Allison saw the Sylvia arrive and figured it would bring the sheriff on his hunt for more damning evidence. They headed toward Osage Cottage to witness the search.

"Think they'll find anything incriminating, Max?"

"Not if Eva has a lick of common sense, but we'll see."

"Then you're not so sure she's innocent after all?"

"I confess that given this business about a possible divorce and her reticence about it, I'm now leaning a bit toward guilty, but I'm still open minded."

Max and Allison could hear the sounds of drawers closing and doors slamming inside Osage Cottage as they arrived. They found Eva Dawkins and Bwana Pete sitting gloomily in white wooden lawn chairs in the front yard, cringing at every sound.

"I just hope those oafs are careful," Eva grumbled. "McCoy told us to stay out here until they were finished. I suppose he wants privacy when wrecking a house."

"Actually,' said Max, "I think it's to keep you from getting upset or possibly interfering. Anyway, I'm sure they'll be finished soon."

"If I'm not finished first," said Eva. She fidgeted, twisting and untwisting a chain necklace she was wearing. Max looked at her and noted that a small and delicate woman like Eva Dawkins might find poison a very practical method if she wished to do away with her husband.

"Max," said Bwana Pete, "just how do you go about finding a poisoner? I mean to say, there's no gun to find and no marks on the body to look for. How do you find a poisoner?"

"You have to find out who has a motive and go from there," Max replied. "So far there are several possibilities, but none of them seem especially strong. Still, it's early yet and I have some more doors to knock on. If Eva didn't poison Bradley, someone else did, and that means there is someone else around here with a motive."

Bwana Pete looked grim, but Eva Dawkins just looked weary.

"Mrs. Dawkins?" a voice came from the porch of the cottage. A skinny deputy with an oversized hat was gesturing toward them. "The sheriff asked if you could come inside."

"Maybe he wants to personally apologize for whatever they broke," said Eva, rising from her chair and straightening her necklace.

Max followed her into the living room, which was in disarray, but not really damaged in any way. The deputy directed them to the stairs leading to the cramped and dark basement. Because of the soil, the basement was only about halfway buried in the ground, but with windows small enough to make it perpetually gloomy.

As their eyes adjusted to the dimmer lighting, they made out the figure of Sheriff McCoy standing over by a storage area lit by a single hanging light bulb. As they got closer they saw several shelves with rows of dusty mason jars and bottles. McCoy pointed to one of the bottles in the back row. Unlike the heavily dust-covered rows in front of it, this bottle looked clean and shiny. The sheriff put a glove on his hand and extracted the bottle.

"You want to tell me what's in this?"

Eva looked at the bottle. It was a small medicine bottle, stopped by a cork. On one side was a paper label.

Nothing was written on the label, only a drawing of a skull and crossbones.

"I...I don't know what that is," she stammered. "I've never seen it before."

McCoy held the bottle up to the naked light and squinted at it. "Looks like it's got maybe a quarter inch of some milky liquid left in it. Guess the rest is in your husband's coffee."

"No..no. I didn't.."

McCoy dropped the bottle in a paper bag. "I think I'll just send this along to Mr. Hurlock's friend out at the University of California and have him check it out. I'll bet you a nickel that whatever's in this bottle will match what's in that coffee cup. Yes sir, I think we might be closer to the end of this case than I thought."

He brushed past them and back up the stairs, leaving them standing in the gloomy cellar.

"But...I didn't put it there," Eva kept insisting weakly.

That night, Max and Allison sat on their porch at the Sans Souci. Eva was too upset to eat, so they had dined alone at the clubhouse. Word of the poison bottle found at Osage Cottage had spread and the other diners were suddenly frostier than ever. Allison felt the cold stares of disapproval, but Max ignored them and ate heartily. He seemed to be in remarkably good spirits considering his client was almost surely headed to a murder trial. Whenever Allison brought up the case, however, Max shrugged it off and changed the subject. Allison knew that this meant he was thinking about it but wasn't quite ready to put his thoughts into words yet.

Later, sitting relaxing on their porch at the Sans Souci with the lights coming on below them and the

Death on a Golden Isle

soft evening breezes in their hair, she brought the subject up again.

"Max, what are you going to do? They found the poison bottle in Eva's basement. Between that and the divorce rumors, they probably have enough to hang her already. So what do you think? Is Eva the killer after all?"

Max sat back in his seat and shook his head. "I admit things do look pretty black for her right now. She has a motive, means, and even a bottle of what I don't doubt will be the poison, but she isn't the killer. That bottle pretty much proves it."

Allison did a double take in surprise. "Proves it? What in the world are you saying? If she isn't the killer, why would she have a bottle of poison in her house hidden away like that?"

"I think a better question," said Max thoughtfully, "is why would she have that bottle around if she is the killer?"

"Explain."

Max leaned over towards Allison and lowered his voice. "Look. If she is the killer, here is the scenario. You tell me if it makes sense. She kills her husband with poison from a small, easily disposed-of bottle that is the only solid piece of evidence that could convict her. All she has to do is get rid of it and there will be nothing solid to connect her with the crime. So does she throw it in the water or bury it in the woods, or smash it on a rock? No! She takes it home and puts it in plain view in her own house where it is sure to be found. Why would any rational killer do that? For a souvenir? Or does she have another husband she wants to get rid of?"

Allison frowned in thought. "Now that you mention it..."

"And why is the bottle so clean?" Max continued, warming to his theme. "I'm betting it's because the bottle has been wiped clean of fingerprints that could identify who really put it there."

"Maybe she wiped off her prints."

"Why? If the bottle is found in her house, what difference would it make if it has no prints? Only if someone planted the bottle would he need it to be clean to remove his own prints and obscure the fact that Eva's prints weren't on it. No, the bottle almost certainly means she didn't do it."

"It makes sense," said Allison. "Now if you can just convince Sheriff McCoy and the entire Georgia court system, you'll be a hero."

"Yes, well, that might be a problem, but I think I have an idea. It's a little unconventional, though."

"Uh oh."

"I've been thinking about the coffee. There were two cups found and only one was poisoned. What if we could prove that someone else brought Bradley Dawkins the poisoned cup and Eva's was clean?"

"That would be great news for Eva, assuming it's true," said Allison, "but how do you prove something like that?"

"It might be possible. As I said, it's kind of a long shot, but if it works it would clear things up quite a bit."

"And if it doesn't?"

"Then we're no worse off."

"High upside potential, low downside risk, as the Wall Street boys like to say," said Allison. "I like it. How do we do it?"

"I have to talk to our good friend Sheriff McCoy. I'm betting he'll be back on the Sylvia in the morning to follow up. I'll have a word with him then."

Chapter 14

Coffee stains

"Question them again?" McCoy almost shouted the words. "Are you out of your cotton-pickin' Yankee mind? My men questioned every person at that dance already."

Max had met the sheriff at the boat dock the next morning as he planned. He thought it was likely McCoy would come back. "Sheriff, I only want you to ask them one additional question."

"I wouldn't even ask them what they had for lunch. It'd be a damned waste of time."

"Like looking for a dismembered body in the dump?" Max asked casually.

McCoy frowned even deeper. "Now don't y'all be bringin' that up. I admit as how you hit the mark on that one and I allow as how you do pretty well readin' clues and all, but.."

"So what's the harm in just one more question?" said Max.

McCoy stopped and thought for a moment. "All right. Tell you what; I won't waste my time with any more questioning of these people, but I can't see as how I'd object to you wastin' yours. I'll give you a list of the people at the dance and you can ask 'em any dang fool thing you like. I'll bring it over with me next time."

"Thanks, sheriff. That's more than fair."

"Now I'm going to look around some more today and I'll be arresting Mrs. Dawkins soons I get the results back from your friend the Berkeley professor."

"Assuming they find poison in the bottle," Max reminded him.

"Oh, they'll find it all right. Then I'll arrest Miz Dawkins and I'll be as happy as a tick on a fat dog."

Max watched the sheriff go, and then turned toward the clubhouse with a guest list Eva Dawkins had provided from memory that morning. It was from memory, but it would give him a place to start, and now he could honestly tell people that the sheriff had approved. The first names were Millie and Phillip Hester and he had just seen them strolling nearby.

"Excuse me, Mr. and Mrs. Hester," said Max, catching up to them a minute later.

"Ah, Mr. Hurlock," said Phillip. "I heard about the poison bottle they found in Eva's house. A damned shame."

"Yes," said Millie. "Poor Eva."

"At this point it is merely a stray bottle," Max explained. "There may not have been any poison in it at all."

"Oh, I hope not," said Millie. "I just can't believe Eva would do such a thing. She's really such a nice person."

"Well, there is something I'm trying to find out," said Max. "The sheriff is providing me with a list of everyone at the dance that night so I can ask a few additional questions. Naturally, your names came up."

Phillip Hester looked slightly guarded. "And just what do you want to ask? We've given the sheriff full statements already."

"Just one question. It occurred to me that in such a crowded room with people moving about, dancing and jostling each other, Eva might have spilled some of the coffee she was taking to her husband."

"Spilled?"

"Oh, not a lot, just a splash or a drip when she brushed up against someone or bumped into another person on the dance floor. She remembers bumping into several people, but she doesn't remember any spills. Still, it's a possibility. And if anyone has the remains of the spilled coffee on a dress or on a suit, the stain could be tested for poison. If there is such a stain and it proves free of poison, it would go a long way toward establishing Eva's innocence."

Phillip was not convinced. "And if there is a trace of poison in this stain? Then what?"

Max shrugged. "Then at least we will know."

"Well, we have found no coffee stains on our clothes from that night, so I'm afraid we can't help you. Still, I wish you luck."

As they walked away, Max drew a line through their names on his list and sighed.

"So how do you like working at the club?"

Allison had run into a young woman carrying a laundry basket and thought she'd get another perspective for her article. The woman she spoke to was in her 20s and had bright red hair pulled back in a bun. She identified herself as Mary Dooley, and looked wary.

"Beggin' your pardon, Ma'am?" The woman had a distinct Irish brogue so thick you could have spread it on toast.

Allison smiled. "I'm Allison Hurlock and I'm researching an article about the club. I'd love to know about what you do here."

The girl looked down at her laundry basket, as if to say 'What do you think I do here?'.

"Oh, I mean beside that. How did you come to be here? Do you live here year round?"

"Saints preserve us!" the woman exclaimed. "I'm just down here with the Woodsons for the season. If I lived here year round I'd go daft."

"Why is that?"

"Well, look around you. There's not much excitement for a young woman. There's no music halls or vaudeville, or even any pubs. What's more there's no Catholic Church except services held in the Faith Chapel behind Crane Cottage. It's nothin' but work and scenery. Oh, they have entertainment for the help now and again, and there's always the beach on your day off, but it's a long way from New York."

"How about men?" Allison asked.

"Men? Well, there's the other white help, of course, but they're just here for the season as well, so it doesn't pay to get too attached to any of them.'

"How about in the Woodson's house?"

"Well, there's Carlos Sanchez, the gardener and butler, but that one's a bit strange I can tell you."

"Strange?"

"Well, look. The help is expected to be loyal and we are, up to a point. I mean, I wouldn't be jumpin' into any fires for the Woodsons' sake, but I do what I can for them. It's only right. But that Sanchez seems to think he's Mr. Woodson's combination body guard and business partner. He gets upset and acts threatening if he thinks anyone is trying to get the best of Mr. Woodson. Sometimes Mr. Woodson takes him along to business meetings just to intimidate people. So I'm not about to be taking long walks on the beach with that one, I can tell you."

"He makes you uneasy?"

"Too right. Why when that Mr. Dawkins got murdered everyone was in a tizzy at the thought of a killer among us. All the help were in a panic, and some still are. But not Sanchez; he just scoffed and said there was nothing to worry about since Mr. Dawkins probably just got in the way of the wrong person."

"What did he mean by that?" said Allison.

"I don't know and I was afraid to ask."

"All right, Mary. Thank you for the information."

Allison turned and began to walk back toward the Sans Souci. Sitting on a bench under a tree by the path was Clarice Bailey. Once again, she was attired immaculately in an expensive-looking dress. She looked up from a small book she was reading and gave Allison a frosty smile. "Hello Allison. Enjoying the club?"

"Most of it," Allison replied.

"And how is Maxwell? He's such a dear."

"He's fine. How is Albert?"

"Albert? Oh yes, Albert. He's all right, but a little dull. I like a man with a bit more excitement."

"Like Bradley Dawkins, for instance?"

Clarice sighed dramatically. "Poor Bradley. He was a dear, too, but he got mixed up with the wrong kind of woman and she killed him."

"Really?" said Allison. "What kind of woman would that be?"

"Oh, maybe a woman with a short temper," said Clarice.

"Or a long memory," said Allison.

Clarice Bailey's face darkened, as did her tone of voice. "Are you suggesting I had anything to do with Bradley's death?"

"You did have a pretty good motive," said Allison calmly.

Allison looked at Clarice and was amazed that such a beautiful face could be suddenly capable of expressing so much malice. "If I went around killing people who displeased me," Clarice said in a growling voice heavy with menace, "this place would look like a battlefield." She snapped her book closed and stalked off.

The air suddenly seemed chillier, Allison thought.

Max walked along the road toward the clubhouse and noticed a young man coming the other way. He was thin and had a scraggly mustache, apparently an effort to look older and more substantial. Max squinted at him a moment. He looked vaguely familiar. Then he remembered.

"Excuse me," said Max. "Didn't I see you at the club dining room the other night? I believe you were with Miss Bailey. I'm Max Hurlock."

"I'm Charles Krauk. My folks live at Cambridge Cottage. You're that detective fellow, aren't you?"

Max started to explain that he was really an investigator, but decided it wasn't worth the trouble.

"I'm glad I ran into you, Mr. Krauk. I'm interviewing people who were at the dance the night Bradley Dawkins died. I understand you were there with Miss Bailey."

Charles Krauk sighed. "Well, yes, but she's been pretty cold lately. I think she's seeing someone else."

Max was sympathetic. "She does seem a bit...spirited. Still, you were at the dance. I wanted to know if anyone in the crowd spilled coffee on you."

"Of course, even when she's with you, she's somewhere else half the time." Charles wasn't finished with the sore subject of Clarice Bailey just yet. "She kept disappearing all night, and it was always for another fella. I'd find her talking with someone different each time I tracked her down."

"I suppose she does get around," said Max. "Now about that coffee spill..."

"One time it was that Albert, and one time I saw her coming in from the veranda."

Max was suddenly interested. "From the veranda?"

"She had been standing around with a cup of coffee chatting with me, and then she says she'll be right back, and off she goes."

"Goes where?"

"I don't know. She disappeared in the crowd, but five minutes later I see her coming in from the veranda, just as cool as you please."

"When was this?"

"I dunno. Nine thirty or so I guess. Maybe a little later."

"Did she still have the coffee with her?"

"The coffee? Uh, no. I don't think so. I guess she left it out there."

As she got closer to the Sans Souci, Allison saw Max coming the other way.

"Hey, Max. Got anyone to confess yet?"

He laughed wearily. "No, but I'm plodding along. I talked to five of the people who were at the dance today but none said anyone spilled coffee on them. What's more, almost everyone has heard about the bottle McCoy found in Eva's cellar by now and wants to know why she's still walking around free."

"Well, Sheriff McCoy might solve that little problem soon enough. He seems to be itching to arrest her as soon as he can confirm there is poison in the bottle. In the meantime, there are a lot more to talk to. Maybe you'll get lucky."

"Maybe I already have. I just talked to the poor sap who escorted Clarice to the dance. It seems our Clarice disappeared with a cup of coffee and emerged from the veranda a few minutes later without it."

Allison let out a low whistle. "The second cup of coffee. So that's where it came from."

"Hold on a minute. He didn't see her go on to the veranda with the coffee. He just said she had it a few minutes earlier. That's not even good circumstantial evidence at this point. I'm afraid I'll have to face the formidable Miss Bailey again and see what she'll tell me."

"Better you than me," said Allison, "I already had a creepy encounter with her just a few minutes ago. With her around they should call this place Jekyll and Hyde island."

"I take it she was giving her charming side a rest today."

"Actually, she has a third side that consists of being formally polite while slipping in the knife; not outwardly hostile, but far from friendly. I said something about Bradley and she showed her nasty side again. Honestly, it's like there are three of her."

"One is plenty," said Max.

Allison frowned suddenly. "Max, I just remembered something. It probably doesn't mean anything, but the Woodson's have a man named Carlos Sanchez, a Cuban. I saw him the other day and he looks like a nasty customer."

Max shrugged. "So?"

"Well, I was talking to another one of the Woodson's help and she says he gives her the heebie jeebies as well. She says he's almost Woodson's bodyguard."

"Interesting, but not very compelling," said Max.

"I know it's a little far-fetched, and you probably don't need another suspect to deal with at this point, but what if Woodson had a quarrel with Dawkins and Sanchez overheard and got a little over protective?"

"A little overprotective? That's like saying the Great War was a little unpleasant."

"Well, I said it was far-fetched."

"That's all right. I've got to look under all the rocks to find the treasure."

At that moment, a voice called out to Max and they saw McHale the gamekeeper coming down the path accompanied by his assistant, Howard Falstaff. McHale was carrying two double-barreled shotguns and Falstaff was hauling a sack over his shoulder.

"Ah, home are the hunters, home from the hill," said Max. "And it appears you've shot dinner for tonight."

"A couple of fine pheasants," McHale replied with obvious pride. "Harold bagged them just as they were rising from the marsh on the north end of the island."

"And they have some good feathers if you'd like some, Mrs. Hurlock," said Falstaff, eagerly. "Just the thing for a nice hat."

"I met Mr. Falstaff yesterday," Allison explained. "He was showing me the impressive feather collection at the gamekeeper's shop."

"I have that Enfield we talked about all oiled up, Mr. Hurlock," Falstaff continued. "Any time you're free for a hunt, you just drop on by."

"That's right," McHale chimed in. "There's nothing like eating a dinner you shot yourself."

"Providing someone else cooks it, I suppose," said Max. "Say, I did want to ask you fellows one thing; do you keep any chemicals around for preserving hides?"

McHale nodded. "Well, just a little tannic acid and maybe a bit of arsenic, but nothing is missing."

"Besides, it's always locked up when neither of us is there," Falstaff added.

"Of course," said Max. "Well, I hope you don't mind my questions, but I'm trying to learn everything I can about this place and the people here."

McHale grinned. "Sure thing, Mr. Hurlock. We all have our jobs to do on Jekyll Island. Well, Harold and I have to get these pheasants to the kitchen. Good day to you folks."

Max and Allison stood watching the gamekeepers go. "Well, I suppose you can at least eliminate them as suspects," Allison remarked. "With their arsenal and experience, either one of them could have shot Bradley Dawkins from a hundred yards away, and made it look like a hunting accident if they wanted to do him in. Poison would be the last thing either one of them would use."

"You could say the same thing about Bwana Pete," said Max.

"Maybe, but he does have a clear motive."

Allison frowned. "You know, Max, seeing the gamekeepers reminded me of something. When Theresa Woodson was showing me around, we stopped by the gamekeeper's shop and only the assistant was there."

"Falstaff?"

"Yes. We surprised him as he was working with his sleeves rolled up. He rolled them down quickly as if he didn't want us to see his arms."

Max shrugged. "Maybe he was just making himself look presentable for you ladies."

"Probably, but I did notice some sort of a tattoo on his forearm, and wondered if that was what he was covering up."

"What kind of a tattoo?"

"I just got a glimpse, but it was mostly a blotch...here, let me draw it."

She took out her ever-present notebook and a pen and started sketching.

"It looked like this, sort of, maybe the size of a silver dollar. As I say, I only got a glimpse. Does it look familiar?"

Max squinted at the drawing. "It looks like a blob all right. Now why would he want to hide it?" said Max. "I guess I'll have to ask. It probably doesn't mean anything but when people appear to be hiding things, my curiosity starts working overtime."

"Mr. Hurlock!" Another voice rang out behind them and they turned to see Jason Williams approaching.

"Hello again, Mr. Williams," said Max. "Allison, this is Jason Williams, the bibliophile handyman around here."

"Pleased to meet you, Ma'am. Mr. Hurlock, I'm glad I ran into you. I was just talking to Sanchez, Mr. Woodson's man."

"Yes, I know of Mr. Sanchez," said Max "What about him?"

Williams looked over his shoulder as if afraid of being overheard. "He brought in one of those cast iron planters to be repaired; said it had fallen over and cracked. Well, I was looking it over to see what we could do and just sort of making conversation when I mentioned poor Mr. Dawkins. Well, this Sanchez fellow just sort of sneers and says that maybe Dawkins did something to deserve it. To deserve it! I said only the worst criminal deserves to be killed by another's hand. Sanchez just sort of kept quiet after that, but it made me right nervous, Mr. Hurlock. What sort of a man would say such a thing?"

Max looked at Allison. "I don't know, but maybe I can have a word with Mr. Sanchez and find out."

"Thank you, Mr. Hurlock," said William, obviously relieved to get the information off his chest.

"Oh, by the way," said Max, "What are you reading, Mr. Williams?"

"What am I reading? Why, one of the great works of Dostoevsky; Crime and Punishment."

"Seems appropriate," said Allison, "at least the crime does. Max is still working on the punishment part."

"The thing is," said Williams, "that this Raskolnikov character kills an old lady pawnbroker in St Petersburg."

"Yes, I remember the story," said Allison. "He's pursued by a detective named, uh, Por something, I think."

"Porfiry," said Williams. "But the thing that's interesting is how Raskolnikov convinced himself he was justified in doing it. He considered himself some sort of superior being. Is that what murderers do?"

"Well," said Max, "let's just say they convince themselves that the rules don't apply to them."

As they walked away, Allison turned to Max. "Do you think there's anything to this Sanchez business?"

Max shook his head. "It's another long shot, but you never know. Still, I'd put Sanchez way down the list. I'll talk to him, but first I need to question the rest of the partygoers about spilled coffee and see if Clarice will enlighten me on just what she was doing on the veranda."

"Talk about a long shot... Well, I've got to go the other direction," said Allison. I've caged an invitation to a ladies' tea at the Crane Cottage. I'm to be the guest of Nancy McCormick."

"She seems to have taken a shine to you."

Allison checked her makeup in a pocket mirror. "Either that or she thinks I'm a kindred anti tradition person. I'll just have to see."

She kissed Max on the cheek. "Anyway, I'll see you at dinner tonight if we don't run into each other before that."

No sooner had Allison disappeared from sight behind the clubhouse annex then Max heard the unmistakable sputtering of a red bug behind him. He turned and saw Bwana Pete. The red bug skidded to a stop on the gravel beside him.

"Ah, Max. There you are. Hop in and I'll show you another part of the island."

"I have my hands full with this part, Peter. I have all these people to look up and question." He showed Bwana Pete the list he was working from and he looked it over.

"Well, that's all right then. I'm going to the beach on the Atlantic side. Many of the people on the list will be there."

Awkwardly, Max got in the passenger seat of the red bug and they were off, fishtailing down the path. "How fast does this thing go, anyway?"

"Oh, not very fast, really," said Bwana Pete. "It just seems fast because of the noise and because your bottom's riding so close to the ground. Still, it gets you where you want to go around here."

They passed a mixed group of bicyclers heading in the same direction. The men were all wearing suits and straw hats, while the women were wearing long skirts, which made the riding awkward.

"So where are we going that's attracting so many people?" Max asked, shouting to be heard over the engine.

"The beach on the ocean side. We're having red bug races today."

"Do you think it's all right to leave Eva alone?"

Bwana Pete shrugged. "I didn't have much choice. She practically threw me out of the house. ..said she had some thinking to do. She was going to take a walk."

"Thinking about what?"

"She didn't say, but it didn't sound like she wanted company, so I made myself scarce. I suppose she has some things to sort out."

"What do you suppose Eva has to sort out?"

"I would have thought that was obvious," said Bwana Pete. "He husband has been murdered and she is most likely going to be arrested and tried for it. That seems to be plenty to think about. Sometimes I wonder how she stands it. Calling you in was her idea, you know."

"Was it?" said Max. "I had assumed you both decided."

"In the end we did, but at first I wanted to hold off and trust justice to run its course. I couldn't believe they'd seriously consider Eva the killer."

"So what made you change your mind?"

"Frankly, I'm not sure I have changed my mind. We'll just have to see what you come up with."

"Thanks for the vote of confidence."

"Don't take it personally, old boy," said Bwana Pete. "It's just that I'm fond of Eva and don't want to see her get in trouble."

"A little late for that," said Max.

The trees were thicker now, crowding in on the edges of the gravel pathway, with an occasional small branch slapping their arms as the red bug zipped past. Suddenly, the path opened into a clearing that opened onto a beach. The gray and restless Atlantic waves washed at the edge of the sand while ragged gray clouds drifted through a blue sky.

Five red bugs were lined up on the beach so they could run parallel to the shoreline. Well-dressed men, women and children were circulating among the vehicles speculating about which was fastest. Bwana Pete pulled his red bug in line and got out.

Max saw several of the people on his list and started to approach them individually. Not everyone welcomed Max's polite question, but answered when Max convinced them he was acting with the approval of Sheriff McCoy."

"Coffee stains?" said Harlan Caldwell. "Don't you think you're going a little overboard on this gumshoe business? I'm as fond of detective stories as the next fellow, but there is a limit. After all, they found the poison bottle in her house didn't they?"

"They found a bottle, yes," Max explained patiently, "but they won't know for sure what was in it until they get the test results back. Meanwhile, they're gathering more evidence. So what about the coffee stain?"

"Neither of us had anything spilled on us that night. It was a genteel affair."

Max checked off another name.

"Why, Maxwell, I feel left out. This is most ungallant of you."

Max turned and saw Clarice Bailey standing with a parasol and pouting.

"Or are you just saving me for last?"

"Last?" Max said.

"I heard you talking to Mr. Caldwell. Don't you want to examine me about the dance?"

Max smiled. He wanted very much to talk to Clarice about the dance, but had decided to lull her a bit before springing his questions about the veranda. "Oh, why yes, of course. First of all, I'm interested in the dress you wore…"

"Oh, you would have loved it, Maxwell. It was pearl gray with embroidered red roses. It had full-cut sleeves and a daringly low-cut bodice. Why Mr. Caldwell couldn't take his eyes off of it."

"I'll just bet he couldn't," said Max, "but all I need to know is if Eva Dawkins might have spilled any coffee on it."

Clarice looked shocked. "Oh, Maxwell, how can you suggest such a thing? Eva Dawkins may have killed her husband, but I doubt she would stoop to despoil another woman's dress."

"I'll take that as a no," said Max.

"Of course, I know you need to be thorough in your investigation. Why don't you stop by after the race and we can examine the dress together?"

"Tell you what," said Max. "You can examine it and let me know if you find a coffee stain."

"Two heads are better than one, Maxwell."

"You're right. Why don't you ask your friend Albert to help you?"

She pouted. "Albert is such a bore. I'll bet he's never solved a crime in his life."

"Most women would settle for a man who's never committed one," said Max, smiling.

Clarice giggled. "Oh, Maxwell; you are the witty one. I could just listen to you all day." She placed her hand on his shoulder in reassuring manner, her fingers actually massaging his shoulder muscles slightly as she spoke.

"Now, Maxwell, you just ask me whatever you like. You will find I can be <u>most</u> cooperative." She was gazing in his eyes in a way that would have gotten her arrested in some places.

"So tell me about your visit with Bradley Dawkins on the veranda that night."

Her hand dropped and she went pale.

"My...visit.."

"Well, you and Bradley were old friends, weren't you? Nothing wrong with dropping in on an old pal to exchange pleasantries. What did you talk about?"

Clarice had still not recovered. Her bedroom eyes were now the eyes of a cornered animal.

"I...I heard he was ill. I...looked in on him. That's all."

Max nodded. "Of course. Very thoughtful of you. So how was he?"

"He...he was doing better, but still not well. I told him I wished him a speedy recovery, then left. That was all."

Max was still nodding encouragement. "I see. Oh, one more thing; how did he like the coffee?"

Her eyes widened. She began to deny it, but realized Max wasn't just fishing. "All right," she snapped. "So I brought a sick man a cup of coffee. Was that a crime?"

"It was if you killed him with it."

Clarice's blue eyes shifted from panic to malice. "Mr. Hurlock, I think you'd do better gathering evidence against the real killer than harassing the innocent."

Max continued smiling. "Of course. It's just that they're so hard to tell apart sometimes."

Clarice turned on her heel and walked away, spinning her parasol, but Max had gotten what he wanted. Clarice Bailey had admitted bringing a cup of coffee to Bradley Dawkins at the dance. The problem now was to find out which one was poisoned.

Within a few minutes, Max had talked to almost everyone at the beach who was on his list. Only Herbert Davis, a Board of Directors member remained. Davis stood off to the side smoking a thin cigar. Max approached him through the sand and nodded.

"Morning, Mr. Davis."

"Ah, Mr. Hurlock isn't it?" Davis replied. "You were the lad who came by our board meeting. We talked about you for a good 20 minutes afterwards."

Max smiled. "I'm glad I made an impression."

"Absolutely. We thought there was much in what you said. The sooner all the facts come forth the sooner this whole sordid business can be wrapped up. You're right of course. A thing like this is bad for the club, and has to be concluded as soon as possible. We can't just let it fester and hope for the best."

"I'm glad you feel that way," Max began to reply, but was interrupted by the race announcer standing nearby.

"All right. Everybody ready," shouted a portly man with a megaphone. "Drivers take your places. Ready, set, go!"

With their engines buzzing like a swarm of bees and their wheels kicking up sand, the red bugs took off down the beach to the cheers of the spectators. They weren't really going all that fast, but they were lively and noisy, and the people loved it.

"They'll go down a couple of hundred yards to a flag we've planted there and then turn and come back here for the finish," said Davis. "It's a bit silly, but it's good clean fun. So what did you want to ask me?"

"On the night of the dance where Bradley Dawkins died, we think Mrs. Dawkins may have spilled some coffee on another member as she was taking it across the crowded room to her husband."

Davis shrugged. "Wouldn't be surprised. It got damned crowded from time to time. You couldn't get from one spot to another without jostling someone. Well, what of it?"

"I'm trying to find out if anyone has a coffee stain on what they were wearing that night, a stain made by the coffee Mrs. Dawkins was taking to her husband."

Davis looked shrewdly at Max. "And if they did, you could have it tested for poison, thereby connecting her with the crime. That's smart, Hurlock. I like the way you think."

"Well?"

"As a matter of fact," Davis replied slowly, as if trying to recall, "Amelia, that's Mrs. Davis, said something about Eva Dawkins accidentally splashing coffee on her new dress, She didn't think anything of it at the time...said she'd have to have it cleaned."

"Where is this dress now?"

"Probably at the laundry. Amelia said something about sending it over there today."

"What does the dress look like?"

The red bugs had rounded the turn and were roaring back, making further conversation difficult.

"Oh, uh..." Davis waved his hands and groped for words, like a blind man trying to describe a sunset. "I think it was sort of a blue color, and it had some kind of a pattern on it; birds or something I believe."

"Thanks," said Max. "Now as soon as my ride gets back here, I can go back and check. I assume you would have no objections to my sending the dress away for analysis?"

"No; of course not. Anything to advance justice."

The red bugs crossed the finish line to the cheers of the bystanders. Bwana Pete jumped out of his red bug and came up to Max.

"Second place this time. Not bad!"

"Congratulations," said Max. "Now let's see how fast you can get me to the laundry."

Bwana Pete looked bewildered. "To the laundry? Well, if that's what you want, but I've never seen anyone so anxious about a clean shirt before."

Although Allison had been told of the luxurious interior of Crane Cottage, she was still not prepared for what she saw as she walked in the front door. Allison found herself stifling a gasp as she took in the scene in front of her. The entire first floor seemed to consist of one huge room with smaller rooms off to each side. With exposed wood beams, rich carvings, tapestries, and antique furniture, the room resembled nothing so much as the great hall of a castle. A double door on the other side of the room opened onto a meticulously manicured interior courtyard with a fountain in the center, reinforcing the impression.

Allison turned to Nancy McCormick.

"Nice place. Has Henry the Eighth arrived yet?"

Nancy chuckled. "It is a bit much, even for Jekyll. One of the board members complained that the cottage would make the clubhouse look small. Oh, but the Cranes are marvelous people. Everyone's just mad about them."

"Well, it's a place to hang your hat," said Allison.

"Come on. I'll introduce you to Florence Crane. She's a dear."

Before they got to Florence Crane, however, Millie Hester intercepted them. She was tastefully dressed for the occasion in a dark green dress, but looked worried.

"Nancy, Allison; I'm glad you're here. Has Eva been arrested?"

"Arrested?" said Allison. "No. The sheriff is still investigating and waiting to hear some lab results, so Eva is still around. What made you think she'd been arrested?"

Millie Hester looked from side to side and lowered her voice. "Oh, you know. First there was that terrible business about the bottle they found in Eva's basement. And now, well, just before I came here, I went to see her along with my husband Phillip and there was no one at her cottage. Phillip was most disappointed."

"Why would Phillip be disappointed?" Allison asked.

"Oh, he wanted to discuss something with Eva about Bradley's business affairs. Bradley was going to use Phillip's bank for his financing, you know."

"Was he?" said Allison. "I thought that was just in the talking stage."

"Oh, no;" Mrs. Hester assured them, "it was all set. They just had to sign some papers."

"That's all?" Nancy asked.

"Yes, and Phillip wanted to make sure Eva would be able to follow through...for her own protection, of course."

"Of course," said Allison, trying to keep the sarcasm out of her tone.

Millie Hester sighed. "Well, I suppose she'll be back, then. I was concerned for nothing. It's just that you don't know from one minute to the next what's going to happen around here."

"You certainly don't," said Allison, mostly to herself.

After she met Florence Crane and complimented her on the cottage, Allison circulated among the women talking and listening for information she could use in her article. Most of the women seemed to love the island, but a few chaffed under the relative lack of excitement. Maybe that was why there was so much interest in the murder of Bradley Dawkins.

"Clarice seems to have taken an interest in you, old boy," Bwana Pete shouted above the sputtering of the engine.

"I think she takes an interest in anything that's not wearing a skirt," Max replied. "She's an attractive woman. Apparently she's found she can usually get away with manipulating men even when it's obvious she's doing it."

Bwana Pete smiled. "That's Clarice, all right. She latched on to me when I first came here, especially when she learned I was close to Bradley. For a while I was infatuated. If she were a hunter, she'd have had my hide on her wall. She's so easy on the eyes a man doesn't always notice the other part."

"The other part?"

Death on a Golden Isle

"She went after Bradley in a big way, but there's only one real love in her life. She sees it whenever she looks in the mirror. She'll be sweet and flattering. She'll hang on your every word. She'll gaze into your eyes like you're the most fascinating person on earth, and make you feel like you're ten feet tall. Just don't cross her. She'll step on you like a bug."

"In her eyes, Bradley Dawkins crossed her, didn't he?" said Max.

Bwana Pete looked at him. "Yes, I suppose he did at that."

"Maybe the poison was her way of stepping on him," said Max.

"I wouldn't put it past her," said Bwana Pete. "She doesn't like to lose and she takes it personally. You keep an eye on that one, Max, and I don't mean because of her looks."

The red bug skidded to a stop on the gravel in front of the laundry building, a frame structure smelling of steam and soap. Max jumped out and opened the front door to see a counter and several dozen bundles of laundry on one side of the room and several piles of dirty laundry on the other. Behind the counter was a middle aged black woman who seemed surprised to see him.

"Good afternoon, suh. Y'all are that Mr. Hurlock, ain't you?"

Max smiled. "That's me. Who are you?"

"Me? I'm Mattie. I sort out the laundry around here. You need something cleaned?"

"No, Miz Mattie. I need something <u>not</u> to be cleaned; not yet at least."

Mattie frowned, trying to make sense out of Max's remark. She was not successful.

"You want something to stay dirty?"

"I'm looking for a dress belonging to Mrs. Davis. They just dropped it off a little while ago. It's sort of blue with some kind of a pattern."

Mattie's face lit up. "Oh, you mean that gown they brought by this morning. That was one pretty dress."

"Yes. Have they started washing the laundry that was brought in today?"

Mattie nodded rapidly. "Oh yassuh. We does the laundry around noon each day. That way we have time to dry it the same day." She looked up at the clock. "Fact, it should be just about done by now."

Max's face fell.

"Almost done? I suppose you use hot water and plenty of soap?"

"Oh, yes, Mr. Hurlock. Believe me, we get out all the dirt and stains."

"All the dirt and stains," Max muttered to himself.

"I can call Rosie out here, Mr. Hurlock. She does the washin' Maybe she can fish that dress out for you."

Max shook his head. "No. I'm afraid it's too late. You see, I needed to retrieve it before it was washed. Thank you anyway."

"Sorry, Mr. Hurlock. I guess we be too fast this time."

Max walked out and found Bwana Pete still sitting in the red bug.

"No, luck, old boy?"

"Lots of luck," said Max, "and it's all bad. The dress was already washed."

"And that's bad?"

"That's bad. I needed to see if it had a coffee stain."

"Ah, the spoor of the killer, eh? Well, that's too bad. It reminds me of the time I tracked a wounded Cape Buffalo in the veldt. I'd plugged him right between the eyes, but the horn boss in that area is very hard and thick, so I didn't know just how badly he was hurt. There was a blood trail, but that could go on for days, so I followed him. Of course, on the veldt, there's not much undergrowth, so it wasn't difficult, just frustrating because I didn't know if the buff was alive or dead. In a case like that, sometimes the first hint you get that the animal is still alive is when it comes charging at you. As it turned out, he was dead, but he traveled a good five miles before he dropped."

"Why didn't you just let him go off to die in peace?"

Bwana Pete shook his head. "Oh no. You can't let a wounded animal go. That's when it's the most unpredictable and dangerous. It would be a menace to anyone in the area. No, you have to track it down and make sure it's dead."

Max nodded. "A good story, but what does it have to do with finding a dress with a coffee stain?"

Bwana Pete slowly lit a pipe and looked at Max. "The way I see it, Max, you're in the same boat. You've got to follow every trail you can find, even if most of them just have a dead buffalo at the end. You've set things in motion and now you're responsible. Sooner or later you'll come to that dead animal, or maybe a live one. Then it'll be up to you to finish it off. Well, must be going. Good hunting."

The red bug sputtered and rattled away. Max strolled to the nearby gamekeeper's shop. One more dead buffalo to get out of the way.

John Reisinger

Chapter 15

Sanchez

As Max approached the gamekeeper's shop, Howard Falstaff emerged with a bag of game he was taking to the clubhouse for the chef. Max fell in beside him.

"You know, Harold, a tattoo is nothing to be ashamed of."

Falstaff stopped and stared at Max. "What...but how did you..?"

"So why are you hiding it?"

"I...I'm not hiding anything."

"But you have a tattoo."

"Oh, that. Gee, Mr. Hurlock, that's nothing. I hid it because some of the members might feel a little uneasy if the assistant gamekeeper has a tattoo. They associate tattoos with criminals and foreigners, so I try to keep it covered up. That's all."

"May I see it?"

Falstaff rolled up his sleeve. On his forearm was an ugly bluish blotch about the size of a silver dollar.

"It was a heart, and it had the name of a girl I was engaged to across it. When she suddenly married someone else, I wanted to get rid of that tattoo in the worst way. I went to a guy who sort of sandpapered it and made a mess. So I finally had a tattoo place inject some more ink so it would all run together and nobody could tell what it was. It was painful and expensive, but at least now I don't have to look at her name every day. That's another reason I'm self-conscious about it."

"It does look something like a heart at that," said Max, squinting at the bluish blotch. "It looks like there was an arrow or something through it diagonally."

Falstaff nodded. "Yes, I guess I went overboard when I had it done. That's why they couldn't remove all of it. Her name was in the middle, but at least you can't see that."

Max nodded. "I understand, but I still think it's nothing to cover up. I've seen birthmarks that are bigger. Still, if that's how you feel, I suppose it's up to you. When I see someone hiding something, I have to ask why. I'm sure you understand. But as long as we're talking about secrets, what do you think of the murder? Do you think Mrs. Dawkins did it? Everyone else seems to."

"Gee, Mr. Hurlock. To tell you the truth, I don't know what to think. Mrs. Dawkins seems nice and all, but.."

"But what?"

Falstaff frowned, as if forcing a thought to come to the surface. "You never know what people are really thinking, do you? I mean, one of the members here is always real friendly to me. He always asks me how I'm doing and all. Well, one day I was delivering game at the clubhouse and I overheard him talking to some other men and he told them I was 'slow'. It kinda cut me like a knife. I tell you, Mr. Hurlock, I haven't looked at him in the same way since. Sometimes people say one thing and are really thinking something else."

Max nodded. "How true. Do you think that applies to Mrs. Dawkins?"

Falstaff shook his head. "I didn't say that, but who really knows what went on between her and Mr. Dawkins?"

To Max it appeared Falstaff's face clouded over as he spoke, as if he was holding something back.

"You know, Harold, I get the feeling you know a little more than you're saying."

"Well..."

"If you know anything, you'd better tell me. Even some small detail could make a big difference."

Falstaff shook his head. "I don't spread gossip about the members, Mr. Hurlock. That's not right."

"I'll tell you what's not right," said Max sternly. "What's not right is withholding information that might be important in a murder case."

Falstaff paused a long time, and then looked around before speaking. "The day before the dance, Mr. Dawkins came by the gamekeeper's hut to drop off his gun for cleaning. It's a service we do for members. Mr. Dawkins wasn't really a frequent hunter, but he hunted once in a while and kept a gun around for varmints that might get in the house or mess up his garden. Alan was out hunting and I was there by myself. Anyway, Mr. Dawson was usually a cheerful guy, but he seemed to be worried about something. I asked him if anything was wrong and he said he'd had a really bad fight with Eva. That's his wife."

"I know who his wife is," Max reminded him.

"Oh, right. Anyway, I tried to cheer him up. You know, just two guys shooting the breeze over a shotgun.

I told him I used to have a girlfriend who'd get mad at me sometimes, but it never meant anything."
"And what was his reaction?"
Falstaff looked around again, and then spoke in a low voice. "He sort of looked away and mumbled something to himself. I don't think he meant for me to hear him, but I did."
"So what did he say?"
"He said 'I'll bet she never threatened to kill you.'"

Allison sat on a bench in the shade of an oak tree and worked on her article. The breeze made soft hissing noise in the branches above her while a swarm of insects hovered lazily nearby. She looked around at the pier, the clubhouse tower, the Sans Souci, the Crane cottage, and several other buildings and thought about what she had seen so far. She unscrewed the top of her fountain pen and began to write in her notebook.

If you've never been to the Jekyll Island Club, you'd probably assume it was a scene of indulgence, a place where millionaires light each other's cigars with lit hundred dollar bills while their wives bullyrag an army of servants to polish up the gold tableware and be quick about it. The actual place, however, is a model of understated domesticity, sort of a summer camp (in the winter) for the wealthy. Oh, it's certainly comfortable, and servants abound, but there is little conspicuous consumption and no decadence. The pleasures are simple; no elaborate costume balls and no dinner parties employing imported French chefs, just a formal dinner at the clubhouse each night, and private get togethers over tea and pastries. Sporting events consist of card games, bicycle rides, beach going, and the occasional motor race. The "cottages" are roomy and comfortable, but devoid of any dazzling display of marble or gold leaf. In short, the Jekyll Island Club is a place where members can relax and be a little bit lazy if they wish.

Allison read her words over. "I'm making this place sound like Atlantic City. Now, what should I say about the murder?"

The recent shocking murder of club member Bradley Dawkins has introduced an unfamiliar element of unease and even fear in this idyllic place. It would seem that even a millionaires club on an exclusive island is not immune to the currents of passion and intrigue that afflict the rest of the world. After all, one can escape from the everyday world on Jekyll Island, but not from human nature.

Allison looked at the article and shook her head. "Well, if nothing else, this article might win some sort of an award for understatement."

Max strolled casually past Excelsior Cottage in hopes of finding Carlos Sanchez, the gardener and suspiciously close servant of the Woodsons. Excelsior cottage was built in the style of an old Spanish mission, with stucco walls and balconies. In a flower garden off to the side, Max saw a tall dark-haired man trimming a hedge with clippers. He walked over.

"Hello there," said Max. The man turned around and nodded but did not reply. He continued clipping.

"Do you do the gardening around here?" Max asked. "It looks immaculate."

"Yes, Senor." Sanchez's voice was deep and rough.

Max looked at him as if he just realized something. "Say, aren't you Carlos Sanchez?"

Sanchez nodded again.

"Well, that explains it," said Max. "I've been hearing about your gardening skills."

Max sat on a nearby bench. Sanchez kept on clipping.

"What I like about gardening," Max continued, "is how it gets you outdoors in the fresh air, a place where you can keep in touch with the world."

No answer.

"So what have you seen, Carlos?"

Sanchez paused and looked at Max. "Senor?"

"I mean, you get around. You deal with a lot of people at the club. I'm sure you have a good sense of what goes on around here."

Sanchez shrugged. "I know a few things."

"I'll just bet you do. So what do you know about Bradley Dawkins."

Sanchez turned to Max and lowered his shears. His expressionless eyes peered out above a black mustache. "I know somebody killed him."

Max looked at him steadily. "Any idea why?"

"Maybe he make somebody mad. Or maybe he make somebody uncomfortable."

"Uncomfortable? What do you mean?"

Sanchez paused for a moment. "This place has many rich men, men who want to stay rich and men who want to get richer. Sometimes one man gets in another man's way."

"And whose way did Mr. Dawkins get in?"

"Maybe somebody's. Maybe that's why he's dead."

Sanchez went back to clipping the hedges.

"Any idea who?"

"No, Senor."

"How did Mr. Dawkins get along with Mr. Woodson?"

"All right."

"I understand they had an argument. What was that about?"

"It was nothing. Mr. Dawkins wanted the pier improved, but Mr. Woodson said the club didn't have the money. That was all."

"You heard all this?"

"Yes, Senor."

Max nodded. "You met Mr. Woodson in Cuba didn't you?"

"Yes, Senor."

"Mr. Woodson has been good to you?"

"Mucho bueno, Senor. He looks out for me and I look out for him."

"And just how do you look out for him?"

"I must get back to my hedges, Senor."

Max was just passing the chapel on his way back toward the clubhouse when he heard a voice.

"Mistah Hurlock!"

He turned. "Oh, hello again, Miz Mattie, How are things at your extremely efficient laundry?"

Hattie caught up, out of breath. "Mistah Hurlock, I been lookin' all over for you. Rosie come out just after you left. Seems that dress you was askin' about didn't get cleaned yet after all. The tub was already full and the dress was put aside for the next load."

Max's face lit up. "Miz Hattie, you are a gem! Where is the dress now?"

"Back at the laundry. I put it aside for you."

"Well, what are we waiting for? Let's get back there."

Back at the laundry, Hattie placed the dress on the counter and Max smoothed it out to examine it.

"Let's see. Nothing here...nothing here...wait a minute. Here it is."

Hattie peered over his shoulder. "What's that, Mr. Hurlock?"

"See that, Miz Hattie? That's what I was looking for. It's a coffee stain; a big beautiful coffee stain. It's a good thing you hadn't cleaned it yet."

Max bundled up the dress and wrapped it in brown paper. He paused in the doorway to tip his hat. "Thank you again, Miz Hattie, and thank Miz Rosie."

By this time, Rosie had come out and was standing by the counter as well, and when Max was gone, she turned to Hattie.

"I ain't never seen a man so happy to find a coffee stain."

Hattie shook her head. "You got to make allowances, child. He's from up north."

"Max! What do you have there?" Allison spotted her husband heading toward the pier with a parcel under his arm. He changed course and came over to her.

"It's a dress with a coffee stain. I finally found one. As soon as the Sylvia gets back I'm going to Brunswick to have Sheriff McCoy send it out for analysis."

"Congratulations," she said. "Hmmm. I never thought I'd be happy to see you running off with another woman's dress under your arm. I suppose it's all right provided the other woman isn't in it."

"Did I hear right?" Allison spun around and saw Eva Dawkins on the path behind them.

"Hello, Eva. Yes, you heard right. Max found a dress one of the wives wore at the dance that had a coffee stain on it from the coffee you were carrying to Bradley. He'll have it analyzed for poison traces. If they don't find any it will prove you didn't poison your husband."

Eva Dawkins looked surprised. "Oh? They can do that?"

"Max seems to think so, but we'll see."

Eva looked thoughtful. "Yes. Of course, someone else could have slipped the poison in before I took the coffee to Bradley."

"I'd say that's pretty unlikely. When you get a cup of coffee for someone, it usually is never out of your sight. You don't just put it down and go powder your nose."

"Well, the room was crowded..."

"Eva, it almost sounds like you're trying to explain away any poison they might find."

Eva shook her head rapidly. "No. Of course not. It's just that I'm not sure what happened that night. It seems anything is possible. I mean, everything else points to me and I didn't do it. They found a poison bottle that I never knew was there, and now they are checking a coffee stain I didn't know was there."

Allison looked at her curiously. "Eva, you almost sound like you're worried about the test."

"Well of course I'm worried. Who wouldn't be? I don't know who is doing the test and I don't know what they'll say they found. My entire life is in the hands of faceless strangers."

"It's the people you know that you should be concerned about," Allison reminded her, "people like Clarice Bailey, for instance. Did you know that Clarice also brought Bradley a coffee that night?"

"I'm not surprised. Clarice never gives up where men are concerned. She usually...wait a minute. If she brought his coffee, maybe she poisoned him.'

"That's a big maybe," said Allison, "but it is a possibility. A clean bill of health on your coffee stain would go a long way toward shifting interest in her direction."

"I can't believe it. Clarice can be vindictive, but murder?"

"A sense of rejection is a powerful motive," Allison reminded her, "especially to someone like Clarice. She probably saw you and Bradley as living slaps in her face. If she killed Bradley and you were blamed, she'd have revenge on both of you."

Eva sighed. "I just don't know what to believe."

"That's why we need evidence," said Allison. "And as soon as Max finds enough of it, we'll all know."

Max caught the boat to Brunswick and returned later that afternoon. He stepped off the Sylvia just in time to run into Robert Woodson who was coming down the path to the dock. He was waving a cane and shouting.

"Hurlock! I want to speak to you. Just who do you think you are, harassing an employee of mine? I pay the man to garden, not to get pumped for gossip by outsider busybodies. You do your gumshoe work at someone else's cottage with someone else's servants. Do you hear me?"

Max smiled. "Ah, Mr. Woodson. Good afternoon."

"Don't you 'good afternoon' me." Woodson was not mollified. "I demand to know why you were questioning Sanchez."

"I would have thought that was obvious; to obtain information."

"Hah! To pry into my affairs is more like it. Well I won't stand for it. You are a guest on this island but the club's patience is not unlimited. I resent this blatant intrusion into my private life."

"Mr. Woodson, I am not especially interested in your private life, but I am trying to get to the bottom of Mr. Dawkins's very public death. I did not ask Sanchez for any personal or financial secrets. I doubt that he would have told me anyway. But someone put poison in the coffee that night and that someone had a reason we have still to discover, so the sheriff and I have to cast a wide net. I'm sure you can understand that. Once the case is cleared up, these inconveniences will be soon forgotten."

"Not by me they won't."

"While we're on the subject of information, do you want to tell me what your argument with Bradley Dawkins was about?" Max asked matter-of-factly.

Woodson turned and walked away without another word. As he left, he brusquely tipped his hat to Allison, who was walking down the path in the other direction.

"Hey, Max," she said as she approached her husband. "What was that all about?"

"Let's just say that not everyone shares my enthusiasm for the quest for knowledge," said Max, shrugging.

"So did you get that coffee-stained dress to the sheriff?"

"Yes, and he sent it off by special delivery to California. We should hear the results in a few days."

"How about the poison samples he already sent?"

"He hasn't heard back yet, but the analysis could come back any time."

"Let's hope so. The season's ending and the members will start drifting away any day now."

Max shrugged. "So, what's a little added pressure?"

"Eva certainly seemed nervous about the coffee stain on the dress."

"What was she afraid of?"

"I can think of a few things. If I didn't know better, I'd have thought she was dreading what that coffee stain might reveal."

"I suppose it could be just a natural fear of uncertainty combined with the pressure she's under."

"Let's hope that's all it is," said Allison. "Otherwise, maybe you'd better make sure you get paid in advance."

Max plodded along for the next two days making little progress. Allison attended several teas and a card game. The investigation seemed to be stuck in place.

Then, after breakfast several days later, Max and Allison lingered outside of the clubhouse a few minutes. A distant put-putting grew steadily louder, heralding the approach of Bwana Pete's red bug. As the vehicle drew closer, Max and Allison could see that Bwana Pete had a passenger, the gamekeeper, Alan McHale. They skidded to a stop.

"Howdy, Allison, Max," Bwana Pete boomed. "Alan and I are rounding up people for the last big hunt of the season. Here's your chance to have some real sport."

"I'm getting plenty of sport chasing down the facts about Bradley Dawkins," Max reminded him.

"Not like this, Mr. Hurlock," McHale joined in. "We're going to the north side of the island to hunt wild pigs. They're destructive if you don't thin the herd once in a while and they're good to eat besides. We've got that Enfield all cleaned and oiled up for you."

"It's almost like big game hunting," said Bwana Pete. "The things will rush you sometimes. Adds a bit of excitement, eh?"

"I'm really busy here," Max began.

"Wait, Max. We've already signed up Colonel McCormick, Robert Woodson, Harlan Caldwell and Phillip Hester," said Bwana Pete. "You'll get more investigating done on the hunt than hanging around the club. What do you say?"

"We'll see." Max was still non-committal. "When is this assault on the local wildlife to take place?"

"This Thursday," said McHale. "Day after tomorrow. Tell you what; we'll reserve a spot for you either way. If you can find the time, I guarantee an experience you'll never forget. We'll supply everything you'll need. The kitchen even packs some food in case we get hungry. We leave around three in the afternoon."

"I'll see if I can," said Max. "Thanks for the invitation."

McHale smiled broadly. "I hope you can go, Mr. Hurlock. It'll be something to tell the folks back home about."

With a roar and a spitting of shells and gravel, the red bug took off down the road. They stood watching it go for a moment, then Allison turned to Max.

"What fun; an assortment of murder suspects thrashing about in the woods with loaded guns. What could possibly go wrong?"

"I didn't say I'd go for sure."

"Oh, you'll go Max. You won't be able to resist. But you'd better keep your head down and your eyes open. After seeing Eva, I don't think being a widow is much fun."

John Reisinger

Chapter 16

Hoof prints

Harlan Caldwell took a horseback ride most afternoons, and Max wanted to talk with him again, so he walked to the stables behind the shops along the road from the pier. He stopped by the gamekeeper's shack to inspect the Enfield they had been reserving for him. McHale assured him it was one of the best guns in the shop. Max picked the rifle up and mounted it to his shoulder. It was a perfect fit. The bolt action was smooth, quiet, and clean, and operated effortlessly. McHale knew how to take care of a firearm.

"Very nice," Max remarked. "You could get off a second shot with this almost before the first one hits."

McHale grinned. "I thought you didn't need a second shot, Mr. Hurlock."

A little farther down the road, Max stopped in to see Jason Williams, who was painting a garden trellis.

"How are you, Mr. Williams?" said Max as he stepped into the doorway.

"Real fine, Mr. Hurlock; real fine indeed." Williams wiped his hands on a cloth. "I finished 'Crime and

Punishment'. Too bad real murderers don't all have Raskolnikov's guilty conscience. Might make catchin' 'em a lot easier."

Max chuckled, then Williams frowned. "That Sanchez came by again. He dropped off this trellis to be repaired and painted. I don't know what you did to him, Mr. Hurlock, but that man was mad. Talked about outsiders askin' a lot of questions and getting' him in trouble with Mr. Woodson."

Max nodded. "I know. I had a little talk with Mr. Woodson and he wasn't too delighted either."

Williams let out a long sigh. "Well, I hope you bein' careful with those two."

"I'm trying to be, but neither of them was happy when I asked about Mr. Woodson's argument with Bradley Dawkins."

Williams looked uncomfortable. "Is that important?"

"The argument? I don't know, but it certainly could be. Why? Don't tell me you heard about it too?"

"Look, I don't go carryin' gossip about the members. They pay for my house and my livelihood. Besides, most of 'em is good people and I don't want to cause trouble."

"Of course not," Max agreed. "And if all you know is gossip, I don't want to hear it, but I've got a feeling you know something a little more directly."

"You gotta understand; members have disagreements all the time. It's only natural. Everyone does. They be rich people, but they're still people."

"So what was Woodson's disagreement with Bradley Dawkins?"

"Well, I was helpin' Sanchez fix a busted pipe to the fountain in their garden one day a couple of months ago and Mr. Dawkins was inside with Mr. Woodson.

Well, the windows were open and we could hear them arguing. Near as I could tell, Mr. Dawkins didn't think the club was controlling its expenditures properly. He said there was money that wasn't accounted for."

"And Woodson took exception?"

"Sure sounded like it. He said Mr. Dawkins was accusin' him of embezzlin'. It got pretty ugly."

"So how did it end up?"

"Mr. Dawkins left and that was it."

"Did they know you both overheard their argument?"

"No, I'm sure they didn't."

"Did Sanchez say anything about it?"

"No. He just looked at me as if he dared me to say anything, but I didn't. We finished fixing the pipe and I left. He never mentioned it. It probably doesn't mean anything."

"Maybe. We'll see," said Max. "I'd better go if I want to catch Mr. Caldwell. Thanks."

Feeling restless, Allison strolled over to the clubhouse and sat on the veranda with her notes. It was curious, she thought, how much activity took place in such a small area. The island was maybe eight miles long, but this little enclave the size of a few city blocks seemed alive with people coming and going. So Allison was only slightly surprised to see Millie and Phillip Hester.

"Hello, Allison," Millie Hester called, a little too loudly. The Hesters were neatly dressed as if on the way to church. Phillip was sporting a carved mahogany cane.

"And where is your husband?" said Phillip. "Questioning suspects?"

"Gathering information," said Allison. "He's trying to learn all he can.'

The Hesters sat down in adjacent rocking chairs.

"Well, I wish him luck," said Phillip, sitting forward with his hands on his cane. "Frankly, though, I'm surprised he's done as well as he has in this place. People can be a bit tight-lipped to outsiders, you know."

Millie waved her hand. "Oh pshaw. I'm sure everyone is cooperating. Has Max formed any opinion on the case, dear?"

"Only that there are a number of loose ends and inconsistencies."

"Ooh, inconsistencies. Do you hear that, Phillip?"

"I'm not deaf, dear. But I wouldn't get too excited. I'm sure there are always loose facts floating around in murder cases, but they seldom change the outcome. I just hope he can wrap this up in time for me to have a little heart to heart talk with Eva about using my bank for her future financing."

"Now, Phillip," said Millie, "this is no time to talk of such things."

"On the contrary, my dear, this is exactly the time to talk of such things. When Eva goes back home she'll be bombarded with opportunists that don't have her best interests at heart the way I do. That's why I hope Max can clear this up soon.'

Millie turned to Allison once again. "By the way, Allison, where is Max today?"

"I believe," Allison said with a slight smile, "that he's seeing a man about a horse."

"Max Hurlock!" called Harlan Caldwell when he saw Max at the stable. Caldwell was tightening the saddle cinch of his horse. "How are you, and where is that charming wife of yours?"

"She's charming someone else at the moment," Max replied. "It's you I wanted to talk to."

"I'm just about to go for a trot. If you'd like to come along, we can talk on the trail. You do ride, don't you?"

"I'd rather fly, but I can stay on top of a horse."

"Wonderful. I'll have them saddle up Jester for you. You ride English, I take it?"

Max nodded and in a few minutes, they were riding a trail in the pinewoods. The air was cool and damp and the only sound was the soft creaking of the saddles. They followed a narrow path that suddenly opened up on the beach where the red bug race had been run. The horses trotted along the wet sand by the water's edge.

"So how is the chocolate business?" Max asked.

"Doing very well; as long as the beans hold out."

"Why's that?"

"So much depends on the cocoa beans, you see. We have several suppliers from Central and South America, and the Caribbean, but with variations in temperature and rainfall, not to mention the occasional revolution, we have to constantly rebalance where we get our product. I have to go south at least once a year just to keep track of it all."

"Was Bradley Dawkins involved in cocoa in any way?"

"Bradley? Not at all."

Max thought of Bradley Dawkins's dying word and tried to fit everything together. He was not successful.

"I like being out on the trails and the beaches around Jekyll," said Caldwell. "Getting away from the club and the routine gives me time to think."

"And have you had time to think about Bradley Dawkins?"

Caldwell nodded. "All the time. I liked Bradley-Eva, too. It's a damned shame she killed him."

"Do you have any idea why she'd want to?"

"Not really. They seemed to get along all right."

"Did Bradley ever mention club expenditures to you?"

"Club expenditures? Oh, he'd get things stuck in his craw from time to time."

"What sort of things?"

"Bradley had an analytical sort of mind. He was always interested in the bottom line. He thought the club wasn't on a sound financial footing. According to Bradley, there are just not enough members to provide the steady flow of income needed to maintain the place, especially in view of the sixteenth amendment."

Max was puzzled. "You mean the sixteenth amendment to the club's bylaws?"

"No. The sixteenth amendment to the United States Constitution. You know, the one they passed in 1913."

"Oh yes. The one establishing the tax on income," said Max.

"Exactly. Bradley thought the income tax would ultimately doom the club because the government couldn't resist constantly raising the rates, leaving everyone with less and less of what they had worked for. With less money to spend, the members would find it harder to keep up the club. Governments crave money the way a glutton craves another meal. Of course he was right. We're all starting to feel the pinch. When the income tax was passed in 1913, it was three percent on a $50,000 income; this year it's 31 percent. A tenfold increase in only ten years! It's a damned outrage. Some members have already dropped out."

Caldwell reined in his horse to a slow walk and turned to Max. "Bradley was worried that the pinch on income might tempt people to find ways to cheat by padding club expenditures and pocketing the difference."

"Was anyone actually doing that?" said Max.

Caldwell shook his head. "I doubt it. Aside from the impropriety of it, anyone caught playing fast and loose with the club's books would have been ostracized."

"Yes," Max had to agree. "It would be a disgrace."

"I told Bradley he was barking up the wrong tree. Still, Bradley was concerned about the constant pressure of the rising income tax rates, so he was always on the alert for anything that didn't seem right as far as the club budget was concerned. He and Bob Woodson used to bicker about it all the time, but nothing ever came of it."

"I'm not so sure," said Max, under his breath. "How did you get along with Eva?"

Caldwell sighed. "A wonderful woman. I admire her greatly. Smart, poised, and a damned good looker. Bradley was a lucky man."

"Up until that fatal cup of coffee, that is," said Max. "Did Eva find you as irresistible as you found her?"

Caldwell didn't seem to take offense. In fact, he laughed heartily. "Few of the woman around here do, I'm afraid, but I keep on trying. Look, it's no secret I appreciate the ladies and I love to flirt. I appreciate a woman with beauty and brains, like your wife, for instance. I know an old dog like me is just being foolish, but I enjoy their company. I'm like a reformed drunk hanging around a bar just to take in the atmosphere; no one's likely to offer me a drink and I'd be afraid to accept if they did."

"So that brings us back to why Eva would want to kill Bradley."

Caldwell pulled up his horse and stopped with the surf gently lapping at the horse's hooves. He turned in the saddle and faced Max directly. "I don't know the answer to that, Max, but I know one thing: there's a lot more to Eva Dawkins than meets the eye."

"Meaning what?"

Caldwell smiled enigmatically. "Just my opinion, that's all. Come on. I'll race you back to the stable."

Chapter 17

Arrest

Feeling a little stiffness in some of his lesser-used posterior muscles, Max slowly made his way back toward the clubhouse. As he approached, he was surprised to see the Sylvia docking. Apparently the club steamboat had made an unscheduled run for some reason. Moving a little closer, Max saw Sheriff McCoy jumping off the boat with a deputy in tow and determination in his step. Something told Max this visit spelled big trouble.

"Sheriff McCoy!" Max called as he got closer.

McCoy spotted Max. "Ah, Max. You got an injury of some sort? Y'all seem to be walkin' funny."

"I'm fine. I just haven't been on a horse for a while."

"Well, here's somethin' that'll get your lasso in a knot," said McCoy with satisfaction. He produced an envelope and handed it to Max. "We just got the lab report from that Professor Heinrich out in Californ-eye-a."

Max felt a sinking in the pit of his stomach.

McCoy continued. "The professor found what I thought all along. The poison in the coffee was the same as what was in that bottle we found in Miz Dawkins's basement. You can't explain that away so easy."

"What about the coffee stain on the dress?"

"Ain't nothin' about that yet. We sent it after the coffee sample, but we'll hear back about that pretty soon too."

"So what are you going to do?"

"Now, Max, I'm sure you can figure that out without my help. Ah'm here to arrest Miz Dawkins for the murder of her husband."

Max didn't reply. He had unfolded the report and read it as they walked toward Osage Cottage.

"Sheriff, did you read this about the poison?" Max said finally.

"What kinda dang fool question is that?" McCoy snapped. "Of course I read it! What are you up to now, Hurlock?"

"I'm talking about the poison," said Max, waving the report as they walked. "It's an extract from the sap of the manchineel tree. It says here this tree only grows in coastal areas in the tropics; places like the Caribbean, Central America and Mexico."

"Yeah, I read that. Very interesting, but what is your point? I've got work to do."

"How would Eva Dawkins get her hands on the sap of some tree that only grows hundreds of miles to the south of here? For that matter, how would she even know about it?"

They were in front of Osage Cottage now. McCoy turned to Max. "Well now, I don't know the answer to that yet, but we gonna have ourselves a lot of time to talk about it over at the Brunswick jail. When I find out,

Death on a Golden Isle

I'll be sure to let you know. Now if you'll excuse us, we got a suspect to take into custody."

Before the deputy could knock, the front door opened and Allison answered.

"Good afternoon, sheriff," she said quietly.

The sheriff took off his hat. "Afternoon, Miz Allison. I suppose y'all know why we're here?"

Allison nodded. "The window was open. I was just having a visit with Mrs. Dawkins. She's in the parlor."

The sheriff and the deputy filed inside. Eva Dawkins was sitting in the parlor looking dejected and fearful. The sheriff took out a warrant.

Mrs. Eva Dawkins, you are under arrest for the murder of your husband, Bradley Dawkins. The deputy and I are here to escort you to the jail at Brunswick where you will be detained awaiting trial."

Eva rose. "Max, would you ask Peter to contact my attorney to see about bail?"

"Of course," said Max.

"I have to tell you, Miz Dawkins, that the judge in town don't usually grant bail in a first degree murder case. We can give you a few minutes to gather anything you want to take."

Eva shook her head. "I'm too upset right now. Allison, could you pack a few things for me and bring them by tomorrow?"

"Sure, Eva."

In a few minutes, the sheriff and the deputy were back on the Sylvia with their prisoner and on their way to Brunswick. Max and Allison stood on the dock watching them go. Eva was standing by the rail, a tiny, forlorn figure surrounded by the sheriff and the deputies.

"Rats," said Allison.

Max was more philosophical. "I'm just glad they took as long as they did. They probably could have arrested her a week ago."

"So what was that you were saying about the poison?"

"Extract from the sap of the manchineel tree, also known as *la manzanilla de la muerte*, the little apple of death. The sap is so toxic it can cause skin blisters if someone touches the bark. It grows green apples that are poisonous. It appears someone made a concentrate of the sap and put it in Bradley Dawkins's coffee."

"How in the world could Eva have done that? And where would she even get it?"

"I have no idea at this point," said Max, "but it occurs to me that there are several others around here who might have had a much easier time of it if they had been so inclined."

"Like that Sanchez character?" said Allison.

Max nodded. "He's from Cuba, so he'd know about the tree and he'd have had easy access to it. It would have been easy for him to bring the poison with him and use it against a man who was pressing his employer about financial irregularities."

"Or maybe Woodson himself did it with poison he got from Sanchez."

"Maybe."

"And Harlan Caldwell?"

"Possibly. He travels to the tropics annually and knows about tropical plants from his business. Maybe he wanted to get Bradley out of the way so he'd have a shot at Eva."

"And that would also account for Bradley saying 'cocoa' as he died. He wanted to point the finger at Harlan Caldwell of Caldwell's Chocolates."

"Of course Clarice Bailey, the McCormicks and the Hesters have possible motives, but no apparent connection with cocoa, not to mention the tropics or exotic poisons."

Max frowned. "No, but there's one other person we know who has both a motive and a connection to the tropics."

Allison's eyes widened. "That's right. Bwana Pete."

"I think," said Max thoughtfully, "we should have dinner with him tonight."

That night, Max and Allison ate with Bwana Pete at the club. Without Eva around, Bwana Pete was dispirited and listless. He poked at his food and sighed softly to himself.

"Do you think she'll get off?" he said finally.

"I don't know yet," Max answered honestly, "but she has some points in her favor. Take that poison for instance. Where would she get something that only grows in the tropics? Or even know about it? It would take someone with a connection with those regions."

Bwana Pete looked at Max suspiciously. "Someone like me. Is that what you're saying?"

Max shrugged. "You tell me."

"It's ridiculous. Bradley was my friend and so is Eva. I can't believe you'd think.."

"Look," Max cut him short, "Do you think I'm the only one who will make that connection? If Eva gets off, they could come looking for you next."

"Do you think she will...get off I mean."

"She does have some points in her favor," Max said cautiously.

"You don't have to sugar coat it for me, Max. I know that she's been the only real suspect from the first. Now she has the poison bottle in her house as well. It'll take a miracle now."

Max was silent a moment, then thought it best to change the subject.

"Are you still going on the wild pig hunt tomorrow?"

Bwana Pete nodded. "Oh, yes. It will get my mind off things. Besides, a hunt is one place where I really know what to do."

"What is it you find so compelling about hunting, Peter?" Allison asked. "Is it making the kill?"

"Making the kill? No, that's just the reward, sort of the medal you get for doing everything that leads up to it. What leads up to the kill is where the real pleasure is for me."

"What leads up to it?"

Bwana Pete looked wistful, as if talking about an old flame. "The kill isn't the important part by itself. If someone just wanted to kill animals he'd work in a slaughterhouse. No, it's the game of wits, really; man against beast. His cunning against your brains. If he's wrong, he dies. If you're wrong, you could die."

"But surely that's not a fair contest," Allison protested. "People are much smarter than animals."

Bwana Pete leaned back and lit a cigarette. Max was glad to see his mind was off of his problem with Eva Dawkins, at least for a while.

"People are smarter in many ways, of course, but in hunting, you're pitting yourself against the one area where the animal is your equal: survival instinct. You can't just go out into the bush and start blasting away. You'd never even see an animal. They'd be long gone, or if you're tracking dangerous game, you could wind up as the prey."

"Has that ever happened to you?"

Bwana Pete exhaled a long stream of smoke before continuing.

"Just once, and it rattled me so badly I almost gave up hunting over it. I told Max about tracking a wounded Cape Buff and finding him dead. Well, finding the animal alive is a lot worse. I was a guide on a safari several years ago in Rhodesia. We came upon a village that had lost one of its elders to a leopard and everyone was jumpy. They saw us passing through and asked us to help. We staked out some bait under a tree where someone had seen a leopard the night before. Leopards hunt at night; you almost never see one during the day. The client was all for it. He wanted a leopard pelt in the worst way and that's almost the way he got it; wrapped around a living leopard.

"We settled down on the downwind side so the cat couldn't get our scent and waited all through that night, and sure enough, a leopard came by just before dawn. Absolutely silent the thing was, and moving like liquid. You can't help but be in awe of a creature like that. It was beauty, grace, and lethality, all wrapped up together to make a perfect killing machine. The lion is bigger, of course, but the lion often gives himself away by growling. Not the leopard. You won't know he's around until he has your head in his mouth. I'd rather face a charging rhino than a leopard.

"Anyway, once the leopard was in the best position, I touched the client on the shoulder to tell him to take his shot. He lined up and fired. In the silence, the noise was deafening, and the leopard jumped. But the shot was off and the leopard was just wounded. Well, you can't let a wounded killer run loose, so I set off after it to finish it off.

"Fortunately the sun was coming up by that time, so I could follow the blood trail; just a line of small red dots in the dust. I knew I was getting closer, so I had my gun loaded and cocked, but I was pretty nervous. I knew a wounded animal is cunning and dangerous, but I was about to find out just how dangerous. Well, soon the blood trail passed under a large tree. As I followed, I could see the drops along the ground going past the tree and into some brush, so I was afraid that was where the leopard might be waiting for me. I was just about to pass under the tree, when I stopped and looked at the ground carefully. I really don't know what kept me from continuing toward the brush, maybe instinct, maybe just fear, but whatever it was, it saved my life. I noticed a small pool of blood just at the base of that tree, and for a split second, wondered how it got there. In that heartbeat of time I suddenly realized the leopard must be up in the tree! I swung my gun up just in time to see 200 pounds of spotted death coming down on me. Somehow I pulled the trigger and the now-dead animal fell on me and pinned me to the ground."

"Yikes," said Allison softly.

"The leopard had doubled back and climbed the tree to ambush me, using his own blood trail as a lure. The only thing that gave him away was the puddle he made as he waited up in the tree, still bleeding. So you see I tend to be very respectful of animal intelligence where their survival is concerned."

"And that's why you like to hunt?" said Max.

"Not that exactly, but the game of wits, reading the signs, figuring where the animal will be and how to get close enough for a shot. I imagine it's pretty much the same thing you do when tracking down a murderer, Max."

"I suppose it is," Max agreed, "and sometimes the cornered killer might arrange an ambush just like that leopard did."

Allison was still wide-eyed. "I assume there is no danger of one of the wild pigs you're going after tomorrow pulling a stunt like that?"

"Not a chance," said Pete. "They're not climbers, although they do have sharp tusks and can charge if you get too close."

"Sharp tusks? Oh, this just gets better and better," said Allison. "Max, why don't you hang out with fellows who collect stamps. I've never heard of anyone being gored by a penny magenta."

Max shrugged. "Unfortunately, in this case, philately will get you nowhere."

Allison was unappeased. "That's my Max; making dumb jokes in the face of death. I'll never look at a leopard skin coat the same way again."

Bwana Pete laughed. "Strange, isn't it? The leopard has spots for camouflage so it will be harder to see in the forest. A woman wears a leopard skin coat because she wants to stand out."

Max frowned. "That's an interesting point. Something that stands out in one place can be concealing in another."

Allison looked at him. "And?"

"Maybe our poisoner is camouflaged in some way. Maybe we're not seeing something that's right in front of us."

"Well, we'd better find it soon; there's not much time left," said Allison.

"Maybe. We'll just have to keep looking up in the trees for that leopard."

John Reisinger

Chapter 18

The Medal

After dinner, Max and Allison strolled by the pier in the twilight. "Well, Max, what now?"

Max looked out at the water. "Things are not quite as I'd like, I'm afraid. My client is under arrest for the crime I'm investigating. There are several people who should be suspects, but I've found no real evidence against them, and the sheriff has little interest in investigating any further. I've got to come up with something to shake loose some fresh evidence, but at the moment I have no idea what that might be. To top it all off, the sheriff is awaiting the lab results on Eva's coffee stain. If they show there was poison in the coffee she was carrying, I'm afraid that's the end of the road for her."

Allison snapped her fingers. "Oh, I almost forgot. Eva asked me to bring a few things to her in jail."

"Like what?"

"Oh, a few dresses, toiletries and unmentionables; things like that. She was too upset to pack anything when she was arrested, so I said I'd bring her some basics. If I stop by Osage cottage and pick them up now I can send or take them to her tomorrow. Why don't you come along? Maybe you'll get inspired."

"Come along and watch you rifle Eva's closet? Sure. Why not?" Max shrugged. "It'll probably be as productive as anything I'm doing here."

The light was fading as they approached Osage Cottage, now standing lifeless and silent.

The front door swung open to an empty house. Allison turned on the hall light and they went up the stairs to the main bedroom. The wooden treads creaked slightly underfoot. The bedroom was furnished simply in blue-upholstered chairs, a mahogany dressing table, an antique armoire, and a comfortable-looking bed. Twin closet doors stood along one wall. Allison opened one of the doors.

"Whoops. Wrong door. This is Bradley's closet." She touched the row of suits. In the silence of the now-empty house, she could almost feel the presence of the dead man.

"It's so sad, isn't it?" she whispered. "It's almost as if he never left, like he was about to...what's this?"

Allison had stopped by a dark blue jacket and was feeling the material. "This looks like his marine uniform. Why would he have it here?"

Max reached over and pulled the jacket from the rack. "This is a dress uniform. He must have worn it to dinner occasionally. Lots of ex-servicemen do. Remember when I wore my navy dress blues to the Odd Fellows Hall dinner in Easton?"

"How could I forget? There was no question just who was the odd fellow that night."

Max was still examining the uniform. "Two silver bars on each shoulder; he was a Captain. And some ribbons over the pocket. Let's see. This red, green, blue and yellow one is the Victory medal. They gave out a lot of these. Even I got one."

"What's that dark blue one with the two red stripes?" Allison asked, looking over his shoulder. "You don't have one like that."

"No. I'm not sure, but I think that's for duty in Haiti."

"Haiti?"

"Yes, we sent the marines to Haiti before the war to try to stabilize the place. Between insurrections and revolving door governments, the place was in need of a firm hand. It looks like Bradley Dawkins was on occupation duty down there after he came back from France."

"Max, you know Haiti is in the tropics."

"So I've heard."

"And I'll bet the manchineel tree grows there."

"Probably."

"So could it have something to do with the murder?"

"You mean some disgruntled Haitian came all the way to the United States and crept on to Jekyll Island with a bottle of poison just waiting for his chance for revenge?"

"Well, when you say it, I admit it seems far-fetched."

Max continued to look over the jacket, "Nothing in the pockets. I guess...hello; what's this? There's an old trunk in the back of the closet. Let's have a look."

He pulled out a small steamer trunk, painted an olive color and fitted with brass and leather. On the top was stenciled the words "B. Dawkins-USMC" in black letters.

"You don't suppose Eva would object if we took a look inside, do you?" said Max, unbuckling one of the leather straps.

"I don't think Eva would mind in the least. After all, what does she have to lose now?"

Max opened the trunk and found some shoes and shirts. "Nothing much here, it seems. Wait a minute. I see some pockets along the side." He pulled out several packets of papers and letters, all postmarked 1919-1920.

"Looks like a bunch of routine correspondence, a report or two, and a few faded photos of military life. Here's the mess hall. Here's a few officers sitting around a camp table. Here's the parade ground. Here are a few Haitians talking to a marine. Here are some marines erecting a tent. Here's a group of Haitians in some sort of fenced enclosure. This one looks like a baseball game. It looks like pretty routine stuff for the most part. This one is interesting. Most of the photos aren't marked, but this one says 'Cuban contractors'. It shows several dark haired civilians installing some pipes."

"Cubans again?" said Allison. "One of them isn't Sanchez by any chance?"

Max shook his head. "It doesn't look like it; not in this picture at least."

"Anything else?"

"Some disciplinary records. It seems some of the marines were put in the stockade for brutality toward the Haitians. One of them, a Lieutenant named Warren McCormick, was even discharged from the service for shooting ..."

Max suddenly stopped.

"Go on. For shooting what?"

Max looked up from the paper. "For shooting suspected cacos."

"Cacos?"

"Allison, remember that congressional investigation last year about conditions in Haiti and the Dominican Republic? I think I heard them use that term, but I didn't really follow it closely."

"Me neither, but Caco is mighty close to cocoa, and did you notice the Lieutenant's last name? McCormick. Could he be related to Nancy and the Colonel?"

"I don't know, but I think we need to do some research on the whole Haiti occupation. Here's something else."

Max was looking at an old folder.

"Jeepers, Max," said Allison. "If you stare any harder at that thing, you'll burn a hole in it. What is it, anyway?"

"It's a report on Lieutenant McCormick. It seems McCormick took out a patrol that captured five Cacaos. McCormick had them hanged on the spot. It looks like that was why McCormick was court marshaled and later discharged."

"So do you think McCormick tracked Bradley Dawkins here and poisoned him in retaliation?"

"It's a possibility, of course. The only problem is that the only people here named McCormick are the colonel and Mrs. McCormick. I'm beginning to wonder if this is connected to who poisoned Bradley Dawkins, but I'm not sure at this point. Even if I was sure, there's no proof anyway."

Max looked at his pocket watch. "I think the club library is open for another hour or two. I think we should find out more about the marines in Haiti."

The Jekyll Island Club library was in a single room. It was surprisingly modest for a millionaires club, but boasted a collection of newspapers from various places.

"Is there an index of these papers?" Max asked. The librarian, one of the members' wives on volunteer duty, said there was no index, since the papers were brought down by members as they saw fit. Max sighed and he set to work with Allison, looking for any references to Haiti and the marines in 1919 and 1920. The lack of an index made the effort hit and miss, mostly miss, but within an hour, they had gathered the information they needed.

"All right, Max," said Allison pushing back her chair. "I think we have a pretty good picture of what was going on in Haiti at the time. Now what?"

"We go back to the Sans Souci and get a good night's sleep. Tomorrow we get Bwana Pete and visit Eva."

The next morning, Max, Allison and Bwana Pete went to the Brunswick jail to visit Eva Dawkins. She met them in the visitors room, a cell-like place with whitewashed stone walls and a metal table.

"How are you doing, Eva?" Bwana Pete asked anxiously.

"Take a look around," she replied.

"Are they feeding you well?"

"The quantity is all right, but everything is pretty bland, and I wish the food came in some color other than brown. Did you get hold of my attorney?"

"Yes," said Peter. "He's contacting the judge about the possibility of bail this morning, but he's not optimistic since it's premeditated murder."

"We're doing everything we can to get you out, aren't we, Max?" said Allison.

"I'm still investigating, but I need any scrap you can give me. I have a few more questions."

"I'll do what I can."

Max turned to Bwana Pete. "Peter, I need to ask a few confidential questions. Nothing personal, of course, but if you could leave us alone for a few minutes, it will make it easier to sort out who knows what."

Bwana Pete looked uncertain.

"It's all right, Peter," said Eva, finally. "I have confidence in Max.

Bwana Pete walked outside and Max turned to Eva.

"Have you ever seen Sanchez around your place?" Max asked.

"That Cuban fellow you told me about? No, I don't think so, but I don't really know what he looks like so it's possible."

"Has anyone pressured you about anything, or approached you with a business deal since Bradley died?"

"Well, Phillip Hester still wants me to use his bank to finance Bradley's company, but he wanted that before. He's a little more insistent now because he says he wants to protect me."

"I'm sure. Anything else?"

"I've been wracking my brain, but I can't think of anything."

"Sure, but maybe you can help," said Max. "What do you know about Bradley's service in Haiti?"

She shrugged. "He mentioned it from time to time. Is it important?"

"We don't know, yet," said Max. "Last night we found Bradley's old trunk in his closet."

"Oh, yes. Bradley kept some papers and mementos in it. I'd almost forgotten about it. What about it?"

"Did he ever mention someone named Lieutenant McCormick?"

"McCormick?" She furrowed her brow, trying to remember. "He did mention him, I think he was drummed out of the marines for shooting prisoners, or something like that."

"What kind of prisoners?"

"There was some sort of local rebellion led by some wild bandit groups in the hills. They called them...." She hesitated, struggling to recall the name.

"Cacos?"

"Yes. That was it. Bradley didn't really talk about it much. That's all I remember him saying."

"Did Bradley ever talk about being threatened by this McCormick?"

"Threatened? No. Not that I remember."

"Do you know if this Lieutenant McCormick was related to Nancy McCormick and the Colonel?"

Eva Dawkins looked surprised. "Related? Oh, I don't think so. How could he be?"

"Never mind. Why don't you talk to Allison while I collect Peter and we have a word with the sheriff and see where he stands. If I turn up anything from this McCormick situation, it would be good to have the sheriff in our corner."

She chuckled. "Good luck. He's licking his chops over my upcoming trial."

"Oh, and one more thing," said Max. "I think it's best not to tell anyone about the trunk just yet; even Peter."

The sheriff's office was in the next building, so Max and Bwana Pete stopped by. Sheriff McCoy was in an affable mood.

"Mawnin'. Good to see you folks again."

"Same here, sheriff," said Max. "What do you intend to do about the Dawkins case now?"

The sheriff looked surprised, as if Max had asked him if he planned on jumping in the river. "Do? Why, I intend to set a spell until I get that lab report on the coffee stain. I figure that ought to nail the door shut on Miz Eva real good."

"You're not still investigating?"

"Why keep lookin' when you already got what you were after?"

Bwana Pete began to object, but Max restrained him.

"I understand what you're saying," said Max, "but you might have to rethink it if that coffee stain comes back negative."

Sheriff McCoy was unfazed. "I'd rethink it if'n my dog learns to sing Dixie, too, but I'm not expectin' it."

"So as far as you're concerned the case is closed?"

"I got the prime suspect who stood to inherit a fortune if the victim is out of the way; I got witnesses that saw her taking coffee out to the victim; I got poison in the coffee; I got the same poison in the suspect's basement. That should be enough for a conviction in itself, but just to erase all possible doubt, I also got proof on its way that the poison was in the coffee she was taking to the victim. Other than a full confession, I don't know what else I could want."

"You realize that if the coffee stain is poison-free that means that the poison was possibly brought by someone else."

McCoy snorted in derision. "Right now I'm not interested in possibilities. I'm interested in facts, and the facts say Miz Dawkins is guilty."

On the boat ride back, Max couldn't hide his disappointment. While Bwana Pete was talking with the captain, Max talked privately to Allison.

"I was hoping something in that trunk would ring a bell with Eva and the whole case would fall into place, but she didn't know much about it. She had heard of McCormick, but apparently he wasn't very important after all. Bradley barely mentioned him to her."

"So maybe he isn't part of this after all," said Allison. "That doesn't leave you with much. Maybe that leopard got away after all."

"Maybe, but I'll still ask the colonel if he's a relation. You never know."

Back at Jekyll Island, Max went to see Colonel McCormick. His wife Nancy answered the door.

"Why, Max. This is a surprise. I've so enjoyed talking to Allison. You two ought to join the club so you can spend more time here."

"Thank, you, Mrs. McCormick. You're very kind, but I need to have a word with the colonel."

"Ah, boy talk, eh? Well, come on in. He's just finishing his lunch."

Nancy McCormick led Max into a bright airy dining room with a heavy oak table. Seated at the table smoking a cigar, was Colonel McCormick.

"Ah, Hurlock. Good to see you again. Sorry about your client, but I can't say I'm too surprised. I'm sure you'd agree that sometimes the most obvious suspect is the correct one."

"Thank you, colonel," said Max. "You've been a big help so far, so if I could clear up one more minor matter, I'll be finished."

"Well, I don't see just what loose ends could be left, but fire away."

"This is probably just a coincidence, but I have to ask anyway. Bradley Dawkins apparently had some dealings with a Lieutenant Warren McCormick in the marines. Was Lieutenant McCormick a relation of yours?"

McCormick shook his head. "Maybe a very distant one, but I'm not aware of him."

Max nodded.

"Just for curiosity, what did this McCormick fellow do?" said Colonel McCormick.

"I didn't say he did anything," said Max.

"Oh, didn't you? Hmmm. So you didn't. My mistake. But why the interest?"

"Bradley Dawkins had occasion to discipline Lieutenant McCormick, so he's another possible suspect."

"You're grasping at straws now. Someone he knew in the marines? Why, that was at least four years ago."

"Still, I feel I have to check it out. One has to be thorough."

McCormick nodded. "Quite right. This is a serious case. You have to run down every alley, even dead ends."

Max rose from the chair. "Well, that's all I really wanted to ask you. It's a small thing, but I need to tie up the loose ends, so to speak."

The colonel looked at him with narrowed eyes. He seemed to want to ask something further, but didn't. "Yes, I suppose you do. Good day Mr. Hurlock."

After he left the McCormicks, Max found a bench under a tree and sat in the cool shade thinking for a long time. People passed by, but he barely noticed them. Finally, he stood up, straightened his jacket, and started off for the Sans Souci.

"So the McCormick in Haiti is no relation?" said Allison. They were in their apartment at the Sans Souci preparing for dinner. Allison was wearing a maroon gown with a pearl necklace.

"That's what he said, but he seemed awfully interested. There could be more than he's letting on."

"So how do you find out?"

"That's the whole problem with this case," Max grumbled. "No one wants to talk because everyone assumes Eva Dawkins is guilty anyway. And that includes our pal Sheriff McCoy."

Allison sat down in the wicker armchair next to the bed.

"Well, you can hardly blame them, can you? I mean, the evidence has pointed to her from the beginning, and finding the poison bottle in her house doesn't help her cause. Besides, they see you as a hired gun determined to help a murderess escape justice."

"You always know how to make me feel better."

"Sometimes a cold slap of reality is just the thing. Max, as a detective..."

"Investigator."

"...investigator, you're the elephant's eyebrows, but sometimes the usual ways just don't work. You've got your nose down following that blood trail Bwana Pete talked about while the leopard is waiting up in a tree somewhere. You have to try something different to stir things up."

Max slipped on his jacket and shot his cuffs. "You're right, of course. I've been thinking the same thing. I gave this case a lot of thought this afternoon after I left the McCormicks, and I believe I finally have it figured out. I'm not certain who did it, but I have a strong suspicion, since it seems to be the only solution that fits the facts. The problem is that, like Bwana

Pete's leopard, this person is concealing the blood trail very well. At the moment I don't have enough evidence and no one is going to help me get it. Even so, I think I can stir things up in a way that just might reveal that leopard. "

"Now you're cooking with gas," said Allison. "What are you going to do?"

"I think I'll try to do as Bwana Pete did on his leopard hunt; set out some bait and wait for the leopard to show up. Only I don't intend to miss."

"Sounds delightfully devious. How will you do it?"

"Well, have you noticed how everyone seems to be following our every move?"

"I suppose we provide something of a change of pace around here, especially now that the season is ending and most of the social and entertainment possibilities have been exhausted."

"Whatever the reason, I think I can use it to my advantage."

"Oh? And how do you propose to do that?"

"I haven't worked out the details yet, but I think it will require you to be in some conspicuous place tomorrow night. Any ideas?"

"I can drop in on the ladies' Mah Jongg game at the clubhouse. Nancy McCormick has been asking me to come anyway. It's very visible and it starts right after dinner. They go on for several hours."

"Perfect. I'll have to make some arrangements, but I think I have a way of looking up in that tree for a very wily leopard. Ready for dinner?"

At the club dining room that night, Max explained his plan.

"Ingenious," she said, "but as I see it, there is one very serious weakness. How will you get Sheriff

McCoy's cooperation when he's pretty much closed the case?"

"As usual, my love, you've put your finger on the nub of the problem, but I think it's worth a try, anyway. Tomorrow morning we'll take the Sylvia to Brunswick again and hope for the best."

Allison looked around at the other diners. "I suppose we've come a long way here, Max. At first everyone in the dining room gave us curious looks, now they ignore us."

"Maybe not for much longer."

The trip to Brunswick the next morning was uneventful as usual, although they noticed several of the seasonal help leaving until next year. The dozen or so people with their luggage were a reminder of how little time was left. Within a few days the members would begin drifting away as well.

They visited Eva Dawkins in the jail once again and Max explained his plan. Eva looked doubtful, but agreed it was at least a chance.

"But will the sheriff go along with it?" she asked.

"He's very understanding," said Max, with more confidence than he felt. "I'll explain it to him."

Allison remained with Eva while Max went next door to the sheriff's office and saw Sheriff McCoy. McCoy was about to leave on another case, but agreed to talk. Max carefully explained what he had in mind, but it did not go well.

"Y'all expect me to waste valuable time and energy on a wild goose chase in a case that's already been solved?"

"You've arrested a suspect," said Max. "That's not the same thing as solving the case."

"It sure as shootin' will be once a jury brings in their verdict. Hell, I know you're trying to help her, but you're lost in the kudzu on this one. For a man who says he chases down evidence, you sure know how to ignore it when it suits you."

"Funny thing about evidence," said Max, calmly, "You can never have too much, but often you don't have enough. All I'm asking is that you help get some more evidence."

"Tarnation, I got 'nuf evidence now to convict her twice over. You're asking me to get some more hounds when the possum already been treed. Well, I ain't gonna do it. The taxpayers would have my hide for wastin' their money. Now if you'll excuse me, I got some boys out in the swamps been runnin' some 'shine to speakeasies in Atlanta and I'm fixin' to pay 'em a little visit today."

"But Sheriff.."

McCoy slammed his palm down on his desk, causing a coffee mug to jump in the air. He made a noticeable effort to control his temper.

"Look, Max," he began in a quiet, but serious voice. "You're a nice fella, and a smart one. I've enjoyed workin' with you, I respect you, and I consider you a friend. But right now, you're getting' mighty close to obstructin' justice. Now you better back off or I'll have you in the next cell to your client. I won't be a part of any damn fool scheme and that's the end of it. The case is closed."

For a moment, they silently glared at each other. The only sound in the room was the slow ticking of an old-fashioned pendulum clock on the wall. Then a deputy appeared in the doorway.

"Sheriff, I'm sorry to interrupt, but you got a phone call."

"Tell them to call back."

"It's a long distance call."

"So who is it?" The sheriff was only mildly interested.

"It's from California. It's that Professor Heinrich. He has the test results and he's sending them to you in the mail, but he knew you were waiting on them, so he's calling to let you know what he found."

McCoy smiled at Max. "You wanted more evidence in this case? Well, here it is; Professor Heinrich's report on the poison in the coffee stain. That's what I'd call good timin'. This is the final piece of evidence against Eva Dawkins and even you won't be able to explain it away. Now you gotta admit she's guilty."

Max shrugged. "I told you I follow wherever the evidence leads."

The sheriff picked up the phone and greeted Professor Heinrich. McCoy listened silently at first, asked Heinrich if he was certain, thanked him, and then hung up.

"What the hell?" he whispered to himself.

"What is it?" Max asked.

McCoy looked up with an expression of bewilderment on his face.

"There was no trace of the poison in that coffee stain."

Max nodded and fought the urge to smile. "So, at the risk of obstructing justice, do you think you could help me get a little more evidence now?" he asked quietly.

McCoy looked at the phone, shook his head, then looked up at Max again.

"What time you want to start?"

Chapter 19

The pig hunt

Max and Allison arrived back at the Jekyll Island Club dock a little after noon. They were pleased to note that at least a dozen people saw them arrive. They had lunch at the club dining room, and then returned to the Sans Souci. They rested and talked over their plans until one thirty, then Max walked back to the clubhouse and sat in a conspicuous place in the main room, under a boar's head mounted over a fireplace. He made a show of thumbing through some papers.

At two-fifteen, an attendant found Max and told him he had a telephone call from Brunswick. Max picked up the phone in the club office and spoke within earshot of several people at the nearby bar.

"Hello? Oh, Eva. How are you? We just saw you this morning, whatever... Yes?...Oh, really? Where is it?....All that?....Why this is wonderful. It's just the sort of break we've been looking for. The next boat back isn't until six tonight and I'm going on a pig hunt in about a half hour, so I'll see you about seven tonight... This is great. Good bye, Eva."

Max hung up the phone and left, grinning broadly, leaving the bystanders to wonder just what Eva Dawkins had told him that made him so happy.

"Afternoon, Mr. Hurlock," said gamekeeper Alan McHale when he saw Max. He and assistant Harold Falstaff were busy making sure everyone had the proper ammunition, game bags, and picnic hampers. The other hunters were standing around sighting down rifle barrels, filling pockets and belts with ammunition, and generally getting ready to go into combat with nature.

"Afternoon," Max replied, looking around. "This is a pretty good crowd, isn't it?"

McHale smiled. "Oh, it's the last pig hunt of the season. It's quite an event."

Max noted with satisfaction the presence of Colonel McCormick, Robert Woodson, Harlan Caldwell, Phillip Hester, and Bwana Pete. They all greeted him courteously. Max was surprised to see that Woodson had brought Sanchez along to be his gun bearer.

"Say," said Max, "how long does this hunt usually take?"

"Usually about two or three hours. Why?"

"Oh, that's fine," Max replied. I just have to be back by six."

"I knew Max liked the cooking at the club," Harlan Caldwell joked.

"Or maybe he just wants to get back to that wife of his," Colonel McCormick added.

Max laughed good-naturedly. "Guilty on both counts, but actually I'm taking the Sylvia back to Brunswick."

"Leaving us so soon?" said Robert Woodson. "Well, can't say as I blame you. It's too bad about your client, but you did your best, I'm sure." Woodson's voice didn't sound the least bit regretful.

"Oh, I'm not leaving for good," said Max. "I'm just taking a trip to Brunswick to see Eva Dawkins. I'll be back around ten or so tonight."

"Didn't you see her this morning?" Bwana Pete asked. "Why go back again tonight?"

"If you ask me," chimed in Harlan Caldwell, "you're just getting that poor woman's hopes up for nothing. The evidence against her is overwhelming."

Harold Falstaff appeared with the Enfield and handed it to Max. Max picked it up and worked the action while the others looked on awaiting his response. He took his time, making a minute examination of the chamber while everyone looked at him.

"There is certain evidence that throws her in a bad light, I'll admit," said Max, sighting down the barrel, "but I believe that's about to change."

The gamekeeper's shop went silent. Even McHale and Falstaff stood staring.

"Well, don't keep us in suspense," said Bwana Pete. "Tell us what's happened."

Max looked indecisive. "I really shouldn't be discussing it. Everyone will know soon enough."

"Just a minute," sputtered Woodson. "Are you seriously suggesting that Eva Dawkins might not be guilty?"

"That is exactly what I believe," said Max, "and I will soon have the evidence to prove it."

"What evidence?" said Colonel McCormick.

"Yes, Hurlock. What evidence?" said Phillip Hester.

Sanchez remained silent, but glared at Max. McHale and Falstaff stood off to the side looking interested, but slightly bewildered.

"I really shouldn't discuss it. My client is..."

"Hurlock, this concerns more people than simply Eva Dawkins," Colonel McCormick reminded him. "This concerns the entire club. Now we've cooperated with you as best we could. We've given you full access to this private club and all its facilities. I think you have an obligation to let us know what is going on."

Max sighed and pretended to be wrestling with the decision. "You're right, of course. I'm grateful for the cooperation you've all displayed, and I wouldn't want to do anything that reflected poorly on the club. I suppose you do have a right to know."

Max paused again, as if searching for just the right words. "It's true I visited Eva Dawkins early this morning, but I got a phone call from her afterwards, just about an hour ago. Being in jail alone and away from her normal distractions gave Eva a lot of opportunity to think. She suddenly remembered that Bradley kept an old steamer trunk in his closet in their bedroom at Osage Cottage. Apparently Bradley Dawkins was a meticulous record keeper because the trunk is filled with papers, letters, reports, photographs, journals, a complete account of his time in the marines, and all of his correspondence up until his death."

The other members of the hunting party looked at each other, but no one commented.

"I believe the key to the murder of Bradley Dawkins is in that trunk, something that had nothing to do with Eva. Somewhere in Bradley's letters and journals will be a direct reference that reveals both the motive and the killer. If I'm right, the information in that trunk will reveal the truth."

"Good heavens,' said Phillip Hester. "If that's the case, what are you doing here? Why not go and examine this trunk immediately?"

"Unfortunately, the trunk is securely locked, and I don't want to break it open for fear of damaging or destroying something vital inside, but Eva has the key among her personal possessions at the Brunswick jail. The Sylvia's next run to Brunswick is at six this evening, so you can understand why I was interested in how long the hunt would be. I'll go to Brunswick tonight, get the key from Eva, and return here on the last run at nine-thirty. Then I'll see what's in that trunk. By tomorrow morning, this will be a whole new case."

"Extraordinary," said Phillip Hester.

The others started talking among themselves until Alan McHale interrupted.

"Gentlemen, we should be going. Mustn't keep the pigs waiting."

With murmurs and a rattle of guns and equipment, the hunting party filed out of the gamekeeper's shop and plunged into the nearby pinewoods.

Max had never cared for hunting and the pig hunt reminded him why. The day was unseasonably warm and the local insects were unusually aggressive. Gnats, flies and the infamous "no-see-ems" swarmed everywhere, nibbling on the hunters for an occasional snack. The Enfield Max carried had been modified with a much lighter stock than the military version, but still seemed to grow heavier with each step. The party proceeded through swampy areas and over stumps and holes in the ground. Someone seemed to stumble with each step and Max prayed everyone remembered the first rule of firearms; never allow the gun to point at anything you don't want to shoot. Of course, the fact that the murderer was possibly tagging along with him in the woods with a loaded gun in his hand didn't do much to sooth Max either.

"So, Max. What do you suppose this mysterious trunk will prove?" The speaker was Phillip Hester, who was now walking beside him.

"Who is the real killer," Max answered simply.

Colonel McCormick had come up on the other side and added his opinion. "It sounds to me like you're putting a lot of faith in a box of old papers."

"I'm not accepting anything on faith, colonel. The evidence speaks for itself."

"What evidence? The fact that she brought him poisoned coffee and that they found the poison bottle in her house?"

"No," said Max. "The idea that a woman with no motive killed her husband with a type of poison she'd probably never heard of and from a place she'd never even been, and then left the bottle where it could be found. And by the way, the coffee she brought Bradley was not poisoned. They just received the analysis that proves it."

Bwana Pete, who was a short distance away, overheard. "The coffee stain had no poison in it? Why, Max, that's fantastic news."

"Yes," said Max, "and it makes whatever is in that trunk even more important."

After trudging and slapping bugs for about 20 minutes, McHale and Falstaff halted the party. They gathered around and McHale spoke in a quiet voice, as if telling scandalous secrets.

"Now the pigs are usually holed up in the deepest, most inaccessible part of the forest," said McHale, "but they forage out some considerable distance for food. Harold here has been placing corn around a clearing a little ways ahead just about this time of day. So let's spread out in a semi-circle and get set up. The wind is coming from that direction." He indicated northwest with a wave of his arm. "So place yourselves downwind. Otherwise the pig'll get a whiff of your scent and take off. Oh, and check your field of fire so you don't shoot another member of the hunt. Just be careful. A wild pig is a powerful animal, and a wounded one can charge, so stay out of its way. Stay near a tree you can duck behind in case of emergency."

The hunters spread out and settled in for a shot at the clearing and Max did the same. He found a relatively comfortable spot on a bed of pine needles and waited. Off to his left and through the bushes, he could just make out the form of Robert Woodson, with the ever-present Sanchez a little behind him. To Max's right, he saw Phillip Hester, sitting on a stump. Nothing happened for about ten minutes, then Max noticed a dark form at the far edge of the clearing. He strained his eyes and the form became a wild pig, with dark brown hair, large humped shoulders, and a pair of nasty-looking curled tusks.

The pig sniffed the air and looked side to side. Satisfied that all was well, the pig slowly walked into the clearing toward the corn that Harold Falstaff had scattered there. The pig swung his head from side to side sniffing the air again, and then began to eat the corn.

At that moment, the woods exploded with gunfire as everyone in the hunting party started blasting away at once. The pig staggered, then struggled to his feet and began to run...right toward Max. Suddenly Max remembered what Bwana Pete had said about the danger of a wounded animal. He shouldered his gun and pulled back the bolt, but realized with horror that he hadn't loaded it! As the pig got ever closer, Max lowered the rifle and fumbled to get a cartridge into it. The pig was just a few yards away now, and still coming strong. Max could feel the ground begin to vibrate slightly with the pounding of the hoofs. He got a cartridge in the breech and pushed the lever forward. He felt the bolt lock the cartridge in place, then he raised the rifle to his shoulder, sighted, and fired. The noise of the shot seemed to fill the clearing as the Enfield kicked against his shoulder.

As the noise echoed away, the pig crumpled into a heap just a few yards in front of Max. Bwana Pete was the first to reach the animal.

"My god, Max. Right between the eyes. Good shot! They'll have pork on the menu tomorrow. Take a bow, old boy."

"I can't;" said Max, "my knees are too wobbly at the moment."

The rest of the hunt was less dramatic. Several more pigs appeared and several more fusillades exploded in the woods. Finally, the party turned back with two pigs to show for their efforts. Back at the gamekeeper's shack, Max said goodbye and turned to get to the club pier. He looked back, but no one was watching him go.

He had learned two things from this particular outing; he still disliked hunting, and everyone on the trip had a strong interest in his investigation. Max just had time to change, meet up with Allison briefly, and get to the Sylvia.

"Remember, when the light comes on, that will be your signal," Max said to her quietly as he stepped onto the boat.

Allison watched the Sylvia pull away and head up Jekyll Creek toward Brunswick.

After a light dinner at the club dining room, Allison joined the Mah Jongg game starting up in one of the meeting rooms off of the main lobby. Three square tables were set up for four players at each one. On each table was a pile of domino-sized white tiles, all scattered. As she stood in the doorway, Allison saw Nancy McCormick at one of the tables.

"Allison. Over here!"

"Hello, Nancy," Allison replied, pulling up a chair. "I thought I'd take you up on your invitation to the world of Mah Jongg. Oh, Hello Mrs. Woodson."

Theresa Woodson was sitting opposite Nancy McCormick.

"Good evening, Allison," she said. "Do you play Mah Jongg?"

"No, but I've been anxious to learn," Allison replied. "Everyone seems to be playing it these days."

"Yes, I know," Theresa Woodson agreed, "but I play it anyway."

"Now it's sort of like a card game," Nancy began. "You try to get combinations of tiles that match those on the Mah Jongg card."

"Oh, you mean this card," said Allison. She was looking at a card with numerous confusing combinations of letters and numbers.

"The tiles have suits, just like playing cards," Nancy continued. "There's the bamboos, (or bams) the dots, the craks, and of course there's the dragons and the winds."

"The dragons and the..."

"And the flowers and the seasons. That's simple enough, isn't it?"

"Well, I suppose..." Allison was trying to keep the terms straight.

"Oh," Nancy continued, "there's also the jokers."

"Oh, well, that clarifies things," said Allison, shaking her head. "And I thought it would be hard to understand. Silly me."

"I wouldn't worry, dear," said Theresa Woodson, examining a stray tile. "It's a bit like riding a bicycle. You can read all you want about how it's done, but you really learn by riding it."

"Well," said Allison, "The suits take some getting used to, but I can play cards, so if that's all there is to it..."

"Not quite all," said Nancy, with the air of someone reluctantly delivering bad news, "I haven't gotten to the dice yet."

"You have *dice* in this game, too?" said Allison, amazed and appalled at the same time.

Nancy nodded. "Oh, yes. And I was about to explain the distribution of the tiles, the trading, the discards, and how to get a Mah Jongg. I'm afraid you may find it gets a bit complicated."

"Gets complicated?" said Allison. "What was it up until now?"

Nancy ran through more of the rules and procedures, and then asked Allison if she was ready to give it a try.

"Sure," said Allison, with more confidence than she actually felt, "Let's get this Asian bicycle on the road and see how long I can ride without falling off."

The game got underway and Allison began to understand what was going on, though it was hard to follow. She strained to keep up with the play, but was distracted and stole a glance at the clock. It was almost seven. She also noticed how dark it had gotten.

"Did Max get the information he needed from my husband?" Nancy asked. "He came to see him, you know, and ask questions. I thought it was extraordinary, seeing as how the case is settled."

"I think Max was just trying to tie up a few loose ends," said Allison. "Wait a minute. I think I have...no I don't."

"There must be quite a few of these loose ends," said Theresa Woodson, passing a tile.

Allison looked out the window again.

"With Max you can never be sure," she said. "He's always looking for evidence. It's an occupational hazard."

"It's more of a hazard for someone else I should imagine," said Theresa Woodson, carefully arranging her tiles.

"He seemed to think we had a relative in Haiti," sniffed Nancy McCormick. "Imagine; Haiti."

"You never know," said Allison. Nancy McCormick give her a brief frown.

"Why, I believe I have Mah Jongg," said Theresa Woodson cheerfully.

Allison looked outside again. The window was still dark.

By eight o'clock, though the Mah Jongg game was proceeding at full speed, Jekyll Island had settled down for the night. Most of the help had retired to their quarters or to some diversion or other, dinner was over, and several dozen members were still at the clubhouse bar or playing cards in other clubhouse rooms. Lights had come on in the cottages, and the members who weren't at the clubhouse had settled in to domesticity for the night. The paths were empty except for the occasional servant out on an errand. Several off-duty help sat on the steps of the unmarried servants' quarters smoking and talking. The chirping of crickets competed with the occasional sounds of birds and the hum of insects.

One or two cottages had already been closed for the season, but lights glowed in the windows of the rest, all except for Osage Cottage. Standing alone, dark and forlorn, Osage Cottage was a black silhouette against the darkening night sky.

At eight-fifteen, two deer grazed on the front lawn of Osage Cottage. In the darkness they slowly made their way across the yard, nibbling, but alert for any indication of danger. Several more minutes passed, then one of them raised his head and looked behind, and they both started and ran off.

A minute later, a dark figure appeared, gliding so smoothly, it appeared to float. The figure silently approached the back of Osage Cottage, paused a moment at the basement door, then disappeared inside. Stillness returned to the exterior of the house.

In the black and dampness of the basement, a lone figure stood motionless for a few minutes listening, but the house was silent. The figure crossed the dirt floor and crept up the stairs to the first floor, then stood listening again. The living room was gray with pale moonlight, but without any other light, no one outside could have seen in. The figure slowly climbed the staircase to the second floor and paused by the main bedroom door. The house was still silent. Downstairs a clock ticked faintly, and an owl hooted somewhere outside.

The figure stood in the darkened doorway looking around the room. The features of the room were dim, but visible in the faint moonlight. The figure paused again, listening, then silently crossed to the closets and opened the first one. With a small flashlight, the figure inspected the closet floor, then moved on to the second closet and did the same thing. Bradley Dawson's steamer trunk was where Max has left it and was plain to see, even in the dull light. The figure pulled out the trunk and examined the stenciled name. Then the figure produced a small pry bar and went to work on the lock after pulling down one of the coats in the closet and placing it over the lock to muffle any sound. With a faint creak of the hinges, the top of the chest opened. The thin beam from the flashlight began to probe the inside of the trunk.

"Put your hands up right now!"

The room was suddenly flooded with light as the switch was turned on. The figure spun around and saw Max Hurlock, along with Sheriff McCoy and a deputy.

"It looks like we've found the real killer, sheriff," said Max. "This is Warren McCormick, former officer in the United States Marines, better known around the club as Harold Falstaff."

"The gamekeeper?"

"Assistant gamekeeper," said Max.

"No," Falstaff protested. "You got it all wrong. It wasn't me. I was just trying to protect the chest until Mr. Hurlock got back."

"With a pry bar?" said McCoy. "Hope you never try to protect somebody's good china. It's pretty clear what you be doin', and it ain't protectin' no chest. Now they don't have a jail on the island, so we'll have to take you back to Brunswick tonight for safekeepin'. Deputy, put the cuffs on this boy and we'll go down to the parlor and have us a little talk."

John Reisinger

Chapter 20

Ghosts of the past

The sheriff grabbed Falstaff's arm in a firm grip and half guided, half dragged him stumbling down the stairs and into the parlor. Falstaff was still looking around in confusion and disbelief. "But you went to Brunswick on the Sylvia," he said to Max. "I saw you."

"You saw me leave for Brunswick on the Sylvia," said Max, "but I met the sheriff and the deputy about half way there. They were waiting in another boat. The Sylvia continued on its way but we all came here and waited for the killer to arrive."

"So it was all a bluff? There's nothing in the trunk?"

"Oh, there's plenty in the trunk," said Max, "enough to give me a pretty good idea of what the crime was all about and figure out your part in it, just not enough to link you with the crime in a way a court would accept. If you had just stayed away tonight, you might have been all right, but you didn't, so now we have enough."

Falstaff didn't reply. He sat slumped on the sofa staring at the floor. In the quiet, they heard someone come up the porch steps and open the front door.

"Evenin' Miz Allison," said the sheriff.

Allison smiled. "I was in a cutthroat Mah Jongg game at the club, but Max told me to come over when I saw the lights go on. He said...Oh, my. Harold Falstaff? Well, well."

Max nodded. "I'm afraid so, but his real name is Warren McCormick, formerly Lieutenant McCormick of the United States Marine Corps."

"Is he related to Nancy and the Colonel? A long-lost son or something?"

"No. I don't think so," said Max. "Just another confusing coincidence it appears."

Falstaff sat on the sofa with his hands cuffed behind his back.

"You got it all wrong. I don't know who this McCormick guy is and I was never in the military."

"I'm afraid you were. The clues were pretty obvious," said Max.

Falstaff remained defiant. "Look, you can't prove I'm this McCormick guy."

The sheriff turned to Max and grinned. "You know Max, ah jus' loves it when they get all defiant and such." He turned back to Falstaff. "Can't identify you? Well, how about this, son? You just been arrested for breakin' and enterin'. That means soons we get you back to Brunswick, we take your fingerprints."

"F...fingerprints?"

"Oh yes. And the Marine Corps no doubt has prints on file for this McCormick boy, so alls we gotta do is compare 'em. What do y'all think we'll find?"

Falstaff suddenly seemed to slump.

"All right, all right. I'm Warren McCormick. But that's all I'm saying."

"Then allow me to fill in some of the blanks," said Max.

"Mr. McCormick here was a Lieutenant in the Marine Corps and was assigned to Haiti. If you'll recall, President Wilson sent the marines into Haiti to stabilize that unfortunate country in 1915. Most of the Haitians were glad we were there to bring some order, but some of the corrupt old guard weren't. In the hills were bands of lawless bandits called the cacos. The cacos had started as escaped slaves many years before, and had sustained themselves by raiding and theft. When the slaves were freed, the cacos were too set in their ways to change. Most of the time the cacos were content to rob villages and travelers, but whenever some group wanted to overthrow the government, they enlisted the cacos with promises of loot and power. So it wasn't long before the marines began to run up against the cacos and they started to clear them out. Soon the marines were pretty much at war with the cacos."

"Scum. That's what they were. Murdering black scum," grumbled McCormick. "They'd cut your throat as soon as look at you. They were vermin and deserved to be exterminated. Sure I had a few of them killed, but I'll bet I saved other people's lives by doing it."

"There's a certain amount of truth in what Mr. McCormick is saying," Max continued. "The cacos were far from being model citizens and the marines performed a great public service getting rid of them. It made life much better for poor farmers and hill people. That did not mean the cacos were to be exterminated on sight, however, especially since innocent farmers sometimes got caught in the net. Lieutenant McCormick was a little too enthusiastic. One day a patrol caught six suspected cacos in a raid in a remote village and he ordered them hanged on the spot. Unfortunately for the good lieutenant, the American press was brewing up scandal about marines murdering cacos at the time, and he was court marshaled. He spent a year in the stockade and was drummed out of the marines. Captain Bradley Dawkins was his commanding officer, and I take it, the man who brought the charges against him. The poisoning was McCormick's way of settling the score."

"But you already suspected him, didn't you Max," said Allison. "Why?"

"When you talked to him about the birds on the island, he referred to a machine gun as a Lewis, meaning the British-made Lewis gun used in the Great War. Someone who'd never been in the service as he claimed would probably not be familiar with that term, but there was more. The tattoo on his forearm was the next clue. He said it was a heart and he had tried to have it removed, but an unsightly bluish blotch remained. I'm no expert, but it looked to me as if the tattoo had only been obscured with ink placed on the skin. Wash the ink off and the tattoo will be revealed. That would indicate the obscuring was to be temporary. In addition, the tattoo was indistinct, but the shape of the blotch seemed to be more like the shape of the Marine Corps emblem of the globe, anchor and eagle. But if he had been in the marines, why deny it? And why try to make that tattoo indistinct?"

"It does seem suspicious," said McCoy, "but it didn't mean he was a killer."

"No, but it told me he was hiding things, especially his possible history as a marine. That seemed to indicate that there was something about his marine service he didn't want people to know about. I also noticed that his glasses appeared to have plain lenses, which would indicate they were only being used as part of a disguise. You see he's not wearing them now. I'm sure the mustache and bushy hair were part of the disguise as well, so Bradley Dawkins wouldn't recognize him."

"I guess it worked," said McCoy.

"Yes. He changed his appearance just enough that Bradley Dawkins never recognized him until it was too late."

"I knew there was something more to Harold Falstaff than met the eye, but I might have never figured out just what. When we opened the steamer trunk, however, there were papers and letters and other files from Bradley's service, including this somewhat faded report."

The sheriff looked it over. "It talks about this McCormick feller, and how he was court marshaled for hangin' them cacos. Wooee. Now this part is interestin'; says here McCormick was mad as a wet hen and said he'd get even. Well now; don't that just beat all?"

"I read the same thing," said Max. "After that, everything seemed to fit together, but there was very little evidence until tonight. I think if we search this gentlemen's rooms we'll probably even find some more of that manchineel tree poison."

"The bastard turned me in," McCormick muttered. "He ruined my life. I was going to be somebody. I was the first in my family to become an officer. I was going to be a general someday. Yeah, I was hard on those murdering cacos, but somebody had to be. Stringing them up is the only thing they understood. You don't get anywhere being soft on them. They'll just laugh at you."

"So what happened?" Max asked.

"We were in the jungle searching for Charlemagne Peralte, the cacos' leader," Falstaff continued, "He was a wily devil, but we were determined to capture or kill him. Well, we captured six cacos at a camp. Maybe another 20 got away. We went through what they had left behind and found a newspaper. Most of the cacos can't read, so we figured some higher up had been with them, maybe Charlemagne himself. We tried to get the ones we captured to talk, but they wouldn't. Then one of them grabbed a marine's rifle and started shooting. Cacos are lousy shots and he didn't hit anything before we cut him down, but I was so disgusted I ordered the rest of then hanged. Then when we got back and Dawkins heard about it, I was court-marshaled."

"So you murdered him," said McCoy, "and tried to frame his wife in the bargain. Here I been houndin' her trying to get her to confess. That really fries my grits. What did that woman ever do to you?"

McCormick shook his head. "I didn't mean for that to happen. I saw him sitting outside on the veranda at the dance and went back to my room and got the poison. I stopped to talk to him and slipped it into his coffee without his noticing. In the dark it wasn't hard. I thought the poison wouldn't be traceable and it would be ruled a heart attack. I never thought they'd arrest her. When I saw the poison taking effect I saw there was no one around, so I couldn't resist telling him who I was. I was going to wait to make sure he was dead, but I saw Jason Williams walking up the path in our direction, so I slipped away before he could see me."

"That's why Bradley Dawkins said cocoa to Williams," said Max. "He was really saying cacos to point the finger at his killer."

"Why not just say Falstaff?" said McCoy.

"We'll never know for sure," said Max, "but I think the poison had made his lips and his tongue numb by that time and to pronounce Falstaff, or even

McCormick, you need to use your lips and the tip of your tongue. Try it yourself."

McCoy and Allison mouthed the words silently. It was true.

"But cacos can be pronounced easily without moving either the lips or the front of the tongue. It would also tell the motive, especially to someone as well read as Jason Williams. Unfortunately, the word was garbled and Williams thought he said cocoa and didn't make the connection."

McCormick nodded. "Yeah, he tried to say something to me, but was having trouble forming the words. That's why I thought he was just a few seconds away from dying."

"What about that poison you used? Did you carry it with you all the way from Haiti?" Allison asked.

McCormick nodded. "Between patrols I visited the nearby village and talked to one of the old men who spoke some English. One day everyone was in an uproar from a man who had staggered into the village and died. The old man explained the man had died from eating an 'apple of death'. When I asked what he meant, he told me about the manchineel tree. He showed me how to make a bottle of poison from the sap. The idea was to kill rats, but I put it away in a duffle bag and never got around to using it. When I was court-marshaled I was mad at Captain Dawkins, but I couldn't figure how to get back at him. Then I remembered the poison and bided my time. I had left most of my personal effects with a friend for safekeeping while I was in the stockade and he wasn't the curious type, so the bottle was still there in that duffel bag when I got out."

"Why didn't you try to kill Bradley Dawkins there?" Max asked.

"It was too obvious. Everyone would know I did it. Besides, they hustled me off to the stockade and I never really had a chance. When I was finally released, I got a job in Baltimore and kept track of Dawkins's company. The Baltimore Sun carried a story about his return and I saw an item in the social pages that said he'd be spending the winter on Jekyll Island. I thought that was the perfect place, because they were more likely to assume it was a heart attack, and there was no John Hopkins Hospital to take him to and save him. I applied for the assistant gamekeeper's job under a phony name and watched for my chance. A few weeks ago, it came."

"What about the poison bottle they found in Eva Dawkins's basement?" Max asked.

McCormick sighed. "I planted it. When they didn't declare the death a heart attack and then you showed up and started asking so many questions, I got nervous. I still didn't think she'd ever be convicted, what with no motive or anything, but I wanted to divert any attention away from my direction."

"It almost worked," said Max, "but it was the first solid evidence I had that indicated Eva's innocence. A real killer would have gotten rid of that bottle long ago, or at least gotten it out of the house. When I saw that bottle, I knew someone was working behind the scenes to get Eva convicted, or at least, suspected."

"Wait a minute," said Allison. "How do Clarice Bailey, Sanchez, and the others fit into this?"

"They don't," said Max. "Sanchez didn't do anything except act sinister, something he apparently does anyway. Several members may have benefited from Bradley's death, but they never did anything to bring it about. As for Clarice, well she did bring him coffee that night at the dance. He drank some, and then placed the cup under his chair where it was later found. Eva brought him coffee a little later, not knowing it was a second cup. He was feeling a little better by then, so that's the one he drank. Unfortunately, that's also the one McCormick poisoned."

"Well, there, Mr. McCormick, or whatever your name is," said the sheriff, "I think we best be gettin' over to the courthouse."

He pulled Falstaff to his feet and the deputy took the other arm.

"You comin' along, Max?"

"That depends. Can we get Eva Dawkins sprung tonight?"

The sheriff nodded. "Yup. I think that there lady's been our guest long enough."

"Very good," said Max. "I'll be coming with you. How about you, Allison?"

"You couldn't keep me away with a club," she replied, "but how about Bwana Pete?"

Max nodded. "I think he's still at the clubhouse. Sheriff, if you could hold off for a couple of minutes, I'll go get him."

When he heard the news, Bwana Pete gave out a cheer.

John Reisinger

Chapter 21

The end of the season

The trip to Brunswick was uneventful, as the fishing boat chugged its way northward. The water was calm and darkness obscured the usual scenery. McCormick sat silently in the stern, staring out into the blackness as if contemplating his equally dark future.

Bwana Pete paced the deck with excitement.

"Max, this is marvelous, but why didn't you tell me what you were up to tonight?" he said.

"I wanted it to be as believable as possible, and I didn't want anyone to let anything slip out ahead of time, so I didn't tell anyone except Allison and the sheriff. There was no need for anyone else to know."

"That's a polite way of saying you weren't positive you could trust me," said Bwana Pete.

"I didn't say that," said Max, but Pete just laughed.

"It was the smart thing to do," he said, "and that's why she wrote to you in the first place; because she had confidence you'd do what was necessary."

"Well, it all worked out, anyway."

"I have to hand it to you, Max," said Allison as they stood watching the distant lights of Brunswick a few minutes later, "You did it. And with a week to spare."

Sheriff McCoy appeared at the rail smoking a Lucky Strike. The tip glowed in the gloom. "He didn't have a week to spare. I was talkin' to the captain of the Sylvia last night. He was tellin' me he has ten people scheduled to leave the island for the season tomorrow. I'll bet you a week's pay our man was one of them. If'n we hadn't gotten him tonight, he'd 'a been gone for good tomorrow."

"I'm not surprised," said Max. "Just after the last big hunt of the season would be an ideal, non-suspicious time for an assistant gamekeeper to say his goodbyes."

"And once that happened, he could disappear forever," said Allison.

Max nodded. "He could as long as we didn't know his real name, but when I talked about Bradley's old marine records, McCormick knew he had to destroy or steal them before he left, just to be on the safe side. They were the only thing that could tie everything together. For all he knew, Bradley might have had a photograph of the two of them together in Haiti. He couldn't take the chance."

She shook her head. "So he went after the bait and fell into the trap. That's one leopard that won't be lurking in any more trees."

The sheriff took another puff.

"Will y'all be stickin' around for the trial?"

Max shook his head. "No. We're heading home in a day or so. You have all the evidence and witnessed McCormick's confession. It shouldn't be any problem convicting him. Besides, you can take all the credit if you'd like."

"Now, Max, I ain't never been one to steal another man's cornpone. You were the one who read the signs right. I thought Miz Dawkins was the killer."

"Well, you weren't alone," said Max, "but as far as I'm concerned, we worked together and came up with the right man. Besides, don't you have to run for reelection in a few months?"

McCoy smiled. "Miz Allison, your husband has a devious mind."

"Yeah," Allison said, grasping Max's arm. "Isn't it wonderful?"

An overjoyed and very much relieved Eva Dawkins was released from the jail that same night. Max, Allison, Eva, and Bwana Pete came back to Jekyll Island on the borrowed fishing boat and said their goodbyes to Sheriff McCoy, who had persuaded the owner of the fishing boat to make one last trip that night. It was well after midnight when they finally arrived back at Osage Cottage.

Max stifled a yawn. "Well, it's been an eventful evening, but it's pretty late. Allison and I should be getting back to the Sans Souci.

"I don't know when I will get to sleep," said Eva. "I'm too excited."

"Should we meet for breakfast?" Allison asked.

"No," said Eva. "I have a feeling that when I finally do get to sleep, I'll be dead to the world to make up for all the sleep I've lost during the last few weeks. I'd never make it to breakfast. How about lunch?"

"We'll come by for you at noon, then" said Allison.

Max and Allison got back to the Sans Souci a little after one AM. They switched on the light and pulled the drapes.

"A good days work, Max," said Allison, slipping out of her dress.

Max embraced her, lifting her feet off the floor. "I work pretty well at night also," he whispered. "How about you? Are you up for a little night work, Allison?"

She whispered in his ear. "As long as I'm working under you."

He reached over and switched out the light.

The next morning, Max and Allison slept late.

"Well, you're looking frisky today, oh great detect..er, I mean investigator," said Allison. "I suppose you're pretty pleased with yourself."

"Oh, I.."

"Well, you should be. Imagine that Falstaff palooka thinking he could fool you. That was bad enough, but it was nothing compared to what he was trying to do to poor Eva. Imagine; first he makes her a widow, then he tries to get her convicted of murder."

"Not very gallant of him, was it?" said Max, tying his tie.

"I hope the crowd at the dining room will treat her a little better from now on," said Allison. "Do you suppose they've heard what happened yet?"

"I'm sure Bwana Pete has told everyone by now. Whether that will change things or not is another question. She may not be a killer, but she's still an outsider."

It was a crisp and cool day under a cloudless sky. Eva was ready and waiting on the porch as they arrived, and the four of them set off for the dining room. In a few minutes they arrived at the club and reached the entrance to the dining room.

"I suppose the members will be surprised to see me back," said Eva. "They almost got rid of me, but now they'll have to get used to me all over again."

When they stepped into the dining room, the buzz of conversation in the room stopped dead as a sea of faces turned in their direction.

"Uh, oh," said Allison softly.

"It's Eva!" someone shouted, and the entire room rose to its feet applauding and whistling.

"They seem to have adjusted pretty well," said Max.

Just when the applause started to die down, someone started up singing "She's a jolly good fellow" and the whole room joined in as tears streamed down Eva's cheeks. Bwana Pete hugged her.

As the song ended, Mr. Woodson came up to the front of the room and called for silence.

"I have something to say," he announced in a booming voice.

"He usually does," said Eva Dawkins.

"Members of the club, I think I can speak for you all when I say how happy we are that justice will be done at last. Mrs. Dawkins has been wrongfully accused, but thanks to the efforts of Max Hurlock and his lovely wife, working hand in hand with our Sheriff McCoy, the cloud has ben lifted. I therefore propose that Max and Allison Hurlock be made honorary members of the Jekyll Island Club."

As voices around the room shouted "Here, here!", Woodson presented Max and Allison with a scroll proclaiming them members in the Jekyll Island Club.

"As for Mrs. Dawkins, she needs no honorary membership. She is one of us and we welcome her back for many seasons to come!"

The room exploded into cheers once again.

"Good job, Max," said Woodson. "We all knew you could do it."

Max just smiled.

"I knew it all along," said Nancy McCormick.

"Me too," said someone else.

"Success has a thousand fathers," Allison whispered in Max's ear, "failure is an orphan."

The Hesters stood by beaming, finally vindicated for standing by their friend. The McCormicks congratulated Eva, Max and Allison with hearty handshakes and pleas for them to stay longer.

"What do you say, Allison?" said Nancy. "We could have some laughs together."

"And you, Max," boomed the colonel. "Why, you bagged that rascal the way you bagged that wild pig. Good thing, too. Can't have some scoundrel disgracing the McCormick name."

Darlene Caldwell hugged both Eva and Allison. Harlan started to attempt to do the same, but a sharp rebuke from Darlene made him jump as if hit by lightning.

The Caldwells cleared away, leaving Clarice Bailey standing with Albert. For a second, everyone looked at each other silently.

"Congratulations, Eva," she said coolly. "I should have known it was one of the servants. They're so unreliable."

She turned to Max and placed her hand on his arm. "You entertained some unworthy suspicions of me, Maxwell, but I just can't stay mad at you."

"You take care of yourself," said Max.

Clarice smiled. "Why, Maxwell, how gallant of you."

"I was talking to Albert," said Max.

Clarice turned to Allison.

"Goodbye, Allison. You take good care of Maxwell. He's an interesting man."

Allison smiled back at her. "He certainly keeps my interest....aroused."

Clarice frowned. "Come along, Albert."

Eva shook her head. "Well, that's the closest I've ever seen Clarice Bailey get to a gracious apology."

"It's still not very close," said Allison, "but I suppose when a pig manages to fly, you can't get too fussy about how far it went."

As they were getting ready to sit and enjoy their meal, Mrs. Woodson appeared again. This time she addressed Max and Allison.

"Max and Allison. When you came here a few weeks ago, you knew very little about the club or its traditions, and I'm afraid I viewed your presence with something of a jaundiced eye."

Max shrugged. "That's what usually happens when we show up someplace new."

Theresa Woodson nodded. "But as I've explained to Allison, Jekyll Island is a special place and is not easily understood by the outside world. Nevertheless, you and Allison showed that you have a better sense of the true spirit of this place than some who have been members for years. It is our great good fortune that you both came here and would be our great honor if you return."

With that, Theresa Woodson hugged Allison like a long-lost sister. As she returned to her table, Bwana Pete stood open mouthed.

"I say, Max, that's the first time I've seen Theresa Woodson ever hug anyone...including her husband."

Max shrugged. "Allison's always had that effect on men. Apparently it works on women as well."

A few minutes later, they were seated and had placed their orders.

"I think it's time Allison and I headed home," said Max. "If I can arrange it, we'll leave tomorrow."

"We'll be sorry to see you go," said Eva. "With you both around I felt safe, somehow."

"Bwana Pete can take over those duties, I think," said Allison. "In fact, it seems to me he's been doing it all along."

Bwana Pete smiled. "Right you are. Don't worry, Eva. I'll be here as long as you need me."

"Thank you, Peter, and thank both of you, Max and Allison. I'm not exaggerating when I say you've saved my life."

"So what will you do when the season ends?" said Max.

"I'll be meeting with Bradley's business partner to discuss the future of the company," said Eva. "Peter has agreed to help me and advise me. He's lining up accountants and consultants to see which way to go."

"Don't worry," Bwana Pete assured them, "Eva will be just fine."

"Yes," said Max, "I think she will be."

After they finished lunch, Max and Allison packed for the trip and Max made some calls to arrange for their return. Finding some extra time on their hands, they took a last stroll around the club.

"It's funny," said Allison. "Remember how strange and forbidding this place seemed just a few weeks ago when we arrived? It almost seems like an old friend now. Do you think we'll ever come back?"

"If you'd like," said Max, "but it wouldn't be the same. We're heroes now, but we'd just be embarrassing reminders if we returned. Besides, I think this place's days are numbered."

"Really? Why? It seems to be doing just fine."

"Yes," said Max, "and it probably will be for some years to come, but its time is passing. With the income tax, there will be fewer that can afford the place, and many will go farther south for the winter. With faster ships and air travel, they could be in Florida or the Caribbean in less time than it takes to get here. The club will eventually wither and die. It's coming. You'll see."

Allison walked in silence for a few minutes.

"It seems a shame. People like Mrs. Woodson have a real sense of duty to the place and those who depend on it. When the club is gone, I think something very special will be lost and the world will be a poorer place. There is something to be said for genteel elegance."

"Mr. Hurlock!" a voice called out. They turned to see Jason Williams in the door of his shop.

"How are you, Jason?" said Max.

"I heard what happened. I suppose everybody on the island heard. You did it. You found the real killer. Congratulations."

"Well, you helped a lot. That cocoa remark clinched it. Besides, you were one of the few that didn't rush to blame Eva Dawkins."

Williams smiled. "What was it that Sherlock Holmes fella said? 'It is dangerous to theorize without all the facts.'"

Max smiled. "Good advice. Too bad more people don't follow it."

"I always said the world would be a better place if people would just read more," said Williams. "Well, I expect you'll be leavin' soon?"

"Tomorrow morning."

Williams nodded. "Well, you have a good trip. It was an honor knowing you both."

Max shook his hand. "The feeling is mutual. You keep on reading, all right?"

Williams grinned. "I was just in there buildin' another bookshelf."

The next morning, Max and Allison had breakfast at the clubhouse, and then took their bags down to the dock. Eva Dawkins and Bwana Pete were there to see them off. They said their goodbyes and got on the Sylvia.

As the lines were cast off, Max and Allison took a last look at the clubhouse tower, poking above the trees. On the flagpole at the peak of the tower's conical roof, the club flag flapped slowly in the breeze as if waving goodbye. As the boat turned and headed north toward Brunswick, they silently watched the Jekyll Island Club slowly recede, then disappear behind them.

Chapter 22

Back up north

On the long train trip back north, Max and Allison could feel the air getting colder. When they finally got to Richmond, Max and Allison were glad to see Gypsy again. The biplane was a little dusty, but none the worse for her period of inactivity.

Max looked at the slate colored sky as he checked the engine.

"Better bundle up. It'll be a chilly flight back."

They took off from a grass field in Richmond and set a course for home. As Gypsy gently lifted them into the cold air, Max and Allison felt a sense of freedom and limitless possibilities they hadn't felt since they had boarded the train heading south.

The sky was overcast, they had a tail wind, and Gypsy was running as smooth as she ever had. Soon they were over the Chesapeake Bay and a little later saw the gray-green line of the Eastern Shore. As the shoreline grew closer, they saw Claiborne and St Michaels dead ahead.

Gypsy made a slow turn over the bare fields near St Michaels and swooped down to a bumpy landing at

Max and Allison's field by the house. After pulling up next to the barn with the familiar "Hurlock's Flying Service" sign, Max cut the engine and sighed.

"Home again, home again, jiggidy-jig," said Allison, rising from the passenger cockpit and stretching. "One good thing about traveling this time of year is that there are no weeds in the garden to deal with when we return. If you'll grab the bags, I'll get a fire going in the house so we can thaw out."

"It's good to be back," said Max, opening the luggage compartment. "It's not a cottage on Jekyll Island, but it's home."

A few minutes later, they were in the house unpacking and Allison found their Jekyll Island Club membership certificate.

"So where do you think we should hang this?" she asked.

"Why hang it anywhere? Roll it up and throw it in a drawer," said Max.

"You really are an incurable romantic, aren't you? Well, I think it's nice to have a few mementos of your cases. You can bet I have a copy of every magazine article I've ever written. We should have a sort of memory place in the house to display some of these things."

Max though a moment. "Not a bad idea. I suppose we could use that spare bedroom for a museum of sorts. You know, like the kind they have at Scotland Yard."

"Yes," Allison said with excitement. "We could display that bootlegger's address book we got from Tim Walsh in the Moorestown case. It helped you solve the crime."

"Not to mention that sensational red flapper outfit you got up there," Max added, "although it loses something without you in it."

Allison looked at him mischievously. "If that's the case, then how come every time I wear it you can't wait to get me out of it?"

Max just grinned.

"Maybe it's just my imagination," said Allison, pretending to be undecided. "I think I'd better try it on again, just to make sure. Now you just relax. I'll be back in a minute."

In the other room, Max could hear the closet door opening. He sat back and sighed.

"Yes sir; it's good to be home."

The End

Notes

The Eva Rablen Poisoning Case

Death on a Golden Isle is fiction, but is based on the Eva Rablen case from 1929. Eva Rablen married well-off Carroll Rablen, an older man who had been left mostly deaf from a war wound. Even so, he willingly took his fun-loving young wife around to various dances and social events. On April 29, 1929, he took her to a dance at the local schoolhouse in Tuttletown, California. During the dance, he waited in the car as his wife cut a rug inside. At one point, she brought him coffee and some cakes, which he consumed gratefully. A few minutes later, partygoers heard him outside screaming in pain. By the time anyone got to him, he was dead.

The autopsy found nothing unusual and the death was attributed to natural causes, but Carroll Rablen's father pressured the local sheriff to investigate further. The sheriff revisited the schoolhouse where the dance had been held and found a bottle of strychnine hidden under a loose plank. The label identified the drugstore where it had been purchased, and the pharmacist identified Eva Rablen as the purchaser.

The sheriff arrested Eva Rablen, but had little real evidence because of the autopsy findings. He decided to ask famed California forensics expert Edward O. Heinrich to examine the evidence again. Heinrich analyzed the stomach contents and found strychnine, just as in the bottle. He also found the poison in the coffee cup Eva Rablen had brought to her husband. Eva, however, loudly proclaimed her innocence, claiming her father-in-law had set her up. Police

Death on a Golden Isle

realized they needed some way to connect Eva Rablen with the poison in the coffee cup, especially since Eva Rablen's defense team was busy trying to disprove the charges.

At this point, Heinrich came up with an inspiration. Figuring Eva might have bumped into someone as she carried the coffee across that crowded dance floor, he asked the sheriff to question the dancers again. Sure enough, one woman remembered Eva bumping into her and spilling some of the coffee on her dress. In a stroke of luck, the dress had not yet been cleaned. Heinrich obtained the dress, analyzed the stain, and found traces of strychnine. Eva had now been connected with the actual poisoned coffee.

When her defense team heard about Heinrich's discovery, they requested a special court session, where they announced that Eva Rablen had decided to avoid the death penalty by pleading guilty.

Chapter 2- The Jekyll Island Club

Founded in 1886, the Jekyll Island Club was a getaway for some of America's richest families. The Vanderbilts, Rockefellers, J.P. Morgan, and Pulitzers all had second homes, or cottages, here. Many members traveled to Brunswick, Georgia in private railway cars, often with servants, and went the rest of the way by one of the club's launches. Once on Jekyll, the members enjoyed the winter months free from the cares of the big cities most came from. Life on Jekyll was simple, consisting of hunting, tennis. bicycling, golf, and various get togethers.

The advent of the income tax made it more difficult for members to retain their wealth, and the Great

Depression caused the membership to dwindle. In addition, the advent of air travel made more distant locations in the balmy tropics more convenient, so the Jekyll Island Club became less attractive as a winter getaway.

The club was finally disbanded in 1942. The State of Georgia took over the island and, after several failing ventures, restored the clubhouse and the cottages, constructed a bridge from the mainland, and reopened the hotel to the public.

Today, the historic district on Jekyll Island, containing the clubhouse, many of the restored cottages, and the manicured grounds is a much-visited tourist attraction.

Chapter 9- Edward O. Heinrich

A chemistry professor at the University of California at Berkeley, Edward O. Heinrich became America's leading forensic pioneer. Combining a natural detective's instincts with a painstaking scientific approach to examining evidence, Heinrich was called in on the most baffling cases of the day, and soon became the terror of defense attorneys nationwide.

Among many other achievements, he is credited with solving the last great western train robbery and the four murders that resulted in 1927 by analyzing an old pair of dirty overalls left at the scene. Heinrich was sometimes called the Wizard of Berkeley.

Chapter 12- The Golden Isles

Mrs. Woodson was both ahead of her time and behind the times in thinking of Georgia's Sea Isles as the Golden Isles. The area was first referred to as the Golden Islands in 1717 when Sir Robert Montgomery used the term in his writings seeking to entice settlers to the area. The term didn't catch on at the time, but was gradually revived in the mid-20th century, and is now the official term for the islands.

Chapter 15- The 16th Amendment

Although various taxes on income had been in effect in the United States since the Civil War, the sixteenth amendment made it a permanent fixture and extended it to more people. The tax started off modestly, with a 1% rate on incomes up to $10,000 and 7% on incomes over $500,000. Just ten years later, however, the rates had been pushed up to a minimum of 4% on incomes up to $4,000, and a maximum of 50% on incomes over $200,000.

Chapter 18- The U.S. Marines in Haiti

President Woodrow Wilson sent the U.S. Marines into Haiti to restore order in 1915 and quell the political violence. (The previous president had just been hacked to pieces by a mob to reintroduce slavery. The rebellion was broken when a team of Haitian Gendarmes, led by two marines wearing lampblack on their faces, infiltrated Charlemagne's camp and shot him. In spite of some noisy congressional investigations into accusations of alleged marine atrocities, the American presence continued until 1934.with machetes.) Haiti had seen over 100 civil wars, coups, assassinations, revolts and other political disorders since its founding and the marines quickly became a stabilizing force.

The cacos, quasi-political bandits in the mountains north of Port-au-Prince were soon in conflict with the marines and fought a series of long guerilla campaigns. The Second Caco War was sparked and led by Charlemagne Peralte, capitalizing on rumors that the Americans planned to reintroduce slavery. The rebellion was broken when a team of Haitian Gendarmes, led by two marines wearing lampblack on their faces, infiltrated Charlemagne's camp and shot him. In spite of some noisy congressional investigations into accusations of alleged marine atrocities, the American presence continued until 1934.

About the author

John Reisinger is a former coast guard officer and engineer. He lives with his wife and research partner Barbara on Maryland's Eastern Shore. John writes and speaks on a wide range of historical, crime, writing and technical topics, and is the author of several books, including Master Detective, Death of a Flapper, Nassau, and Evasive Action.

And don't miss other adventures of Max and Allison Hurlock as they investigate murder and mayhem among the well-to-do in the Roaring 20s.

Coming soon!

Death of a Flapper

A late night visit from an old friend plunges Max and Allison into the baffling case of a New Jersey society couple found shot to death in a locked room. Along the way they encounter flappers, bootleggers, speakeasies, and a future TV star in a case that has more questions than answers. To make matters worse, the killer strikes again and the suspicious local police arrest Max for the crime!
And that's all in the first few days.
Now Max has to find the real killer, if he can just stay out of jail long enough to do it.
Based on a real case, Death of a Flapper is a roar through the Roaring 20s.

For more information, visit
www.johnreisinger.com

John Reisinger

Other books by John Reisinger....
See www.johnreisinger.com for more detail

Master Detective:

The Life and Crimes of Ellis Parker, America's Real-life Sherlock Holmes

The story of America's greatest detective and his tragic role in the Lindbergh kidnapping investigation. He obtained a signed confession but went to prison for his trouble.

"*...thoroughly researched, well-crafted biography ...Gripping.*" Booklist

"*Fascinating reading for true crime fans and mystery buffs alike.*"....Max Allan Collins, author of The Road to Perdition.

"*...a masterpiece of a biography.*" ... Troy Soos, author of The Gilded Cage.

"*...a story powerfully told.*"...Roger Johnson, in the newsletter of the Sherlock Holmes Society of London.

"*Very well done...an important and entertaining book. ..great accomplishment.*" Jim Fisher, author of The Lindbergh Case

Evasive Action:

The Hunt for Gregor Meinhoff

A tense manhunt through WWII Canada for an escaped German POW with an explosive secret that could change the outcome of the war.

"Fast paced, well-constructed...a first-rate adventure yarn." ... John Goodspeed, Easton Star-Democrat book review.

Nassau

Civil War blockade runners turn a sleepy tropical port into a boomtown as they await their next runs through the fire and steel of the deadly Union blockade.

"the final chase scene was among the most exciting things I've ever read." ... Dr. Ken Startup, history professor and VP for Academic Affairs, Williams Baptist College.

Reading group guide

Death on a Golden Isle:

As the story progressed, what character did you suspect was the killer and why?

How does the story make Eva Dawkins's possible guilt seem uncertain?

What sort of red herrings appear in the story and which are most convincing?

Why does Max try to gain the confidence of the local sheriff and how does he go about it?

How would the investigation of the murder have been handled differently with today's technology?

John Reisinger

In what ways are Max and Allison a reflection of the 1920s and of their backgrounds?

Discuss the dynamics of the Jekyll Island Club and its effect on the local economy and culture. Could a place like the Jekyll Island Club exist today?

How do Allison and Max work as a team and how do they sometimes come in conflict?

What are some of the ways Max and Allison went about prying information out of the islanders?